THE MINOAN MANIFEST

THE MINOAN MANIFEST

NICK THACKER

WANT FREE BOOKS?

HEAD OVER TO NICKTHACKER.COM/FREE-BOOKS to download three full-length thriller novels!

PROLOGUE

6,000 YEARS **ago**

Weddell Sea

The molten pine resin spilled up and nearly over the sides of the great bowl. Rusa gasped and lunged forward, grabbing the sides of the wooden bowl to steady it just as another massive swell tipped the entire vessel to the side.

He strained against the force of gravity, but the swell was too large to fight against. The bowl toppled, spilling the hot, slow liquid onto the linen floor covering. Steam immediately escaped into the air, the brutal cold of their surroundings once again taking a victim.

This time, the victim had been some of their most essential supplies.

"Rusa," the young man behind him yelled. "The waves are too much! We must turn back to sea!"

Rusa watched as the linen became soaked with the resin and the waters outside of the craft smashed into the hull once more. As his father used to say, 'once spilled, the resin cannot be returned.'

Their last jar of pine resin had just been spilled onto the floor of their ship, and Rusa knew they would not be lucky enough to find any trees to replenish their supply once they reached their destination.

If we reach our destination.

The resin was a crucial element in sailing — Rusa's own cousin, a master shipbuilder, and his team had crafted the ship. They used the age-old Minoan technique of joinery, connecting the many hardwood strips together at the sides, bending and shaping the hull and drying it, constantly tightening until a singular, solid shape was formed.

A painting of heated pine resin was applied, then finally a layer of linen cloth, forming a smooth floor of hardened lacquer through which water could not enter.

In this way, the Minoans like Rusa had accomplished the extraordinary task of world-spanning travel, learning to defy their sea god a step at a time until Rusa's ancestors had become the world's best seafaring nation.

But there was a problem only those who ventured *far* from home discovered: the colder seas to the north, and their bitter counterparts to the south, where Rusa and his men were now, caused the ship's wood to contract.

The water-soaked underside of the ship had not expanded enough to counteract the contraction because of the frigid waters they now found themselves in — the pine resin had been warmed atop the stone-floor pit near the bow, and they had painted over the worn linen with new resin, hoping to stop the incessant leaks.

And now their last bit of resin was spilling around the fore section of the ship. Fine to reinforce the seaworthiness of the floor there, but Rusa knew there would not be enough of the glue remaining for future repairs.

And, worst of all, they were only halfway through their journey — this was a round-trip affair, but they hadn't made it even to the end of the first leg yet.

Their actual destination was near — surrounding them on three sides — but it seemed there was no safe shore for landing. Earlier that morning and for the rest of the day, until Rusa could barely see the hardened, cold outlines of the black rocks of the shoreline, he had examined this land. The jagged rocks cut up through the water, tempting his sailors with a reprieve from the endless sea while simultaneously threatening their lives.

The mountains loomed above him, surrounding this narrow bay. To make matters worse, the sea had not calmed when they had entered this place — on the contrary, the sea god seemed more furious with them than ever. Had they gone too far? Perhaps there were still, somehow, places man was not destined to journey.

No, he thought, shaking away the sinister thoughts of damnation and terror. *We were* told *to come here. It was fate that allowed it to happen.*

He knew they must continue; they must push forward.

Their journey had been long — longer than any journey any of his men had ever embarked upon. Six new moons before they had found the tiny speck of ice bobbing on the horizon. Another half-moon of traversing the coast. The icy speck had become a veritable mountain of frozen water, and it was not the only one they had come across.

Rusa had been instructed to come here by the gods themselves. The elders in his village had chosen him for the role, knowing that he was a fine sailor and leader of men. *And they will need to be led,* they had told him. *There will be mutinies to quell, hunger to stave. It will be the most arduous journey of your life, and there will be lives lost.*

"Nashuja is growing sick," the younger man said to Rusa. Rusa had let go of the bowl and returned to his post at the bow of the low ship, looking out over the frigid waters at this unknown land. Smaller pieces of ice dotted the bay in front of them, each swelling up and over his line as the waves fought with one another for dominance.

"He will recover," Rusa said, without taking his eyes from the coastline. "There is nothing else for him. No alternatives."

"And if not..."

Rusa turned to face the younger man, the brother of a friend he had back home. He had done a favor for the friend in bringing along the young sailor — to return safely would earn the man a lifetime of payment and reward. "And if not," Rusa said, "we will press onward. His sacrifice will help spread the rest of our supplies."

Their food had been caught from the sea, at first smoked over the fires that had burned through their supply of wood during the first three moons of their journey, and then taken raw. They were not malnourished, but some were close. Nashuja was a powerful man, but the sea god was ruthless. A sickness here would be death.

Rusa narrowed his eyes, trying to make out the shape of the coastline in front of him. The waves danced up and over his vision, playing with him the same way a mirage played with a man's eyes in the desert, but when the sea fell again, he smiled.

"There," he pointed. "Enough beach to land."

There was a sharp and steep crag between two towers of rock, spilling out onto an equally narrow beach. The beach was white, covered in snow, and Rusa only hoped there were no dangerously sharp rocks hidden beneath the calm and inviting covering of white.

It didn't matter. They needed to land; they needed to rest and recoup and prepare for the next leg of their journey.

Before they could turn back for the long, grueling journey over the sea and return to their homes, they had instructed Rusa to do one thing, and one thing alone:

Find the Ancient Ones.

PROLOGUE

6,000 YEARS ago

Weddell Sea

Rusa and Pamesijos, the scout, set off at daybreak. The night had been long and cold, and the seven remaining men of the expedition had huddled together for warmth, covering themselves with a few of the massive hide blankets their women had sewn together.

Rusa had left the crew with a single instruction: protect the boat, and ensure she was seaworthy. He was to return in three days' time. The foodstuffs Rusa and Pamesijos brought was bare, but enough for that length of time: the last bits of smoked fish and octopus, some dried seaweed, and a few fresh specimens of a mussel-like shell they had found in the waters near the shore.

The trip up and through the crag was treacherous, and both men nearly slipped on the ice and fell to their deaths, but after a half-day of climbing, they reached the top.

The wind at the higher altitude was strong enough to make both men wish they had stayed back at the boat, but Rusa tugged his hides tighter around his face. The elders had instructed them to bring more clothes than they thought they would ever need. Rusa had laughed at the order but obliged anyway, assuming they might lose some overboard.

He had not expected the cold to be what it was. In fact, he had never known cold such as this, nor had any of the elders explained it well. They had simply informed Rusa that the seas to the south were not of the same waters as their island home; the seas where he was going would be 'chilled.'

They had told him nothing of the frozen, uninhabitable rock on which they now clambered on. They had told him nothing of the deep, unending pain of the biting cold.

And how could they? None of his people had ever, to his knowledge, *experienced* cold such as this. Sure, the winter months in his home brought chilled air from the north and east, but the waters, even then, were swimmable.

Here, however, the land seemed to be stuck beneath a terrible blanket of wet and cold. It was unrelenting, and the first day of their expedition atop the mountain pass was nearly bad enough that Rusa thought of turning back.

On the morning of their second day, Pamesijos, walking at the front of one of two lines, finally pointed down at something. "A ridge," he said, exclaiming over the howls of the unrelenting wind. "We can climb into it. Perhaps it is warmer there."

Rusa only nodded. It would be warmer, but only slightly. However, he saw toward their navigational star that the ridge opened later, bending back to the north.

They climbed down slowly, hoping for some reprieve from the cold, but found none until they were almost at the bottom. Pamesijos hopped from the last rock to the floor of the valley they were now in and waited for Rusa to finish his own descent.

There, at the bottom of the cliff, Rusa looked around.

The valley wall on the opposite side was oddly shaped, as if someone had cut pockets from the rock, tiny enclaves that stood in dark contrast against the surrounding white. They were spaced perfectly, and Rusa wondered what fantastic god had designed this place.

They turned and walked up the valley toward the bend, neither man speaking. Rusa thought of his men, wondering if they could find anything to burn for warmth. He had not seen a tree or bush since they had landed. Perhaps here, in this valley, life had continued.

Pamesijos walked faster, and Rusa stretched his legs to keep up. After a day of traversing knee-deep snow and slick ice, their progress along the valley floor seemed remarkably fast. They reached the bend and continued following it.

The shapes on the cliff walls grew, and Rusa thought of the tiny birds of his home island that used to build their dwellings in the muddy hills along the coast. But there were no birds here; there was no life at all.

We are at the end of the world, Rusa thought. He was an educated man, trained in the ancient ways of navigation and seafaring, and knew their world was spherical. Start in one spot and sail forever in a line, and you will return to the place you originated from. His elders and teachers had guided him in these ways, just as many thousands of generations of Minoans had.

Yet he had not understood just how vastly *large* it was, standing here in a place so very unlike every place he had known. He could not remember even reading or hearing of a place like this. Covered in white, the cold powdery substance — snow, he knew it was called — at once beautiful and deadly in its constant suppression of heat.

The valley lurched back in the opposite direction. South. They continued following it, each man silent. Rusa thought of warmth, thought of the summer sun and waves warm enough to bathe in. He thought of his wife and son, the two he loved most in the world, and the two he could not wait to return home to.

Around another twisted section of the valley, Pamesijos stopped. Pointed. Rusa stared.

"What is it?" he asked.

"That shape," Pamesijos said. "It is stone, yes?"

Rusa nodded, not seeing what the man's point was.

"But does it seem… unnatural?"

Rusa examined the shape, finally understanding. The structure was stone, and it was difficult to see the edges of the thing against the white backdrop, but after a few seconds of focus, Rusa knew what he was looking at.

"It is a building, Pamesijos."

"It seems so."

Rusa was about to say more when his eyes drifted to the right, noticing for the first time *more* of the shapes, each half-hidden against the snow and ice-covered cliffs.

"There are… there are many," Pamesijos said.

Rusa nodded again. "I count at least ten."

"Could this be the site the elders told us about? The place where the Ancient Ones finally came to rest?"

Rusa did not know. He did not want to decide without more information. This place was clearly a settlement of some sort. But how? In this climate?

And it seemed to be deserted. There was nothing but the buildings to give the two men the impression that anyone lived here. That anyone *had ever* lived here.

Pamesijos and Rusa marched forward, trudging through the snow as it grew deeper, approaching the first of the small buildings. Much like the constructions of his own people, whoever had built these had used rock, carving larger pieces into stone blocks, and affixing them together somehow. The roofs were flat, but Rusa could not see what they were made of.

The first structure was now merely steps ahead, and Rusa noticed that a door had been left on one side, but a hanging sheet covered it, long since frozen solid. He reached out for it, hoping to nudge it gently from its moorings.

Instead, it fell from the ceiling, sharply landing on the stone floor and cracking into a thousand fragments. Pamesijos reeled, and Rusa stepped back. They waited. The sound of the cracking door echoed through the hard-walled valley, but then again, the air fell silent.

Rusa took a breath, watching it coil and float up, then freeze and fall to the ground.

He stepped back onto the stone foundation and into the building.

Pamesijos was right behind him, and Rusa moved forward another step to let his scout into the structure. It was a single room, small, no larger than the boat itself, had it been the same shape.

Rusa took in the dark, icy walls, his eyes finally falling toward the floor of the place just as Pamesijos gripped Rusa's arm. He heard the man suck in a breath.

Rusa's eyes fell to the floor. Saw the bed-like pile of stones in the corner. Saw the twisted, disfigured shape of the thing laying on top of it—a person, and yet not human.

And Pamesijos screamed.

CHAPTER 1
EVGENI

THREE WEEKS **ago**

Weddell Sea/Ronne Ice Shelf, Antarctica

Evgeni Volkov pulled the 4x4 close to the other two. The large, modified cruisers were powerful enough for short-distance travel over snow and ice, and in this location there were plenty of both. Volkov's partner, Luka, sat behind him on the cruiser, watching and waiting.

Evgeni pulled his gloves higher over his hands. It was a warm day today — around 0 degrees Celsius — but the sun was going to set in about an hour. He nodded at the four occupants of the two other cruisers as he stepped off the vehicle.

"This is where you found it?" he asked.

Tatiana, the team's physician and climatologist, nodded. Evgeni sucked in a breath as the beautiful woman spoke. He tried to hide his face so she wouldn't notice if he started blushing. "Yes, over there." She pointed toward a sharp crag — the tip of a mountain peak. "There is a cliff, but it is not steep. We came to the edge and examined the valley across from here. The object is jutting out of a glacier, about fifteen meters above the valley floor."

Evgeni nodded, stretching his shoulders out wide. He knew she was focused on her work, careful not to allow any unprofessional behavior, but back on the *Rezak*, he thought he'd seen her looking. Perhaps there could be something there, or perhaps he was just crazy for attention.

He turned back to his own observations. Without better gear, they could not test the glacier and the actual age at the depth of the object until the *Rezak*, their team's research ship, returned from its own expedition across the bay. It was scheduled for tomorrow morning, but there were also signs of inclement weather that could postpone the *Rezak*'s return.

Which meant there could be more nights of sleeping in the tiny, claustrophobic pods.

The pods were the latest and greatest invention of the Russian science community — fully isolated, self-contained living quarters that could house a single person. The pods could be connected via tunnels made of the same vinyl-reflective material as the pod shells, and the floor throughout all of it was attached via Velcro to the walls and tunnels.

They were testing the units for the Roscosmos, the Russian Space Agency, to see if they proved to be a viable method for building a colony on Mars.

So far, Evgeni's laptop journal recording his thoughts were that the tests proved exactly what Roscosmos needed to know: the pods worked flawlessly, were cramped as hell, and were miserable to live in for any length of time. A near-perfect score in their world.

His team had lived in the pods now for going on eight days, since they'd disembarked from the *Rezak*. They had set up the pod village in a star-shaped array, connecting each to a central, larger 'hub' and then each side to another pod. The central hub was large enough for three people, so there were no communal dinners or gatherings — most of their interactions during the hours they were holed up inside happened via web conferencing.

The ironic part of their isolation here was that Evgeni had faster internet connectivity than he did back home. While the service was satellite-based, there were no other humans besides his team members in a five-hundred-mile radius to clog up the connection points. Their web conferencing with one another was lag-free, and even his calls home to his family were relatively high-speed.

"Can we investigate, Evgeni?"

The voice had come from Mila, a beautiful twenty-something who had somehow impressed the powers-that-be enough to land a role on Evgeni's team. Her doctorate was in applied chemistry, which was not exactly a useful skill for this fieldwork, but she had a brilliant mind and played well with others.

Evgeni nodded. "I believe so. We have the climbing gear, and the weather seems it will hold. What is the estimate to reach the object?"

He turned to another man on the team, who spoke up as he strode toward Evgeni. "I think it will be only an hour. As Tatiana said, the cliff is not steep. In fact, I believe there is a perfect course already, cut into the side of the mountain."

He followed the man's finger as he pointed downward.

"I see," Evgeni said.

The team worked together alongside the mountain, but as they had predicted, the route was not treacherous. Evgeni knew they would enjoy the distraction. It was this or parsing data back in the pods, alone and bored. Even Luka, the resident glaciologist, in a world surrounded by the things he loved the most, had grown tired of the data-gathering experience.

When they reached the bottom and crossed the narrow valley, Evgeni took in the details of the mountain pass, appreciating a new perspective. He was an expert in the geology of Antarctica, and though every area was different, providing vastly rich topographies and exciting revelations, the entire continent had suffered from the same devastating calamities.

This valley seemed to add to the story.

At some point in recent history — Evgeni believed it to be around 10,000 years ago, give or take 2,000 years in either direction — Antarctica had finished its journey south, ending up over top the South Pole and growing an enlarged coastline made of pure ice. The actual continental land was now hidden beneath that sheet of ice, and it likewise hid the history of the place just beyond obvious recognition.

The continent was dotted with volcanoes — nearly 100, scientists had recently discovered — most no longer active. Each had formed as the landmasses had shifted over crustal hotspots along its route.

This valley, at first glance, seemed to have been caused by the two neighboring mountain peaks shearing over some geological frustration, forming a deep, narrow crevasse. The ice and glaciers on both sides had continued to press onward and downward, the massive forces of universal law ongoing and never-ending.

It was a beautiful sight to behold, and it was even more miraculous that Evgeni was standing in it now, in a spot likely no human had ever stood in.

And yet, against all odds, the object they were now chasing seemed unnatural, as if humans had, in fact, reached this valley in the past. When his team had discovered it, he had written it off as a trick of the eye, an illusion. A joke of the fates, often played on the normally discerning eye that had been cooped up for too long inside a Russian science experiment.

But now, standing on the valley floor and looking up at the thing, it seemed his team was correct.

This object had been made by humans.

It was impossible, for sure, but Evgeni could not shake the truth away, even with reason and logic. He was staring at a *thing* jutting from the ice about three-hundred meters away, and that *thing* seemed, incredibly, to be manmade.

"We need to get closer," he said, fiddling once again with his gloves. The temperature on the valley floor, even though protected from the high winds up on the plain, had dropped a few degrees.

They marched toward the object, and Evgeni added the details of it to his mind's database as he drew nearer. *Black or dark. Pointed, but rounded base. Or rounded top. Some sort of —*

"Volkov!" a man shouted. Evgeni's heart raced. The team used first names by default. Only in times of stress, excitement, seriousness, or another heightened state of emotion did they revert to their 'official' names and titles.

He hustled to the spot Tatiana and Mila were standing in. Directly beneath the object. He could see now that it jutted out almost three meters, about halfway across this narrow valley.

It was, in fact, pointed. *And* rounded. The tip of the thing rose upward and then sloped back into the glacier's wall, and it widened as it fell into the ice as well.

"Evgeni, it appears to be —"

The scientist did not finish her statement. She didn't need to. Evgeni was staring straight up as well, seeing the same thing the others were seeing. It was hard to believe, and yet it was impossible to deny.

Evgeni knew, even from fifteen or twenty meters below, that he was looking at a boat jutting out of a block of glacial ice on the continent of Antarctica.

"Could it have been lifted from the depths?" Luka asked. "Perhaps pulled along and formed into this ice when it came to rest on the shoreline?"

An impossible thing, Evgeni knew. "No," he said. No need to explain. This glacier — like all the glaciers they had come across during their trip — was as much a part of Antarctica as the earth deep beneath the ice. The glacier had moved, shifted over time, but there was no mistaking that the only way *this* object could have come to rest inside the glacier's hull was that it had been here when the glacier had formed.

"I do not believe it," Mila said, breathless. "It seems impossible."

"It *is* impossible," another scientist said.

But Evgeni did not agree. While their knowledge of this place, of history itself, had so far proven something like this impossible, he knew that the impossibility of a claim relied on the absence of no new, contradictory information.

"It seems to be old," Luka said. "Not even of this century."

And this is certainly what I would call contradictory information, Evgeni thought. He tried to make sense of it, of the thing's presence here.

He nodded. It *was* old. They would need to wait for the *Rezak's* return to test cores from the glacier itself, but if what they were looking at was authentic, and not somehow an elaborate and wasted trick, those cores would only affirm his suspicions.

He turned and spoke to his crew. "I do not understand how it came to be here, or why, but I know exactly what this is. I have seen this type of ship before."

"You do?"

He nodded. "The boat is reminiscent of a civilization I have studied a bit, or it is at least closely related to it. A Mediterranean civilization that ceased to exist almost 2,500 years ago. What we are looking at, my friends, seems to be a ship built by the Minoans."

"I... I just... I can't believe you wouldn't even, like, call."

The sentence was, technically, complete, but Ben's mind parsed it slowly, as if an old-school tape machine with dying batteries had uttered the words.

"You — you hear me?"

Ben nodded, and the world went sideways. He pulled his eyes forward, trying to get both to commit to looking the same direction, but he still saw three people in front of him.

Three Reggies.

Of course, there was only one. He *knew* that, but it was still...

"Hey," Reggie said again. "You, uh, I got, uh..."

Reggie tried to stand and stumbled to the side, one foot nearly tripping over the other. All Ben saw were three blurry, out-of-focus men stumbling their way in sync toward the small kitchen. Ben did not know if Reggie was going to make it or not.

It didn't matter — there was no way Ben was going to stand up and help. Instead, he chuckled, which turned into a full-on laugh, which turned into a roar of amusement matched by Reggie himself.

Ben opened his mouth to answer the question he assumed

Reggie was asking, but while his lips moved and his chin fell, no words came out.

He felt as though he were thinking clearly, yet the world around him seemed odd, unrealistic. It was as if he were sitting in a vat of clear goo, viewing his surroundings through a viscous fluid.

It was going to feel like hell tomorrow, but tomorrow was many hours away.

Reggie yelled from the kitchen of the small apartment. "So? What... what are you drinking? Same... thing?"

They had already been at it for two hours, wasting little time after Reggie had picked up Ben from the airport and driven him to his girlfriend's place in the city. Dr. Sarah Lindgren was currently at the nearby university, preparing for three back-to-back presentations, the last of which would be tonight at 7 pm.

Reggie had already heard the presentation a few times, so she had informed him he was off the hook and could stay at her apartment with Ben while he was in town. Ben had just returned from Switzerland, stopping off in Anchorage for a week before heading down to St. Louis to visit Reggie.

The bottle of bourbon Ben had purchased for Reggie sat on the end table in the living room, still unopened. While Reggie was just as much a fan of trying new bourbons as Ben was, lately the man had branched out into slightly more obscure flavors.

The two friends were currently making their way through a selection of Jamaican rums Reggie had picked up over the last few months. Sarah, being part-Jamaican, had turned him on to the fruity, gamey spirit. Usually found in mixed drinks and rum punches, which Jamaica was famous for, Reggie had taken to mixing a bit with any fruit juice they had on hand.

They had already downed the last of the orange juice and were working their way through the pineapple and a strawberry banana concoction he'd found at the back of the fridge.

Ben smiled, trying to stifle the laughter, but noticed one eyeball seemed to droop consistently to the left, creating even more Reggies than had existed before. He did his best to speak. "I, uh, the pineapple..."

His head dipped, and the sentence was indeed short, but Reggie apparently got the message. He brought Ben a tall glass of half-rum, half-juice, and held up a pink-looking beverage to toast. "To... to us," he began. "I mean... to what, to who we... and Julie and Sarah and stuff."

Ben clinked Reggie's glass, and both men took a sip. "I couldn't... have not... wouldn't said it myself, better."

Ben felt his phone vibrating in his pocket and frowned, trying to push away the surreal numbness surrounding his face. He placed the drink on the end table next to him, his tongue poking out of his mouth as he tried to guide the dangerously unstable drink onto the coaster that Sarah had placed there. She was laid back, but Ben knew she had a few pet peeves. Water rings on her brand-new furniture was certainly one of them.

His phone had finished vibrating, but he pulled it out of his pocket anyway and pulled his eyes together to focus on the tiny screen. He blinked a few times, working his eyebrows down and up to make sense of the text message.

It was from Julie, that much was clear. The rest, it seemed, was completely indecipherable.

"Just got..." Reggie began, pulling his own phone out of his pocket. He didn't finish the statement, and Ben glanced up to see all three Reggies concentrating feverishly to make sense of his own message.

Ben unlocked the screen and navigated to the message, hoping that the bright background would help with his comprehension levels. It did, to an extent. He pulled the drink back up from the coaster and held it to his lips as he focused on each word, one at a time.

"From Julie," Ben said. "Wants... need to meet..."

He closed his eyes. It was no use. Whatever the message, it would have to wait until tomorrow — likely until tomorrow afternoon. He told Julie he and Reggie were going to just spend the next couple of days hanging out and catching up, and she had agreed that he needed a few days off to relax and recoup from his adventure in Switzerland.

She can't already be calling me back in, he thought. He knew she should have flown to St. Louis as well, to see Sarah and hang out with the rest of them. It was too easy for her to get into her own head about work.

Reggie grunted something in response, and Ben looked up at him. Reggie's head — all three of them — was moving in slow circles. Or maybe it was his own head; Ben couldn't be sure.

"Not Julie," Reggie said. He met Ben's eyes. In a moment of clarity, Reggie looked down at his phone, read the message once more, and looked back up at Ben. "JSOC."

Ben frowned, but even as he did, he noticed Reggie was correct. It was a message requesting a meeting, but it had not been sent from Julie. His eyes — and his mind — had played a trick on him. He had seen the 'J' and assumed the rest. Reggie was right.

"What — who is that?" Ben asked, his words slurring.

Reggie was already working his way to his feet. "JSOC — United States Joint Special Operations Command."

CHAPTER 3
SARAH

DR. SARAH LINDGREN'S heels clicked on the tiled floor as she hustled from the tiny office to the lecture hall. Her skirt was comfortable; the stockings she had donned underneath them for their conservative appearance were not. Her shoes, single-buckled monstrosities she'd purchased just for this lecture circuit, were even worse.

She blew a puff of air from her bottom lip to move the stray bob of curls back to the top of her head, where she knew it would rest for precisely seven seconds before falling once again in front of her eyes. She had a proper dataset to prove: it was a process she'd already repeated about forty times that day.

Her three lectures today were back-to-back. First, a talk she'd given only a few times before, on the history of religion — mostly based on research she'd developed with her friend and peer, Victoria Reyes. Second, the talk she'd just delivered was on a subject she could yammer on about in her sleep: Ancient Philosophies of Prehistoric Civilizations. It was a fun speech, but it was also something no one in her field could actually call her on. Philosophy itself wasn't something that was easy to pin down, and since 'prehistory' literally meant 'all that happened before humans started keeping track,' talking about beliefs and philosophy of human life before anyone was recording tended to be a straightforward job.

Her third talk was set to begin in thirty-seven seconds, and she was at least one minute away from the university's second lecture hall she was scheduled to appear in. Unfortunately, that lecture hall was in a completely different building. Why this place had moved Anthropology into the Chemical and Biological Sciences building, she would never understand.

She slowed down and took a deep breath. She was going to be late either way — no reason to stress herself out and elevate her heart rate about it. Anyone in attendance had come to see her and hear her talk; they could wait an extra minute.

She felt her phone buzz in the tiny pocket of her skirt, but she ignored it, pressing the button on the side of the device. She had meant to leave it in the office she was borrowing, but she wasn't sure if the shared space would be occupied during her lectures.

Sarah blew the fuzzy piece of hair out of her eyes once again, continuing her clacky route through the hallways. She'd spent more than enough time in university buildings all around the world, and she could never understand why all of them had decided to build lecture halls on the top floor and near the back of each building.

The daughter of an esteemed archaeologist, Dr. Graham Lindgren, Sarah was no stranger to college and university life. At a young age, she had excelled in academics, both in the classroom and in the political realm most professional educators eventually found themselves in. She was a driven, hard-nosed woman, but she had a delicate, sweet side that allowed her to endear herself to her male counterparts more often than ostracize herself from them.

The double doors to the lecture hall were standing open, and she could see a packed audience inside. A few of the students in the front row turned and saw her coming, whispering amongst themselves. She knew half of the people here would be here only to earn credit for attendance, but those in the front row were more likely here because they actually cared to hear her speak.

Her phone buzzed again, and she tapped it quickly as she entered the lecture hall. *Not a good time*, she thought, immediately stepping up the three stairs and onto the stage once she had entered the room. The teacher's assistants who had prepared this lecture in this building had done well: a full bottle of water sat atop a table next to the podium, the cold contents creating condensation on the outside of the plastic container. The microphone had even been bent to her height, either a small touch that spoke volumes or just a serendipitous stroke of luck that she was the same height as the previous presenter had been.

She stepped up to the podium and cleared her throat, quickly working through her main talking points once again. Since her experiences with the Civilian Special Operations her boyfriend, Reggie, was involved with, she had become quite an in-demand speaker. Two book publishing contracts and over fifty speaking engagements later, she was becoming quite the expert at public speaking and discourse.

Her father's fame in archaeology circles certainly didn't hurt, but she was proud that most of the reason she was in demand was because of her own success. She had put in the work for years, earned her stripes, and now she had the experience to boot.

She looked out over the crowd, the individual faces turning into shadows and then blackness after the fourth row. If they didn't turn up the lights, Q&A would be difficult. She was about to launch into her opening statements when she felt her phone buzz once again.

Seriously? Reggie knows exactly where I am. What the hell does he

—

She pulled the phone out of her pocket, intending to set it on the podium upside down, but when she looked for the name of the caller, her eyes widened.

It wasn't a *caller*, but a text message. She couldn't help but scan the message; her eyes darting over the short text string.

>> Urgent: need your help with matter of extreme importance. Potential issue of national security.

The phone number of the sender was one she didn't recognize.

She frowned, her mouth moving, but no words came out. It had to be a joke. Some sort of text spam or junk message.

Satisfied this was the answer, she placed the phone-face up on the podium and began her discussion.

"Good evening, and welcome. My name is Dr. Sarah Lindgren, and I know why you are all here: it's an easy credit."

She paused for the prepared five seconds of chuckles and laughter, mostly from the students in the front row, when her phone buzzed again. This time, her phone vibrated loud enough on the podium that the microphone picked it up, and she heard the reverberation of the buzzing through the speakers in the room.

Her eyes once again could not ignore the message flashing onto her screen, but she saw immediately that if it were a joke or some sort of spam message, the sender had taken it to another level.

>> Gareth Red and CSO already en route to HQ. Please respond ASAP.

Rather than continuing her introduction and making her way towards the meat of her presentation, she took a step back from the podium and grabbed her phone. "I — am sorry, I... apparently I need to take this."

One of the teacher's assistants sitting in the front corner of the room jumped up and began walking toward the stage. He asked if she was okay, but Sarah was already down the opposite stairs and heading out the door, the phone up to her ear.

CHAPTER 4

ROLLINS

GENERAL NATHANIEL ROLLINS forced a smile as he stood, hands clasped behind his back, in front of the Director's desk. He hoped the permanent frown worn by most generals and other military men of his stature wasn't wasted on the Director, but Rollins had the faint sense that anything but the sound of the Director's own voice would be lost on him.

Director Stephen Williams, a career politician, stared up at the general with eyes that told Rollins exactly what he needed to know. *You serve at my discretion, and any insubordination in any way will be met with immediate political consequences.* Unbeknownst to SecDef Director Williams, however, General Rollins cared little for political maneuverability.

A decidedly *non*political career military tactician, General Rollins cared for results and results alone. For matters of national security, he wished nothing more than for the seat of the second-highest command to be filled by someone who at least understood what it meant to serve his country.

But that was a battle that couldn't be fought here today. Instead, general Rollins's battle was something slightly more articulated and intentional.

"If I am to understand you correctly," Rollins began, "you intend to invade enemy territory without the consent of Congress or the president."

Williams squeezed his eyes shut and ducked his chin, then looked back up at his military commander. "It's not an *invasion,* per se. No one owns the land, and if we move quickly and quietly, no one will know we are there."

"I assume the people who are already there will know we are there," Rollins said.

Williams blinked twice. He ignored the comment entirely. "And as for the President's involvement, he would rather focus on his golf game than worry about certain artifacts finding their way to American soil."

"Is that a statement admitting ignorance or plausible deniability?"

"Does it change your operating procedure, General?"

Rollins smirked. "I guess it does not. But no procedure is ever as clean as we hope or intend, Director. No plan —"

Williams raised a hand and waved it around in the air dismissively. "I know, I know. 'No plan survives first contact with the enemy.'"

"That's not what I was going to say," Rollins said. "Nevertheless, you are not wrong. No plan survives *most* contact with the enemy, especially when, at least on paper, there *is* no plan, and there *is* no enemy."

Williams smiled, then chuckled a bit, then finally stood and strolled around his desk. General Rollins stood almost a head taller than the short, stocky man, and he felt himself tighten up and extend to his full height as the Director approached him. It was an involuntary display of power, a 'measuring up' of sorts.

"General Rollins, you've served this country well. No one will ever dispute that. Your brand of leadership is a 'boots on the ground, missiles in the air' sort of leadership. That is undoubtedly helpful in many situations. However, it is not the only brand of leadership needed to run a country."

General Rollins could feel the lecture beginning to roll off the lesser-qualified man's tongue, and yet there was nothing he could do to stop it or to ignore it.

Williams continued. "*My* particular brand of leadership, if you will, is just the opposite: I prefer to handle things behind a desk, to sign memos and send emails and make things happen without ever really having to lift a finger. I understand it comes across as laziness, but what I need *you* to understand is that it still gets the job done. *Without* having to wake up a sleeping Congress and a tired military force."

"I get that," Rollins said. "But tell me *who* exactly is going to fight your little war for you? If I'm not sending a battalion anywhere, and I'm not asking my counterparts in the Navy to reposition a carrier group or two, who do you intend to go in?"

Once again, Williams smiled. Of all the games Washington liked to play, Rollins liked this one the least. It was one he called the 'I know something you don't know, and I've been hoping to have the opportunity to dangle it over your head' game.

"There is a group based in Anchorage, Alaska, that I'm hoping will take the job."

Rollins frowned. "A private security firm? Mercenaries? You can't just—"

Once again, Williams's hand raised and faced Rollins. And once again, Rollins felt himself die a bit inside as he cut himself off and allowed himself to be interrupted by this plebeian.

"Whoa, slow down, General. No one said anything about private security or paid-for-hire killers. No, what I'm talking about is a different group entirely. It's a group that refers to itself as the Civilian Special Operations."

You can't be serious, Rollins thought. "*Civilians?*"

Williams nodded. "We have had representatives from the armed services on their board of directors for some time now, although they are nonvoting roles. More like advisors, but they also help to keep a pulse on what the group is currently engaged with. You may not believe it, General, but this group has shown incredible promise in their dealings, and they've racked up success after success in solving certain problems the US government would rather not be involved with."

"So, it *is* about plausible deniability?"

"Isn't it always?" Williams asked. "If you can get the things done you want to get done and need to get done without ever having the chance to be blamed by someone else for foul play, wouldn't you do it that way?"

General Rollins understood the man's point, for once. But he still couldn't grasp the idea of civilians running an operation such as this. "Are they trained? How? If they're good at something like this, I imagine a smaller, surgical military unit would only be better."

"Yes, it would be if a smash-and-grab were all that was necessary. But you've read the brief. You know, there is a lot more nuance to the situation than just running in, guns blazing. Even a surgical operation, something the Rangers might pull off, would send the wrong message if word got out."

"Still, I think —"

"I know exactly what you think, General, but the issue is out of your hands. We don't need *soldiers*; we need *scientists*. A healthy mix of both is exactly what the CSO offers."

Rollins bit his tongue. While the Director pissed him off supremely, it was hard not to admit that Williams had a point. If such a group existed, and if it were as good as Williams claimed, it would be a perfect group for the mission at hand.

He extended an olive branch. "Okay, it sounds promising. *If* what you're telling me is true. I'd like to read up on them, although I have a feeling you've already pulled the trigger on this."

"I like to get things done, but I'm not a dick. Understand that my hands are tied here. JSOC has already been working to put a team together for the past few hours. They're going to expect me to say something about it, so I suggest we assume our involvement. Yes, I've already made the decision, but you'll find a lengthy proposal and description of this group and their past successes on your desk. My assistant is already on his way down to drop it off."

Rollins shrugged. "Fair enough. What do you need from me, then?"

Williams hesitated, looking out the window at the campus, then finally turning back and sighing deeply before speaking again. "I need you to do what you do best, General. Let's cut to the chase: the CSO group is good; I believe in them. But what we're asking them to do — what we *think* we might ask them to do — is at best a harebrained and half-baked plan we are forced to put into play without enough time to test alternative options, and at worst, a full-on suicide mission."

General Rollins nodded. Finally, he understood the gist of what the Director was asking.

"I need you to prepare those alternatives. Test them if possible, and if time permits, but no matter what, be prepared with those boots on the ground and those missiles in the air."

Rollins smiled again, only this time meaning it. "The old 'if America can't have it, no one can' routine?"

Williams, however, was not smiling. "You've read the brief, but there are more details you need to be filled in on. There is a lot more at stake here than what a cursory glance might suggest. I need you to be ready for all options, General."

CHAPTER 5

PETROKOV

VLADIMIR PETROKOV STOOD in the room's corner, at attention, while his supervisor delivered his practiced monologue. The man was irate, but Petrokov was not sure what about. He watched as spittle formed on the corner of his mouth, watched as the man continued, not even taking the time to wipe it off.

He wanted to smile. All this political bullshit used to make him angry, but now it was simply theater — poorly acted theater, but theater nonetheless.

His boss finally finished, staring down his ambassador for the project that was now known as simply *The Project*.

"Do you understand me, Petrokov?"

Petrokov nodded. "Of course. You have made yourself clear. There was to be no revelation of *The Project* until you and the board signed off on its completion."

The man stared bullets.

"And you have *not* yet signed that proclamation."

"No, Petrokov," his boss said. "I have *not*. Nor will I for another *year*, at least. I thought you understood that."

Petrokov sighed, glancing down at the floor, then back up at the man seated behind the massive desk, the one that Petrokov couldn't help but admire for the way it made his boss seem that much smaller. "I understand that Mr. Mikhail. However, as my report on the matter stated, this 'breach of conduct,' as you insist on calling it, was no such thing — their mandate down there has been to study and explore *in addition to* the stated mission objectives for *The Project*. And since the upload and dissemination of the information was not, in any way, associated with the actual —"

Mikhail held up a small, puckered hand. It was hook-shaped, as he had suffered from a debilitating disease as a young boy that had left part of his body disfigured. He was small and somewhat grotesque-looking in Petrokov's mind, but where Petrokov saw a lack of physical strength, the rest of his country saw political clout.

Thanks to his family's money and their connections to Vladimir Putin himself, Mikhail had risen through the ranks of the Russian bureaucracy and had landed in a coveted, protected position at the Kremlin. He was now in charge of many arcane, top-secret projects that were deemed to be in the interests of national defense.

The Project was just such a thing. A slippery, oddly shaped array of tasks and goals that had little to do with one another, in Petrokov's opinion, all wrapped up in a massive ploy that was known only to a few. The entirety of the project was likely known to one man alone, and Petrokov was interacting with that man at that very moment.

"Petrokov," Mikhail interrupted, "that is where you are wrong. I do not hold you *personally* responsible for the oversight, as the information regarding this facet of *The Project* is not within your purview. Suffice to say that I want the matter resolved. I expect you to resolve it, and I expect it done swiftly and quietly."

Petrokov's eyebrows danced on his forehead. "I see." In all his years as a Russian patriot, he had trained for many jobs and challenges. He had not, however, had much training in playing unknowing subordinate for a man who could never be his equal. "If you were to give me more details of this 'facet,' perhaps I could — "

"I have told you what you need to know: I have a problem with the scientists revealing the information about their discovery of the Minoan artifact, and I need that problem solved."

"They will be in custody within a day, Mikhail. What else is there for me to —"

"They *will* be in custody," Mikhail said. "But *they* are not my concern now. I have a team ready to collect them from the *Rezak*, but it is the party they may have *alerted* that has me concerned."

Petrokov frowned. "The Americans?"

"Who else?" Mikhail smiled, an evil-looking grin from just the side of his mouth that mixed dental implants with real, decaying teeth. "They no doubt saw the live stream of the *Rezak's* presentation, as well as a copy of the initial report the crew uploaded to Moscow's university servers."

Petrokov shrugged. "Fine. But what am I supposed to do, simply walk around America and hope someone mentions *The Project*? I have no leads."

"No," Mikhail said, his voice lowering. Petrokov knew the drill. He knew what his boss was about to say. "You *don't* have a lead — because *I* have a lead, and I have not yet given it to you." He sniffed and wiped his nose. "Consider this a warning, Petrokov. I need this job completed on time, without delay, to move to the next phase. There can be *no more* questioning, no more breaches of conduct — or trust.

"I will give you this lead for you and your team to seek out and destroy the American involvement in *The Project* before it gets off the ground, but — and I cannot stress this enough — I need you to understand that this is *my* project. It will always be *my* project, Petrokov. Your cooperation is appreciated, and yet it is also completely at my request. Understood?"

Petrokov wasn't surprised to be receiving a formal dressing-down. He'd expected as much as soon as he'd received the summons. But he was very surprised at how strongly worded Mikhail's argument had been. Petrokov had done nothing wrong — he had allowed

information from the scientists' discovery to be released online —
but now he knew that was unpalatable for the powers-that-be.

Fine. He could live with that. Top-secret, eyes-only, codenames
for everything. He'd operated that way before.

But it was Mikhail's *delivery* of the order that had surprised him
most. He wasn't angry.

Mr. Mikhail was *scared*.

He was working for a man who was *also* working for someone,
and that someone was *very* interested in producing a result that
succeeded without a hitch. That someone had expressed their dissat-
isfaction in Mikhail's treatment of *The Project* and Mikhail was
simply passing it down the chain.

Petrokov would receive the details of Mikhail's lead before
leaving the office. It would be sent directly to his secure line, over an
encrypted cellphone, as always, one he would toss into the trash as
soon as the call ended. It would give him a direction, a target.

This part was simple, and it was the part he enjoyed. He would
receive the last known location of an operative or a cell, and it would
be his job to remove those pieces from the playing field.

Petrokov was *very* good at this part of his job.

He left the office, pulling the phone up to his ear to call his
second-in-command: his best friend and a man he trusted with his
life.

"Brother," he began, "get the plane prepared. We are going to
America."

CHAPTER 6
BEN

BEN'S CALL to Julie had gone quite the way he'd expected. To be fair, he had expected little — he was still reeling from the effects of the alcohol he and Reggie had consumed, and he knew it was going to be at least four or five hours before he could likely put a sentence together.

Julie, for her part, hadn't seemed impressed. She had also received the message from JSOC, which Ben had discovered had been verified and routed by Mr. E and his communications team run by his wife. Ben had discovered from Julie that the message was legit and that whatever the reason for it, it appeared urgent.

Ben had done his best to explain his stupor during the call, but most of the words that had come out of his mouth had been singular, one-off, sporadic spurts of language. He wasn't understanding much now, and he got the feeling Julie wasn't understanding anything he was saying, either.

Reggie seemed to have fared better with his call to Sarah. She had walked out of the beginning of her presentation and called him, and the two had chatted for the better part of half an hour. By the time they finished the phone call, Ben was nearly asleep on the couch and Sarah was a minute from home.

Reggie did his best to tidy up the house and fluff the many pillows on the chairs and couches in the small space — including the ones they hadn't even sat on — and he collapsed into his previous spot on the couch just as Sarah opened the front door.

Ben stood, working his way to his feet slowly and methodically and standing there like a fool, trying to decide which direction to walk.

Sarah smiled at him and waved her hand. "Sit, sit," she said. "We don't need to hug. It's great to see you, Ben. Glad to see you made it safe and sound and could relax a bit."

She tossed her purse and bag on a table in the entranceway and entered the living room. Ben noticed Reggie seemed to relax a bit as well, realizing that his girlfriend was in high spirits. He opened his mouth, but Sarah shushed him.

"Nothing out of you, Red," she said, smirking. "You, unlike Ben, have *not* just flown halfway across the continental United States to come see me, so there is no excuse for *you* to be acting like an idiot."

"But we just talked," Reggie said, then stopped. He frowned down into the dying remnants of his drink and tried again. "He didn't come to see you, he came —"

"Are you going to just sit there like your tongue just fell off, or are you going to make me a drink?"

Reggie smiled, then nodded. It took him a few seconds to get back to his feet, but the maneuver was successful. He planted each step carefully on his way back to the kitchen.

While he was gone, Sarah turned to address Ben. "JSOC, huh?" she asked.

"Apparently so," Ben said.

"I'm surprised I got the message as well."

Ben shook his head. "Don't be. Whatever it is, it's serious if they are reaching out to us like this. And they don't really know who we have on payroll anyway, so Mr. E was probably informed to send it to all of us."

"Did I miss anything?" Sarah asked, pushing a large coil of hair back up over her ear in a way that made Ben think she had been doing that exact motion all day. "Did they send anything else?"

"No, and they probably won't. It's government stuff, military. You know how it works — *when* it works, it works slowly. They're probably still putting together a brief and arguing about who oversees this whole thing."

Reggie returned with three more drinks, which made Ben's heart sink. He wasn't sure if he could handle more, and he knew it was probably not in his best interest to try.

He reached for the glass, feeling the cold comfort of a brand-new concoction awaiting him inside.

"This one is an Appleton Estate 25-Year," he said. "It's worth at least a taste. Definitely not as funky as the rest of the stuff we've been messing with."

"You both seem a lot more sober than when we talked on the phone, Reggie," Sarah said.

Reggie shrugged. "Something about the presence of gorgeous women allows us to turn on our swagger," he answered.

She raised an eyebrow, taking a sip of the drink. Then her eyes closed, and she basked in the satisfaction of the new rum. Ben followed suit, finding that Reggie had, in fact, held out on him. Whatever was inside his glass was *far* better than what Reggie had been serving him prior to Sarah's arrival.

"Swagger, huh?" Sarah asked. "Red, you go to the bathroom recently?"

"I, uh... I just peed, why?"

Ben and Sarah looked over at the man now seated on the couch across from him.

"This 'swagger' you think you have — does it prevent the ability to zip up your pants when you're done?"

Ben laughed and watched as Reggie struggled with his pants. Sarah turned back to him. "What's the plan now?" she asked.

"Regardless of their disorganization, I'm assuming they want to meet soon?"

"Well," Ben said, "They want to meet as soon as we can all be in one place together. Julie and Mrs. E are still in Anchorage, but we're almost at their doorstep. They're coming from North Carolina, and they'll be here tomorrow. Meeting is set for 3 pm tomorrow afternoon, brief to come tomorrow morning as soon as they can get it completed."

"Doesn't sound like they're very disorganized at all," Sarah said. "I'm assuming Julie is going to fly over here?"

Ben nodded. "Yes, exactly. Which means Reggie and I have the rest of the night to hang out and drink."

CHAPTER 7

BEN

BEN LOOKED across the table at Reggie. From what he could tell, Reggie was completely fine. Either he was an excellent actor, or the alcohol had burned off sometime between yesterday and today.

Ben felt like he'd been hit by a truck.

"Mr. Bennett," the voice returned, "can you tell me a bit more about the CSO?"

He frowned, then shook his head. "S — sorry, I —"

"I can jump in, if that's okay," Julie said. She squeezed his hand from under the table.

Ben was seated at a conference room table at the same university Dr. Lindgren had given her presentation the day before. She'd been able to explain her situation to the department head, and when some high-ranking military official by the name of General Rollins had followed up with a cryptic yet intriguing explanation of their meeting request, the dean herself had swooped in to make things happen.

The meeting was described by the black-tied men who'd prepared the room as a "closed-door, no-comm, ears-only" event. Apparently, that meant no notetaking, no computers or phones, and the single camera in the room had been taped over with black electrical tape.

"The CSO is a group dedicated to the preservation of humanity through the exploration of —"

The man seated across the table from them — previously identified by one of the black suits as a three-star general — raised his hand, and Julie fell silent. "Cut the crap. I appreciate the effort, but I'm going to need you all to spare the bullshit and cut to the chase."

Ben looked at Julie, noticing that he'd moved his head a bit too quickly. He blinked away the fatigue and hangover.

Julie didn't budge. She set her jaw and stared down at the tall man across from her. "Cutting to the chase, *sir*, would require you and your team to actually *explain* what the hell it is you hope to accomplish during this meeting."

Ben met Reggie's gaze, and he found his best friend ogling Julie as she dropped the comment. Ben understood; Reggie had, at one point in time, been a career Army man. A sniper, best of his class, hotshot, sought out, all of that. His service time had been cut short by a poor decision and mission gone awry, but Ben knew the soldier was always going to be in him.

And a soldier *always* knew when to follow orders.

Ben wasn't questioning Reggie's loyalty; he was on the side of the CSO no matter what. But Reggie also couldn't help feeling uncomfortable at Julie's immediate and nonchalant defense.

Ben chuckled. Julie — and the rest of the CSO — was *not* military. He had no intention of showing disrespect, but he also had no qualms about standing his ground. His wife, Jules, would feel the same way.

The general considered her statement for a moment longer than normal, but then he sucked his teeth and turned to his aide — one of the black-suited men who'd accompanied him.

"We, uh, right," the aide started, obviously feeling out of his element sitting simultaneously next to a man who controlled a generous portion of the United States Army and a group of what he had to think were nothing but common miscreants. He cleared his throat and started again. "As you can imagine, this subject is one that may imply a certain matter of national —"

"'May imply a certain manner of national security?'" Reggie said, interrupting. He giggled.

"*Matter*," the man said.

"Right. Matter. Whatever."

Ben shot him a glance. *So maybe it's* not *Reggie's ingrained military rhetoric that's keeping him on edge,* he thought.

The general swung his head around and glared at Reggie. Before the esteemed military commander could speak, Reggie opened his mouth again. "I'm just saying that we haven't even gotten... gotten into the *meat* of it — of this... this shit — and you're already being vague and 'government-speak'y."

Julie seemed shocked. Ben had to admit it was a bit off-the-cuff, even for Reggie, whom he knew had always been borderline abrasive.

Sarah leaned over and grabbed Reggie's arm, but he shook it off. "You come in here," he started, but then lost his train of thought. "You come in here and start... I don't know. Start talking government talk to us without —"

"Reggie," Ben said, coughing loudly to attract the attention away from his flailing friend. "Reggie, I think we should just hear them out." Ben's head was swimming, but at least his words seemed to be strung along in the correct order.

The suit cleared his throat once again, no doubt annoyed and flabbergasted at the behavior of these people. "Thank you, uh, Mr. Bennett," he began. "Despite your, uh — *friend's* — awkward way of coming to a point, he is correct. The specific details of the reason for this meeting are sensitive because we aren't sure yet what, exactly, we're dealing with."

Ben nodded. Across the table, Reggie did as well, albeit with a half-smirk still smeared across his face.

The suit continued, the general frowning along with every word. "One of our constituents received word approximately two days ago that an anomalous occurrence at coordinates we will reveal at a later date —"

The general slammed a fist on the table. "Enough!" he barked. "We got word that there was something real — and if you don't mind the pun — *fishy* out in the ocean. Down south."

The black-clad suit-wearer glanced around as if the mere mention of nondescript details on his watch would earn him time in the slammer.

"How far south?" Sarah asked.

"As far as south gets," the general said.

Reggie's eyes drifted toward the table. Ben wasn't sure what to think, so he looked over at Julie.

Her gaze was still pointed directly at the general's forehead. She leaned in, her breasts pressing against the table. "Like, *Antarctica* south?"

"There a problem with that?" The aide asked.

Ben looked around, blinked a few times. "We... uh, we've already been there."

"This isn't a vacation we're offering you, son." The general locked eyes with Ben. "This is a US-sanctioned militaristic exploratory and fact-finding mission."

Ben swallowed. "Right, it's just... yeah, bad memories there. Doesn't matter — what's the job?"

The general paused a moment. He was a man of practiced nuance, and he waited for everyone in the room to lean in, involuntarily awaiting his next words.

"The job, admittedly, is a long shot," he began. "We found something, and we're not quite sure what it is. But we can't justify sending a logo-clad squad or even covert forces there, for fear that it will cause unwanted scrutiny. Instead, we want to send a team of trained professionals, under the guise of researchers, aiding a team of specialized construction workers. The goal, of course, will be to do some poking around for answers to a few specific questions."

He looked once again around the table and saw that everyone's eyes — even Reggie's, which were drooping and bleary — were on him.

"We want to send someone who can get the job done but make no mistake: if it *doesn't* get done, there's probably no coming back from this one."

CHAPTER 8

SARAH

THERE'S *no coming back from this one.*

Dr. Sarah Lindgren heard the words from General Rollins' mouth and immediately looked over at Reggie. If there was a time she wanted — *needed* — her ex-military boyfriend to not be inebriated, this was it. Instead, he looked back at her with a goofy grin.

She shook her head as she listened on to Rollins' explanation.

"About three days ago, we received satellite imagery of a region between the Antarctic Peninsula and Coats Land," the general began. He nodded a quick, serious-looking face toward the black-suited aide seated to his left, and the younger man quickly jumped up and walked over to a briefcase.

Sarah watched him open it and extract some stapled documents.

"This area, which includes the massive frozen sea known as the Ronne Ice Shelf, extending from the South Pole to the ocean, is British-claimed territory."

Ben frowned. "I thought it wasn't possible to 'claim' an area on the continent," he said.

The general grunted. "Yes, very discerning. So you're all familiar, Jacobsen here is passing out documentation, including maps and legal explanations of exactly that. Yes, Mr. Bennett, you are correct. Since 1961, there have been 53 signatory countries involved with the Atlantic Treaty System, or ATS. The ATS governs — albeit loosely, in my professional opinion — the ability for any nation to control certain stakes based on the continent of Antarctica."

Sarah felt a five-page printout with a top-left corner staple being placed into her hand. She saw that the cover page simply read: *US DEPARTMENT OF DEFENSE: ANTARCTIC COMMISSION.*

It didn't need to be stamped with '*Top Secret:*' she wasn't about to be the person who leaked whatever this meeting was about.

"You'll see essentially what I'm describing now on the second page of the handout. Suffice to say, although it is technically against the rules of the ATS, the United Kingdom and six other nations *have*, in fact, claimed territory for themselves."

Reggie wobbled a bit, but he seemed to slide out of his stupor. "How — how did they manage that?"

"Well," the general said, "the same way you claim anything: they simply decided it was theirs, and they told the world. The signatory countries in the ATS, of which England is a part, argue against the claims of their peers and for their own, but as there is really no enforcement arm of the treaty..."

"It's theirs to claim," Ben finished.

"Indeed. One provision of the treaty is that there shall be absolutely no military involvement on the continent, from *any* nation. And although Argentina and Chile have been most outspoken about Britain's claim in Antarctica, there's not really any international interest in kicking them out. After all, Antarctica is inhabited only by temporary scientific communities and folks waving around research grants. It's not like the UK is oppressing anyone by having two research bases in the area."

Sarah nodded along, and when there was a lull in the general's monologue, she spoke up. "So, what exactly *is* the problem?"

The general looked her over and grunted again, this time half-covering a slight chuckle. "Page three," he said, taking a long sigh. "As usual these days, the problem is another nation entirely: Russia."

She flipped to page three and saw a subtitle on the top of the page: *POSSIBLE RUSSIAN INFILTRATION*. She frowned. "I thought the Russian Federation was a signatory as well?" she asked.

The aide, Jacobsen, had returned to his seat and cleared his throat. "Yes, they are. And since the British can't actually claim territory in Antarctica for themselves, Russia is technically free to explore and research in this area as well. In fact, the ATS itself states that, 'all areas of Antarctica, including all stations, installations, and equipment within those areas... shall be open at all times to inspection.'"

"The problem," the general continued, "is that it's *Russia*. They're notorious for political sleight-of-hand, and even more notorious for trying to sneak in military assets where they're not invited. A few days ago, we caught a research vessel called the *Rezak*, a Russian polar research ship, off the Ronne Coast, heading toward the peninsula and Rothera Base."

"And you have a feeling these Russians *aren't* researchers?"

"No, we know they are. But it appears Russia has a much *larger* interest in the area. When we pulled information on the *Rezak's* manifest, it turned out they weren't new to the area."

"What do you mean?" she heard Ben ask. "Russia's been poking around for some time in that region?"

"'For some time' is an understatement," Julie said. "Check Page 4. '*Satellite imagery appears to show multiple Russian Federation ships and assets near the Ronne Shelf.*'"

"I see," Ben said. "So, you want us to go see what they're looking for."

The general cocked his head and grinned. "Not really. The British themselves sent a team of researchers that way, about 150 miles from Rothera over the pass to the opposite coast."

"And?"

"And we haven't heard from them since."

Sarah's eyes flicked up. "That sounds like a big deal," she said. "And I'm surprised we haven't already heard about it."

"You won't, outside of this room," the general said. "And that's by design." He paused, leaning back into his seat and looking at each of the people in the room. "Listen, folks," he began again. "I've been a military man all my life, and my father and grandfather were before me. There are certain ways I'm used to doing things, and that rarely involves starting in the civilian sector for help."

He sniffed. "That said, I *also* know pretty damn well when there's something brewing, something real suspicious. I'm not sure what it is, but I'm already past the games and diplomacy. Russia is doing *something* down there. The British are trying to contact their lost team, and we've got satellite imagery of Russian Federation ships all over the place.

"They're screwing around with something, and they're keeping their lips sealed about what it is. I don't like that sort of thing, and I want to end it."

Ben waited to see if he was going to continue before speaking. "So, you need us to find out how to stop what they're doing."

"Officially, yeah," the general said. "It's you, as civilian researchers. *Unofficially* — and no offense — I think you'll need some help. That's what Page Six is all about."

Sarah felt concern falling over her face as she flipped to the end of the packet. "But there are only five pages here."

The general looked at her, then nodded ever so slightly. "That is correct. I think we're done here. Page Five discusses your next steps and timing. I'll be in touch, but I want an answer before the end of the day."

CHAPTER 9
EVGENI

THE EXTRACTION PROCESS was going about as well as Evgeni Volkov would have expected. Meaning, of course, that it had not even begun.

His country was like any other modern nation — there were piles of bureaucracy countless low-level government officials needed to wade through before anything would be removed from the ice here. The ship remained fixed in the glacier, and it would stay there until someone high enough in his government deemed it important enough to remove.

Evgeni sighed. At least they were no longer in the pods. His research team had retired to the warmer and more spacious quarters onboard the *Rezak*, where they were joined by the vessel's eight-man crew. The captain had come down to debrief with them, but instead of intermingling, the researchers and crew had so far stayed apart.

It gave Evgeni time to review his notes on the find. He was confident it was from a pre-Greek era, though he couldn't be sure without seeing more of the ship. He also was no expert in that sort of thing, so one thing he'd requested during his debriefing call the day before was for someone trained in ancient maritime history and oceanic navigation.

Still, it was strange that they had found the object *here* of all places. Every search he could find with the ship's limited internet access had turned up only documents 'proving' that no pre-civilization had even come close to circumnavigating the globe. While the peoples of the Mediterranean had traded amongst themselves across their relatively large sea, most experts believed that prehistoric seafaring civilizations had been limited to float-like boats, useful for moving short distances.

And that didn't explain Evgeni's bigger question: how had the ship come to rest where it now lay? His team had taken a few cores from the ice near the ship, and every sample had come back with an age approximating 6,000 to 7,000 years ago, with a tiny margin of error for each result.

It was uncanny — somehow a seafaring people had come to this continent millennia before it had been 'discovered' in the modern age and had then gotten stuck halfway in a frozen wall of ice. That could only be possible if, at the time of the boat's arrival, there *wasn't* a wall of ice there.

The mystery was curious, but Evgeni was excited to study it. His life's passion was learning. Study, exploration, science, history — these were the reason he had become an Antarctic scientist. He was about to move to his computer and once again continue searching for whatever he could find about this boat when a knock at his cabin door startled him.

He answered it, finding the captain standing outside. "Someone is here for you, Volkov," the gruff, sea-hardened man stated.

Evgeni frowned. "Who is it?"

"Someone from the Federation Exploratory Commission, I believe. I told him you would meet him in the forward mess in five minutes."

"Right — sure," Evgeni said. "Did he — did he say what he needed? And where did he come from?"

The captain narrowed his eyes. "All questions you can ask him yourself. He is waiting now."

The captain turned on a heel and left, his girth nearly hitting the walls on both sides of the narrow passageway as he strode back toward his bridge.

Evgeni slipped on a thick sweater but didn't bother with a coat or jacket. He wouldn't have to go outside to reach the mess, and the temperature inside the vessel was at a reasonable level.

He walked in silence, wondering who the person was and what they wanted. And why they hadn't emailed him beforehand. It was strange to simply show up on another ship off the coast of Antarctica without warning.

He reached the mess and saw immediately that the man waiting for him was not accustomed to meeting in locations such as this. He wore a suit beneath an overcoat, and besides the thick wool cap and heavy gloves sitting on the table in front of him, he seemed utterly unprepared for Antarctic weather.

"H — hello," Evgeni said, stepping into the room. "The captain informed me that —"

"I am to remove you and your crew from the *Rezak* and return you to the *Aleandra* within the hour. A helicopter is waiting."

"A helicopter?" Evgeni asked. "I did not even hear it arrive. It is on the deck now?"

He couldn't help himself. The first thought he had was: *Where is Tatiana?* He wanted to check on her, to see if she was safe.

The man nodded, already standing up. "Can you have your crew ready in ten minutes?"

Evgeni was about to nod, but then stopped himself. "I — uh, no. That is not enough time to even get a piss. What's this about? And what is the *Aleandra*?"

"A tanker about five nautical miles from here. There is an important message from our leadership awaiting you onboard."

"If it is so important," Evgeni said," why not send it along with you? Is it that sensitive that you must —"

"You now have nine minutes. The chopper is warm, but the weather is closing in. My pilot will leave, with or without us. I, however, will not leave without *you*."

Evgeni swallowed. *Federation Exploratory Commission*, he thought. Now that he considered each word in turn, slowly, he realized he had never heard of it before. *Is this some kind of joke?*

Evgeni Volkov stared at the man standing in front of him, feeling out the situation. He noticed out the small porthole window that the weather was indeed closing in. Blackish clouds were forming over the long, flat expanse of white, and they were slowly creeping out toward the sea. The *Rezak* could weather any storm Mother Nature intended to throw at it, but he knew a chopper would fare considerably worse.

Whatever this is, it seems serious, he thought. *And I want to find out.*

The learner and explorer in him won out over his better judgment. He nodded at the newcomer. "I will have my crew on deck in nine minutes."

"You have eight minutes now, Mr. Volkov."

CHAPTER 10
SARAH

DR. LINDGREN HUNG up the receiver. Her cellphone was charging on the nightstand in the small hotel room, so she'd taken advantage of the free long-distance calling feature and dialed her father.

The conversation was brief. He had used the excuse that he was preparing for his own lecture series to cut their time short, but Sarah had known her father to be more than happy to deliver a mini lecture to her whenever prompted.

No, Sarah knew the *real* reason the man had been excited to get off the phone: he was dating, and she had seen on his TownHall profile earlier that day that he had dinner planned that evening with a 'lady he quite fancied,' in his own words.

He had always been an exceptional wordsmith, favoring puns and word games to puzzles and jokes, and ever since she was a child, he had taken time to write hand-written letters to her, opening each with an incantation or invocation from some historic quote or another, and signing them with a long, verbose postscript.

She smiled as she thought of her father — an incredibly gifted educator and orator, world-renowned for his discoveries and theories, and generally considered the world's best living archeologist.

And, according to Sarah, the world's *worst* dater. He wore his hair in a disheveled, careless way, his shirt was often half untucked, and his socks rarely matched. He was charming yet clumsy—the epitome of an accomplished professor who didn't spend enough time with the fairer sex.

After her mother had passed away, Sarah didn't think the man *could* even date. They had been a model of love and adoration, and it had nearly killed him when her mother had succumbed to the illness. But she — and him, no doubt — had been pleasantly surprised when he had mentioned to her a few years ago that he 'may once again consider exploring the possibilities of interaction with the female kind.'

As she rolled off the hotel bed and to her feet, the door opened. It was Reggie, sharing the room with her while they were in St. Louis. Even though she lived in the city, the CSO had decided it wise to collect its members under one roof until they had planned and embarked on their Antarctic journey.

She still wasn't sure if there would be one, but Reggie seemed confident Ben would help the general. There wasn't really another option, he'd explained. The US government itself rarely got involved with the CSO's affairs, but when they did, Reggie had said, it was usually best to listen.

Ben himself had just returned from Switzerland, but Reggie and Julie were raring for some more action. Sarah had to admit that getting a quick break from the lecture circuit did sound nice, even if her idea of a 'quick vacation' wasn't to someplace like Antarctica.

She was a trained anthropologist, and Antarctica typically lacked for subjects to study in that field.

"Hey," Reggie said, stumbling into the room.

"Are you still drunk?"

His eyes widened. "I was *never* drunk, my dear. Just *happy* to see you. And no. I tripped over the rug. Why do these places think putting a three-inch-tall rug right in front of the door is good design?"

She rolled her eyes. "Any word from Ben?"

He grinned. "I tried to knock, but the room was quiet. I'm assuming he and Julie are busy *discussing it.*"

He raised an eyebrow to underline the innuendo as if he thought it necessary to explain.

Again, she rolled her eyes. "Well, I'm hungry. Want to grab a bite downstairs?"

Reggie shrugged. "I could eat. Restaurant here is right off the lobby, so if Ben and Julie decide to join us, they'll see us in there."

She nodded. "Sure, but I sort of thought it would be nice to enjoy a meal with *just* you." She batted her eyes at her boyfriend.

He stiffened, straightening his back, and blinked a few times. "Oh," he said. "Right, I — I think that would be nice. And then we can come back up here, and, uh... *discuss* things?"

She clicked her mouth and looked up at the ceiling, then tossed the stray strand of hair that had been giving her grief over her ear. "You always know how to ruin a good time, Red," she said.

He laughed as he followed her out of the room. "Baby, I *am* the good time."

He was still laughing at his joke when they reached the restaurant. It was a quaint, small place, but the hotel had done well to appoint it to appear luxurious. A maître d' greeted them with a gigantic smile and asked for their party size, and just when Sarah was about to follow Reggie into the restaurant, she heard a voice calling his name.

"Red?" a man asked. "Gareth Red?"

She spun around and was immediately forced to suck in a breath. Standing directly in front of her was the *largest* man she had ever seen. Rock-solid from head to toe, his face and neck chiseled out of granite. His eyes were a piercing blue, and his hair was close-cropped and combed over toward his left ear, a long, hard part down the right side from front to back.

"I, uh..." she said. She had to remind herself to close her mouth.

"I'm Red," Reggie said, stepping up next to her. She felt him lean into her slightly, as if protecting her.

Or as if proving his relationship to me.

The man pushed out a hand. He was wearing jeans and a plaid long-sleeved shirt, both correctly fitted yet still pushing tightly against his bulging muscles, and she saw he was wearing army-issue boots.

"Name's Freddie," he said to her. Then he looked at Reggie and added, "Corporal Frederick Grant, Marine Corps, head of the assault weapons team General Rollins ordered. He said I might find you all here."

Sarah frowned as they shook hands. "General Rollins sent you?" she asked.

He tipped his forehand. "Yes, ma'am," he said. "Told me you should expect me."

Reggie smirked. "Did he, now? I'm assuming you and your men are staying in this hotel as well, at least until we give Rollins our confirmation?"

Freddie nodded, a whole head-bobbing that seemed to move his chin more forward than down. "That's right."

"Interesting," Reggie said. "I didn't think we would have much help on this little mission of ours."

Freddie smiled. "Oh," he said. "Yeah, don't worry about it. It was all on Page Six."

CHAPTER 11

BEN

BEN JUMPED the last two stairs and hurried across the lobby toward the restaurant.

"Ben," Julie said. "Wait up. They're not going anywhere."

Ben heard her, but he ignored the comment. He wasn't moving too fast, and he wanted to make sure he didn't get stuck waiting for the gaggle of tourists that had turned up in the lobby.

He reached the restaurant, and a smiling young man asked him a question. "I've got an appointment," he said. "Inside."

The kid was about to argue, but Ben was already past him and into the main atrium of the restaurant. He saw Reggie and Sarah sitting across the table from what had to be the world's largest, strongest man.

The guy had a plaid shirt on, the sleeves rolled up as high as they would likely go: barely past his wrists. Still, Ben could see the bulging beneath the shirt as he rested his elbows on the table.

Ben finally slowed and allowed Julie to catch up, and she grabbed his hand as they neared the table.

Ben thought of the message he'd gotten from Reggie: *Breaking news: giant marine here to steal our women.*

It was funny, but Ben was more concerned that General Rollins had forced their hand. He had told the man that *he* would decide if the CSO would help the government with their Antarctic problem. The general had agreed, informing Ben that they had until the end of the day to decide.

So, what was this? Ben had thought. *He's sending in backup to persuade us?*

Ben came up to the table, expecting the monster of a man to eye him down, size him up, and play the testosterone game. Ben wasn't a small man, and he could hold his own in a fight. And sometimes guys like this seemed to be almost looking for a reason to take a swing.

What had Rollins told him? That I was stubborn? That we'd be holdouts, and he needed to play hardball by sending in a sinewy, ripped-up Marine?

Instead, Ben was greeted with one of the warmest smiles he'd ever seen on a human male. The kid — and he was certainly a kid, no older than thirty — rose and stuck out his hand.

"You must be Mr. Bennett," the guy said. "How's it going? I'm Freddie."

Ben frowned, but he pulled a chair out for himself and Julie, and they sat. "Thanks," he said. "Ben's fine."

"Ben. Great. Well, General Rollins wanted me to meet you tonight. I'm sorry for barging in, but I'm excited to get going."

Reggie leaned in. "Yeah, it seems weird that a *general* is giving you direct orders, huh?"

The kid shrugged. "Sure. Yeah, maybe. I'm just a corporal, but I got sent to a detachment that ended up here, under his direct authority." He shrugged. "I mean, it's the Army. I'm a Marine, but it's not really any different — anything can happen when you rank high enough."

Reggie seemed enthused by this answer. "I know a little about that," he said. "So why you, then? I mean, you seem... like a capable guy, but you're..."

"Young?"

"Yeah."

"Right," Freddie said. "Well, two theories on that."

Ben looked at Julie, who had a silent grin on her face. Ben wondered if she knew it or not. The kid was charming, he had to admit.

"First, this whole thing — a 'restricted operation,' we call it — it's pretty off-the-books. At least my involvement. Yet it's more precautionary, or so I've been told. Can't go sending in SpecOps all the time, especially when there's a strict no-military posting for the entire continent. Wouldn't take much to notice a bunch of SEALs or CCTs amidst a bunch of nerd researchers." He chuckled, and his entire frame shifted six inches upward and back down. "Even though CCTs are sort of, by definition, supposed to be undetected..." he trailed off.

"Yeah," Reggie said. "We can pick them out of a crowd."

"Right, exactly."

"...But I think we can pick *you* out of a crowd just as easily, son. You're what? Six-seven?"

"And a half, yeah," Freddie said. "Momma said it was this or basketball."

"She *told* you to join the Marines?"

"Well, kinda. I was a freshman when 9/11 happened, and she said, 'well damn, someone ought to do something about it,' so here I am."

Ben couldn't help but smile at the kid's easy slide into his southern drawl when articulating his mother's words.

"I'm sure that's what she meant," Reggie said. "Anyway, the point is, I'm not sure anyone your size has ever *been* to Antarctica. Aren't you a little worried people will ask the same questions as if we just sent a bunch of Green Berets in?"

He shrugged. "Maybe. But I'm pretty good with computers, too. I can probably pretend I'm just a programmer or something. I suppose they always need computer help down there."

Julie coughed, and the waiter brought over a round of waters.

Ben was tempted to ask for a glass of bourbon, but he wasn't sure how well his system was prepared for another bout of drinking, and he wasn't sure what protocol was right now — whether they were on the clock.

"Anyway," Freddie said, "I think they wanted a team that wasn't high profile. Easier plausible deniability, that sort of thing. People won't be missing a corporal as much as a colonel, you know?"

It was sadistic, but Ben had to admit it was true. Leave it to the US government to send in the best-qualified yet most disposable units. It was a mild surprise Freddie was a Marine, and not just some run-of-the-mill soldier.

"What's the second reason?" Julie asked. "You said you thought you were tapped for one of two reasons?"

"Oh, right," Freddie answered. He leaned in a bit, as if not wanting to share this delicate morsel of information, yet the smile returned to his face. "It's probably this one, but I don't know. Anyway, General Rollins has always kinda had a thing for propping me up. He'd never admit to preferential treatment, but he is my uncle, after all."

Reggie almost spat out water. "He's your *uncle?*"

Freddie laughed. "Yeah. Well, step-uncle, or whatever. If that's a thing. But he's family. I guess that might have something to do with it."

Ben shook his head slightly. He wasn't sure now whether Rollins had sent this kid here to babysit *them*, or if they were now supposed to babysit *him*.

CHAPTER 12

BEN

BEN ROSE FROM THE TABLE, handing the check to the restaurant's manager, who had come by to ensure their meal was satisfying. They had only shared drinks and a few light appetizers, and Ben paid the tab with the company credit card.

Reggie and Sarah pulled back from the table and stood, as did Julie and Freddie. Ben noticed how Freddie stood about two heads taller than his wife, and how rigid and well-formed his arms and upper body were. He couldn't help but think that he wouldn't stand a chance against this monstrosity of a human, whether on the battlefield or in a game of picking up women.

Ben shook the feeling off — there was no reason to suspect Julie was interested in anyone but him, and he had to admit that Freddie seemed rather young to be meddling with the affairs of older women.

Still... there was a part of Ben that wanted to sit the kid down and explain how it was going to be — that he was in charge, and no matter what —

A cracking sound caused everyone around the table to look up and toward the front door of the restaurant. Ben reacted to the sound of gunfire before his mind truly registered it. To his left and right, tables shook with the impact of sizzling rounds hitting their tops.

Patrons screamed and jumped up, only to duck and fall to the floor in fear. Julie screamed, and Reggie grabbed her wrist and pulled her aside. Ben and Sarah fell to the ground as well, and he caught sight of Freddie out of the corner of his eye.

The big man was crawling underneath tables toward the welcome station near the entrance. Ben looked up and saw that there was a man standing there, holding a subcompact machine gun that looked like an Uzi, glaring into the depths of the restaurant.

It didn't take Ben longer than two seconds to understand what it was the man was looking for.

He's here for us, he thought.

Freddie crawled forward, and Ben turned to Reggie and Julie and delivered an order. "You all stay here. Get a table flipped over when you can; I'm going to flank this asshole and keep his eyes away from you and Freddie."

He wanted to make sure the gunman was paying attention to him as he crawled forward, rather than to the man sneaking up toward him and the rest of the CSO group corralled into the corner. The man seemed to be looking for a target, but he wasn't approaching their table.

Ben found that odd — the man had opened fire almost immediately when entering, and the shots had landed around the CSO's table as they stood, paying their bills.

Ben knew the man had seen them, or he wouldn't have opened fire.

Which meant...

Shit.

Ben started crawling faster, keeping tables, restaurant patrons, and other objects between him and the shooter, hoping to remain unseen. But he now realized why the man at the front of the restaurant hadn't moved from his position.

Because he's not the only shooter.

Ben pressed forward, reaching the end of a row of booths near the center of the hotel restaurant, where he could get a better view of the space. There had been about five or six other parties in the restaurant when Ben's group was preparing to leave, and most of them were parties of two. Those people were now cowering beneath tables, behind pillars, and near the doors to the kitchen with other restaurant staffers, all wide-eyed and terrified.

Ben felt the anger rising in him. He'd been shot at, beaten, and battle-hardened, and while he was worried about his own safety, he was more pissed off at the blatant terrorist attack and fear it would cause in the other innocent civilians here.

And then he saw him. The *second* man, the one who had *actually* shot at the CSO group when he'd entered in front of his teammate.

This man knew exactly where he was aiming — right toward the CSO's table, waiting for one of their heads to pop up. He'd missed the first shots, run into the center of the small restaurant, then turned to re-target the group. His partner, standing at the entrance, would also aim toward the section of booths in the corner.

Neither man was looking toward Ben.

Ben would approach the shooter from the side rather than from fully behind him, but it was better than nothing. He hoped to at least get the attention of both shooters to give Freddie a chance at a counterattack. The bear of a man was — hopefully — still crawling silently underneath the tables, using chairs and draping tablecloths to stay out of sight.

Three more seconds, Ben thought. He was about to reach the edge of the rows, putting him in range to sprint toward the first shooter before the man could get his gun up and aimed properly. Ben prepared for the twenty-foot sprint by rising to a crouch and stretching one leg back like a runner on a starting block.

And then he heard a commotion to his right.

The gunman in front of him turned to the side just as Ben

brought his head up to look. Freddie had closed the distance between the tables and his target — the second gunman — and was completely consuming the smaller man's position.

Freddie collided, knocking the man back and out the doorway to the restaurant. The first shooter started running.

Ben followed, cutting him off at the intersection of two rows of tables. He tackled the shooter, and both men fell to the floor.

Ben crawled up and on top of the man just as he was reaching for his weapon, which had landed a few inches away from his outstretched arm. Ben maneuvered over him, pressing his hand down on the back of the man's head and onto the hard tile floor.

The shooter grunted in pain, and Ben repeated the move, pulling on the man's hair to give him some distance before smashing it down once again.

This time the man sighed, and his eyes went dark. Ben rolled off of him, just as Reggie and the others arrived.

Julie began glancing around at the other patrons, asking if everyone was okay, and Sarah joined in. So far, no one had been shot.

Ben looked down at the unconscious shooter, wondering what this was all about. He was used to parties working against his own interests, but those attacks usually began well after the CSO team embarked on their mission.

This time, it seemed, the mission had come to them.

CHAPTER 13

BEN

BEN DRAGGED the unconscious shooter toward the front of the restaurant. Reggie had offered to help, but Ben preferred the dragging; it would only end with the man getting more injured, so Ben was happy to oblige his anger and yank on the man's arm, careful to hit every upended chair and table leg with the man's head on his way.

Reggie chuckled, walking behind the man and enjoying his friend's handiwork. When they reached the front doors of the restaurant and entered the hotel lobby, they were greeted by four other men.

The first two Ben saw were hotel security guards, holding the batons affixed to their waists and frowning at Ben. The other two were Freddie and his new captive, the second shooter who had entered the restaurant.

The man's eyes were bulging out of his head, and he stood, arms twisted behind his back, directly in front of Freddie. Freddie's mouth was neutral, an even line across his face, but Ben saw the tightness in his biceps and knew he was applying plenty of painful pressure to the shooter.

The man's gun lay off to the side, a few feet away. Neither security guard seemed to care much.

The security guard on the right addressed Ben. "Sir, we're going to need to ask you to step over here while we —"

"Restaurant's clear," Ben said, interrupting. "There are people inside who will need help. Reassurance. That's your job."

"But, sir, we need to —"

"These guys aren't working alone, but they're also not here for anyone else. They wanted *us*, and considering that *us* is still all accounted for, I believe our best move is to leave and find another place to sleep tonight."

"You know who they are?" the guard on the left asked.

"No idea," Reggie said, picking up the conversation from Ben. "Started shooting and then waited for us to pop up and look around. They won't be any more trouble, and I doubt they'll start talking, but if you can call in the big boys to haul them off, we might get something —"

Before Reggie could finish, more gunfire erupted from behind Freddie and his captive shooter.

Ben felt himself dropping to the ground, launched toward the dropped Uzi before he knew he was reacting. He pulled closer to it and reached for it with a hand, just as Freddie and his man fell to the floor as well.

More screams from the restaurant as the patrons, thinking themselves safe, reacted to the new shots.

Ben saw Freddie pull his hand around toward his lower back, wincing in pain.

Three more shots sounded, and Ben saw the first shooter's torso light up with red mist. His eyes widened in surprise, but he fell forward and onto the floor.

The unconscious shooter, whose arm Ben had dropped when he'd left the restaurant, was lying on the floor three feet to his right.

Ben grabbed the gun and pulled it up, but he was too late. Another burst of gunfire ripped through the lobby, echoing off the hard walls and floor, and sailed into the shooter.

His body lurched with each impact, and immediately a spot of blood underneath him began pooling outward toward Ben.

Ben pulled the gun toward his chest and pushed back with his legs into a seated position against the glass wall near the restaurant's entrance, trying to see the *new* shooter.

All he could make out was the silhouette of a man holding a similar-looking weapon, outlined by the bright exterior of the hotel from the rays of sunlight falling in.

Nothing but a shadow.

Ben aimed.

Before he could fire, the new gunman turned on a heel and ran out the open doors of the hotel lobby. Within five seconds, he heard screeching tires and saw the shape of a van disappearing around the hotel's curved drop-off in the front parking lot.

Whoever it was, they were about to be long gone.

"Get someone out there!" he yelled. "They're getting away. Now — the police should have been alerted, right? They're going to be —"

"It's okay, brother," Reggie's voice said. "They're gone. We need to regroup, figure out what just happened."

Ben was seething. Julie and Sarah had still been inside the restaurant during the second attack, but they were standing, wide-eyed, near the entrance now. The two security guards looked completely out of their element, likely having never been trained for such a situation. The one on the left, looking no older than twenty, had a slack-jawed expression on his face. His partner was fumbling with his phone.

"They — they came for us," Ben said, trying to piece together the events that had just transpired.

None of it made sense. None of it seemed to have a purpose, but Ben knew there was one — they just didn't understand it yet. Why they had been targeted. Why now?

And then Ben saw him. *Freddie.*

The kid was lying on his side, his hand pushed back behind his torso. There was blood around him, but Ben wasn't sure if it was his blood or the blood of the first shooter he had been holding.

His eyes were closed.

Reggie rushed over, and Ben followed, dodging the two security guards in the center of the lobby.

Reggie tapped on Freddie's arm, just as the giant opened his eyes. He blinked a few times, then looked up at Ben and Reggie.

"Hey there," Reggie said.

"'Sup."

"Nice moves, but it seems you forgot to dodge the bullets. Isn't that Battle Shit 101?"

Freddie's mouth broke into a huge smile, one rivaling the size of Reggie's, and he rolled over. Before he spoke, he gagged. Ben and Reggie jumped back. "I think it just grazed me, honestly," Freddie said.

"You — you're okay?" Ben asked.

"Oh, I'm fine. Turns out I'm actually *terrified* of blood." Freddie shrugged, still lying on the floor, and he brought his hand up to cover his mouth. "It's a weird thing, really. I'm not *scared* of it necessarily; it just really makes me want to retch."

Ben snorted, and Reggie shook his head.

I guess we do *know who's here to babysit whom,* he thought.

SARAH WAS HUNCHED over the sofa in the hotel room, tending to a miniature wound in a leg that was the size of a tree trunk. Freddie was grinning from ear to ear as she worked, and she noticed that Reggie, standing in the opposite corner of the room, was not grinning at all.

"Pull the shorts up a little higher if you need to darlin'," Freddie said.

Sarah held the gauze pad she'd been using to wrap his leg tightly in one hand and then flicked the wound with her other. Freddie's upper body shot up, and he seethed in pain.

"Damn," he said. "Why'd you gotta do that?"

"First of all," Sarah answered, "you might be twelve feet tall and built like Angus beef, but my boyfriend back there's handled a few studs like you before." She pulled the gauze around the elevated leg once again and then tightened it and tucked the end under itself. "Second, call me darlin' again, and you'll find out how well *I* can take on a stud like you."

Freddie's grin disappeared, and Reggie snickered.

"Okay," Ben said from behind her, addressing the room. "These guys were Russian. All here for us specifically. Anyone want to challenge that assumption?"

Heads shook.

Ben continued. "So, the next logical leap is that they came here to *prevent* us from getting to Antarctica."

Julie stepped in. "And *that* means there's absolutely something down there they don't want us to see."

"Right," Ben said. "But how'd they find us? How'd they even know about us?"

"Doesn't matter," Reggie said. "They were here to kill us. That means, in my book, they're dead."

"Sure, but it would help to understand everything behind the motivation to take us out."

"It would," Ben answered, "but we don't have that information right now. What we have is an order — General Rollins wants us wheels-up ASAP. Has a plane already fueling and waiting."

"So, we're going to roll out *now*?" Reggie asked. "I thought there would be, I don't know, another briefing or something?"

"There will be," Julie said. "Mrs. E is sending over any helpful information about the destination, but we can brief for the actual mission on the plane. We've got two hours here, then we're heading to the airport. Hopefully, our *booboos* will be all healed up by then?" She swung her head over toward Freddie.

Sarah hadn't wanted them to be harsh to the newcomer, but he could handle it. Plus, it felt nice to have another woman have her back.

Freddie swung his massive leg off the sofa and stood up. He gave a feigned wince as he put weight on the foot, then smiled. "Good as new," he said. "Truly appreciate it, ma'am."

Sarah winced, and hers wasn't feigned at all. "You can add 'ma'am' to the same list as 'darlin.'"

"Noted, ma'am — sorry. *Sarah*," he said. "Anyway, I'm ready to go. My bag's still at the bellhop counter. Just a duffel for me."

"An Antarctic trip with just a duffel?" Reggie asked.

Freddie shrugged. "Never been there. Is it chilly?"

Sarah grinned, and Ben laughed out loud. "We've got a plan for that," Ben said. "Your uncle is providing military gear, including proper cold-climate outdoor clothing. Should have all our sizes; we just need to get to the airport."

"Any reason to suspect more of these Russian operatives on the way?"

"To the airport?" Ben asked. "I doubt it. This was a targeted attack, and if they'd had more operatives prepared, they'd have sent them. I think we're good until we're on the ground in Antarctica, but — as always — let's stay vigilant. Who knows where they'll come from next?"

Sarah nodded along, but she couldn't help but feel the rising anxiety inside her. She was an anthropologist, not a soldier. With the CSO, she'd seen more action than most actual soldiers, and she wasn't sure how she felt about it. Ultimately, she wanted to *research*. To discover new things, new possibilities, uncover new threads of ancient history.

Somehow, against all odds, the CSO had provided her with that opportunity. She enjoyed her academic career, but she had to admit there was something compelling — something real and immediate — about the missions she was taking on with her boyfriend and his friends.

If this mission was like the others, she knew it would be one she'd hate to have missed. She wasn't interested in guns and battles and fighting for her life, but if what the general had described was true, there was something in Antarctica the Russians wanted to get their hands on, and she wanted to help find it.

And the general had requested her presence as well — she wasn't an afterthought. That meant he didn't think of her as a useful yet minor tool in a toolbox. Her presence there was key, and he knew it.

As the team prepared to march through the hotel and catch their rides to the airport, she wondered where this mission would end up.

CHAPTER 15

PETROKOV

"REPEAT THAT," the voice said.

Petrokov sighed. "The Americans are on their way to the airport."

"You were tasked with preventing that from happening, were you not?"

Petrokov pulled the phone away from his ear for a moment. He wanted to curse, to tell this person on the other end how he *really* felt about him. This man was no soldier. He did not understand the mindset of a trained killer, how these things — no matter how much preparation went into a mission — always had a large helping of randomness.

"I was," he said.

The man on the other end made a sound of disapproval. *"That is unfortunate."*

"It is."

He wondered how long he would have to keep up the charade. How long he would have to pretend to answer to this fool. Petrokov had been given a task to accept this man's word as law, to provide him support, no matter where or when or what it was. He was told to act as the man's subordinate.

Sure, there was no actual chain-of-command between the two men — that would be uncouth. This was an off-the-books project, just as Petrokov's *actual* boss had described. It was a bit of political maneuvering from the state. They wanted a job done, but they wanted it done in a very specific, controllable way. Yet they *also* wanted full plausible deniability. If anything came out about this man's mission in Antarctica, Russia would be quick to deny knowledge of the project.

Petrokov's role was to play ambassador between the two parties. He was charged with getting this man on the phone whatever he needed to complete the mission on the ground, and then report back to headquarters at the Kremlin about the goings-on down there.

It was a pedantic, annoying role, and he hated every aspect. It was government at its finest — miles of red tape and paperwork that was nearly undecipherable, with one caveat: nothing was actually *written down* anywhere. The entire project was kept so dark that not even an email between agents was allowed. It all needed to happen via encrypted burner phones, replaced daily. The last call of that day — this one — served as the update, during which the new numbers would be exchanged.

This call was also the last scheduled call for some time. Service where this man would be in Antarctica was going to be impossible. The military had refused to allow the use of satellite communications for fear that any relay from the continent would fall into enemy hands. The United Nations was already suspicious of Russia, and they had their ear to the ground. If they heard any Russian chatter from the southernmost landmass, they would be up in arms.

And it did not help that Petrokov's brother had failed *his* mission. Now, there were Americans heading to Antarctica, scheduled to arrive in two or three days.

"I have the flight information. I will get it to you soon."

"It is too late," the voice said. *"We cannot email the data, and I*

must begin the next phase of the project here. Our ability to call one another will end.”

"I know this," Petrokov said. "But it is good information. Information you can use to —"

"We do not need it, Petrokov. There are no planes that fly here. We will notice any that do.”

Petrokov waited, hoping he could get a logical jump on the man to prove his worth once again. He hated this, having to prove himself to a lesser man, in order to get into the man's good graces once again.

All politics, he thought. He needed this person to be on his side, if only to convince their superiors that Petrokov was worth a promotion. *One promotion,* he thought, *and then this ends. Then I can have actual power.*

"Fine," Petrokov said. "I am here for whatever you may need, as always."

"Our relationship ends here, Petrokov. At least for the next few days. The mission is nearing completion, and the machine cannot be stopped once it is engaged.”

"But I may be able to offer —"

"Your support ended with a spectacular shootout and the deaths of Russian agents, Petrokov.”

"And one of those deaths was of my own brother."

"I am sorry for your loss. It was poor planning to include family in a mission such as this.”

Petrokov placed his hand over the flip-phone microphone and swore. *This rat-bastard,* he thought. He wanted to scream, to tell this *civilian* how useless he truly was to the Motherland. Russia didn't need him or his stupid project. Whatever it was — whatever the *true* goal of it was — Petrokov was sure it was but a pittance compared to the long-term plans of the state. This was a simple science experiment, meant to obtain some natural resource that would be valuable for trade.

But that was it. Petrokov could not imagine what else could be so important there, so worth the secrecy and subterfuge. The risk with the United Nations was great, which meant the reward had to be that much greater. But Petrokov did not know why they had begun this project this particular way, why they had chosen a civilian scientist to lead the project instead of a military man like himself.

"My brother was a great man," Petrokov said. "He died for his country."

"And he will not be forgotten, Petrokov," came the reply. *"It does not change the mission parameters, however. Nor does it change the schedule, although it creates some problems."*

"You have a plan to take care of the Americans?" he asked. *Why wasn't I made aware of this?*

"We do. All will be well, Petrokov. Please send my update at your earliest convenience."

Without another word, the line was disconnected. Petrokov had not even told the man the number for his new phone. It was an abrasive, callous display of arrogance. One that his superiors at the Kremlin would not appreciate.

He pulled the phone in half, breaking the hinge connecting the two pieces, then tossed them into the trashcan in the hotel room. He was hungry, and he needed to think things over.

He could use this — he could use this man's arrogance against him. He just needed to think about it, to figure out exactly how.

CHAPTER 16
BEN

TWO DAYS **Later**

Ben hated planes. He didn't like the idea of defying the laws of physics, hurtling through the air tens of thousands of feet above the hard earth in a metal tube, propelled by super-flammable liquid. It just seemed... wrong.

He had never been in a situation that would have taught him this fear; it was simply because of his understanding enough about how the world worked and yet not quite enough about science. It was an intuitive fear, something he couldn't control.

And it didn't matter now, as he was currently hurtling through the air inside of one. He was terrified whenever any plane he was on took off, but landings were the worst. Aiming for a tiny strip of concrete, barely wider than the plane itself, and resting the entire massive behemoth on tiny little air-filled tires, all while slamming on the brakes and hoping the whole mess didn't just careen off the other side of the runway and into traffic.

Or as would be the case today, careen off the ice pack they would try to land on to concrete and into a mountainous crag of rock. Or worse yet, off the edge of an ice cliff and into a frozen sea.

The CSO team had been joined by Freddie and two of his

buddies, both well-trained and experienced soldiers who had served with Freddie before. The three soldiers, joined by Reggie, Sarah, Julie, and Ben, were all nearing their destination after three days of travel: they were about to touch down at Palmer Research Station off the coast of Argentina.

From there, they would depart for their actual destination: Antarctica.

They had been there before two years ago when trying to track down a communications signal picked up from an area near the South Pole. They had almost lost their lives while there, and they had lost excellent soldiers during the nightmarish mission.

And what they had found there had been nothing short of terrifying; it reminded Ben that left unchecked, evil would somehow always find a way to prevail.

He hoped what they were dealing with this time was something far simpler. Something that could be handled with words and diplomacy rather than guns and soldiers.

And yet, he had enough experience in his life to know that there was usually a reason these entities opted to set up shop at the far corners of the globe. There was usually a reason people wanted to hide.

There was usually a reason groups like the CSO would be called to find those people.

He glanced back at Freddie and his friends. All good men, capable. All smaller and shorter than Freddie, but far larger than the average human male. Each had sinewy muscles poking out beneath tight t-shirts, and each had the jawline of a G.I. Joe. They were laughing and joking amongst themselves a few rows back. Ben couldn't hear the conversation, but he remembered being their age and what topics might come up. They were most likely talking about girls and guns and video games.

He smiled and shook his head. *Damn, how old have I gotten?*

He glanced over at Julie, seated directly next to him in his row.

She smiled back and gave a minuscule nod. Whenever they boarded a plane, Julie turned into a sort of caring mother, making sure Ben felt safe and secure. Nothing she could do would really help, but it was cute, and Ben enjoyed the attention.

"Doing okay?" She asked.

He nodded. "About as well as I could expect. I think my anxiety's coming back because it knows we are about to land."

"Yeah, I feel some butterflies as well. A little of that turbulence over the ocean didn't help, either."

Ben swallowed, then looked out the window. The vast expanse of blue had turned into a vast expanse of white. Their travel had been clear of poor weather, so he could see all the way to the mountain range jutting up in the distance. For a continent as large as Antarctica, there was no place on earth as desolate and depressing.

He looked down, trying to discern one bright-white feature on the ground from another. It was impossible to survive here, and the scientists and researchers that called this place home still only served six- to twelve-month terms, cycling out with other coworkers so as not to be claimed by the depressing and pounding desolation.

"When we're wheels down, we'll have to disembark quickly," Julie said. "The brief the general wrote has us meeting with the head of the research station here within the hour."

Ben nodded. "Yeah," he said. "Seems like the general is trying to turn us all into little soldiers, whether we like it or not. I have half a mind to show up late to the meeting, just to see what the old man's going to try to do from 3,000 miles away."

Julie arched an eyebrow.

Ben held his hands up. "What?" he asked. "I'm kidding, but still. Sheesh."

Julie tossed her head backward toward Freddie. "It's not for us, Ben. It's for him. Good a soldier as he is, he's the man's nephew. There's no way in hell he's going to let down his guard when it comes to his nephew's safety."

Ben shrugged but nodded. The same protective instinct Julie had when watching Ben struggle through a takeoff and landing was probably the same feeling the general had for his nephew. Sure, the man had been trained to keep things professional and calm no matter what, but he was still human at the core.

Maybe.

The plane jostled a bit, and Ben inadvertently and involuntarily gripped the handle of his chair a bit tighter. The last time they had flown into Antarctica, they had been in the back of a cargo plane. While this cargo plane looked the same on the exterior, its interior had been retrofitted with seats, the material matching the colors of the commercial jetliner they had been purchased from. They didn't quite fit the space, either — there were nets and webbing all around them, holding gear and equipment for the scientists and researchers, as well as crates full of weapons and ammunition for the soldiers — but at least the seats were more comfortable than sitting on the hard, metal floor or in a jump seat along the curved walls of the aircraft.

It was far from luxurious, but it was a step up from their experience last time, and Ben hoped for many such step-ups this go around.

Ben heard a whistling sound, something far off and seemingly from outside of the plane. He felt the interior of the cabin go silent, even the roar of the engines seeming to lower their volume a bit. It was as if everyone on board had heard it at the same time, recognizing that it was not a normal sound, and were now all holding their collective breath.

Suddenly, the whistling stopped.

Ben perked his ears up, and exactly one second later, a section of the fuselage exploded inward, and an entire ten-foot chunk of plane simply vanished.

BEN

BEN DIDN'T REACT — he tried but couldn't. He tried working his jaw. His eyes twitched, but no words would fall out, and he couldn't blink. As soon as the hole had been ripped open, things moved outward.

...From inside the plane to the space beyond.

Crates of gear, netting, a broken row of seats. The whistling sound returned, but this time it was more intense, more like the sound of a screaming banshee. The roar of the engines whined as they increased in pitch. There was cold all around.

A sucking, life-ending cold.

Julie gripped Ben's hand in a vise, and Ben squeezed back, still unable to keep his eyes off of the gaping maw on the opposite side of the plane. The howling wind continued in a fury he had never experienced, and he felt the plane's starboard side dip.

His stomach lurched, and Julie screamed.

No, no, no. This was it. His absolute worst nightmare.

The plane's bow then dipped, turning their flight into a steep descent immediately. When he thought his stomach had jumped as far as it would go, he now found that it could ascend the entirety of his esophagus and end up in his throat.

Ben felt himself choking, trying to swallow his insides back down to where they belonged. Julie screamed louder, and he heard men's voices joining in the cacophony. One was shouting what seemed like orders; the others were simply screaming. None of the notes were in harmony. A chorus of tritones added to the mix of blistering wind and roaring engines.

Ben heard a crackle come through the aircraft's onboard speaker system. It was distant, faint. The pilot's voice cracked through tidy, poor speakers that were not in any way prepared for combating noise such as this. If the pilot had just explained to all of them how they might hope to stay alive in a plane crash, Ben hadn't heard a word of it.

It didn't matter. Ben knew the statistics. His nightmares had reminded him — day in and day out — of the chances of survival of a plane crash.

The plane dipped again, now almost vertical, and he noticed one row of seats across the aisle and behind him lift forward, then come completely unbuckled from the floor. The bolts must have worn, and the motion and impact of the explosion were too much.

It was a row with one of Freddie's soldiers and it.

The kid was wide-eyed, terrified, as he tried to click apart his seatbelt restraint. Ben couldn't focus on him — he was riveted, facing forward — but out of the corner of his eye, he saw the kid nearly break free, finally deciding to extricate himself from the seat without unbuckling his belt.

He was standing now, halfway out of the row, when the seat tumbled again, end over end in a roll, heading toward the open gash in the aircraft. Small items, paper and debris and duffel bags were still being sucked outward from the interior of the plane, and it was toward this gaping outward blast that the kid and his row of two seats tumbled.

Ben couldn't hear him, amid all the egregious noise. It was as if everything else in the world was completely silent, replaced by this monstrous turbine-like sound.

Ben watched as the kid in the tight t-shirt ripped and pulled at the tumbling row of seats, his face bloodied and smashed from an impact with the floor as it rolled once again end-over-end.

And then... they were gone. The kid, the seats — all of it.

The soldier, Freddie's friend, had simply disappeared into the white fog outside the plane.

Ben choked again, this time his own scream reaching his ears. Julie was gripping his right hand with her left, but her right hand was frantically working on something next to her. Ben wasn't sure what it was, but he knew it was hopeless. There was nothing within reach — nothing on the plane at all — that would have any hope of saving their lives.

Ben squeezed his eyes shut as he felt the roar and whine of the engines pummeling upward and forward, screaming against the never-ending onslaught of gravity. The tip of the plane pulled up, and Ben felt his stomach pushing back down into his chest, landing closer to where it actually belonged. The chaos and nightmare were everywhere, unrelenting, and the cold had finally worked its way into Ben's core. He wasn't sure if it was because they were flying thousands of feet in the air or because they were in Antarctica. Perhaps it was both.

In the split-second, before everything went black, Ben had the fleeting realization that if they somehow *did* survive this incident, the cold would surely kill them shortly thereafter.

He finally could move his head, slowly ratcheting it over to the right to look at Julie. She was staring back at him, her eyes wide, her right hand having given up whatever task it had been trying to perform.

For a moment, their eyes locked, their gaze steady amidst the tossing and tumbling world around them.

CHAPTER 18

BEN

THE BLACK NOTHINGNESS was overwhelmed only by the severe cold that had now penetrated deep into and through Ben's body. He felt like he had become one of the many trillions of pieces of ice that made up the landscape.

Ice.

There was ice here. *In the plane.* The snow had gathered and somehow entered the plane. He felt it piled on top of him, around him. He was blanketed by it, and though it was dark and he could see almost nothing farther than a few inches in front of him, he knew there was snow.

That means I'm alive...

He wasn't dead. Somehow, against all odds, against every understanding he had of aircraft flight, he was alive. The pilots had somehow lifted the nose and skied the plane onto an embankment of snow, smashing out windows and ripping off shards of fuselage and allowing snow and ice to seep into the interior of the massive cargo jet.

But he was alive.

He opened his mouth to speak and felt a horrible soreness in his throat. He tried turning his head, felt it held in place by some sort of metal bar, so he focused on his extremities instead.

Fingers, toes, all wriggling free and able to move. Cold, but no pain.

He tried his hands. One wrist ached, but there didn't seem to be anything broken. One elbow felt as though it had been crushed, but upon further examination, he realized it had just slid under the space between the window and the armrest and smacked hard against one of them during the crash.

So far, all the outward parts of his body were working and in fine order. He used his hands to feel around his torso and legs, trying to get to the spaces he couldn't reach with his eyes, as his head still couldn't move from its perch between the bars.

He slid his hand up his left side, feeling cold and ice and then —
Wet.

Blood? Ben stabbed around with his fingers, poking into the soft parts of his stomach and gut until he found it.

And it didn't take much of a poke for him to lurch, his body flying upward in the seat and smacking his shoulder against the bar that was still holding him in place.

The pain was excruciating. He clenched his jaw and poked again; a bit higher up. Again, excruciating pain.

He decided to rest, to try again later. This barbaric form of self-diagnosis was probably not helping anything, and all he needed to know was that he was injured. He had no idea how badly the injury was, but he assumed that the only reason he was not in constant pain was the fact that he was crunched into a sitting position in his chair.

Pushing aside the pain for a moment, he turned his attention to the more important question: *Where is Julie?*

The bar that was holding him in place had jostled a bit when he had involuntarily lurched upward, so he used his right hand to reach upward and push against it. With a bit more force than he had wanted to expend, causing more grief to his injury, he could push the bar up and back enough to get his head free.

He immediately felt a welt forming on his forehead and a bruise on his shoulder where the bar had been pressed against him. He must have rattled against it quite a few times as they had landed, but in the whole scheme of things, he was willing to take a welt and a bruise over something far worse.

It was still dark, so he couldn't see much of anything, and certainly not enough to get his sense of bearings about where they had gone down and in what configuration they were all in. He thought he heard a crunching sound from somewhere farther away, but he focused again on the task he had intended.

Find Julie.

With one final heave, he pulled himself forward in the seat but then groaned in agony as the deep gash in his side seemed to scream back against him. Defeated, he gave up and sat back down, panting heavily. He wasn't going to be able to move, at least not on his own, at least not right now. There was an inkling of an idea, deep in his brain, that told him he was going to die from this injury long before he died from the cold, but then he argued with himself about it.

Maybe the cold will set in first, and I'll freeze to death in less than a minute.

He truly did not know how cold it was, knowing that adrenaline and dopamine were shooting through his veins, keeping him awake and alert and alive.

For now.

He knew those chemicals would recede, leaving him very much at the whim of the elements. Elements that were not particularly keen on keeping humans alive.

He shifted sideways, eliciting yet another scream from his injury, but he was able to work his right hand over to where Julia's seat —

No.

It wasn't Julie who was missing — Julie's *seat* was gone. The entire metal frame, once attached to Ben's own chair, had been ripped away. He felt the sharp spots where it had been connected to his own only moments ago, felt the empty space as his hand hung down in the absence.

His panting grew heavier. He was going to hyperventilate — surely not a good thing for his injury. He tried speaking, but only whispers of the first half of her name rolled out. "Ju —" he croaked.

"Julie," he said it a bit louder. The pain was immense, and it was going to be the end of him. He could not continue calling out for her, not like this. He felt tension in his heart, the tightness that preceded a panic attack, much like what heart attack victims felt before the throes of cardiac arrest set in. In that moment, he would have longed for a heart attack to just take him and end it all.

He would have hoped it could have taken him *long* before the plane went down, for that matter.

Now he had cruelly survived the plane crash, only to end up barricaded in his seat in the dark, icy wasteland of Earth's southern-most continent.

Alone.

He reached down with his left hand again and felt his torso. There was more blood there now — he was able to poke at it and get blood all over his fingers without causing any pain, which only told him he was bleeding out — whatever he had done had just quickened the pace.

He wondered what it would feel like to die of blood loss. Perhaps it was like dying of exposure? Perhaps it would take him quickly. He would simply close his eyes and fall asleep, and everything would just cease to exist.

Or perhaps it was like drowning. Excruciating minutes of pure agony as he thrashed for survival against an unrelenting force that permeated his very being, and then — and only then — a final few seconds of calm, sweet bliss.

Either way, the end was inevitable. Julie had been sucked out of the plane, much like Freddie's soldier friend, and now Ben had been left here to die a slow and painful death while he thought of both of them.

And what of Reggie and Sarah? What of Freddie and his other friend? The pilot and co-pilot had to be around here somewhere as well, didn't they?

Ben almost chuckled as he imagined each of them, independently dying a slow, agonizing death only feet from each other and unable to call out for help. It wasn't funny, but in this moment, Ben wasn't thinking clearly.

He reached again for Julie's seat, feeling the tears pooling in the corners of his eyes. They hurt — almost frozen as soon as they found open air. But he didn't blink them away.

As soon as they broke free from his tear ducts, they rolled a few inches down his cheeks and completely froze in place. He saw his breath now. Whether there was actually more light or his eyes had finally adjusted a bit, he wasn't sure.

But it was there. His breath, like the tears, froze. They fell gently forward and then died, falling as droplets of ice onto his lap.

He wondered if freezing his wound was a way to postpone blood loss. He didn't know. He had never studied medicine or first aid beyond simple field-dressing of a wound. He put his hand over the spot on his side that was causing the most pain. The searing jolt of warmth hurt, then felt immediately better.

Ben dropped his head back onto the hard metal bar he had just moved out of the way and closed his eyes. He would not let this environment steal his tears for Julie, nor was he going to let it take his blood any faster. There was little control he had of the situation, but he did the only two things he could think of.

It was futile; he knew. But it was something. And he had always known he'd go down fighting.

He closed his eyes and imagined a better place. A warmer place, one with Julie alive and next to him, resting her head on his shoulder.

They were at a beach, on a honeymoon they never got to take, an imaginary vacation that had to be cut short by yet another mission.

They had argued about it, but they had both known they would take the mission. They would do the job, forgoing their own comfort and pleasure for the greater good.

It was his — and now Julie's — way of operating.

It was a shame he couldn't tell her that.

As he drifted off into the eternal sleep, a small smile grew on his face, and the tears froze his eyes shut.

CHAPTER 19

JULIE

JULIE'S EYE was plastered shut, the blood and swelling keeping it from providing any visibility. The eyeball itself wasn't injured, and it would heal in time, so she wasn't concerned about it.

She still had one good eye, and it fed more than enough information to her brain to tell her that what she was seeing was an absolute shitshow. Strewn out on the ice and snow as far to the left and right of her vision as she could see was a yard sale from hell.

The plane's fuselage had cracked and ripped down the middle, sending shards and chunks of metal and seat cushions in every direction, a few of the larger sections of seating directly in front of her now. The gash in the plane had widened as the aircraft had slid over the sharp ice, the insides of it now mostly on the outside.

There were bags and busted crates half-buried in the snow, along with streaks of dark-colored liquid that had frozen into place, forever marking this location. Likely oil, though she couldn't tell.

The pilots — both now dead — had brought the injured aircraft down on a relatively flat section of ice in a long, narrow valley. Because the runways in Antarctica were simply flattened and smoothed-down strips of ice anyway — essentially long, skinny hockey rinks — the landing hadn't been terrible. The aircraft had perished along with its pilots, but they had managed to get two of the three sets of landing gear down to at least provide a relatively safe landing.

The landing had not *felt* safe, however, and Julie had nearly broken her neck from the whiplash. Still, she was alive.

Except for the poor soul who'd been sucked out of the cabin and the two unfortunate pilots who had a front-row seat to the destruction, so were the rest of her team.

Freddie had pulled Reggie out of the aircraft, and Sarah had been able to retrieve Freddie's other soldier friend they'd met at the airport. Julie had seen the shocked, devastated looks on their faces when the two soldiers had disembarked from the crumbled mess, but in a small show of mercy, the body of their friend had landed somewhere far away.

Julie and Ben, sitting farther up in the craft, had been nearly crushed as the fuselage collapsed under its own weight, and it had taken Reggie and Freddie a lot of work to get her out. They'd ended up having to search the boxes for a tool, and finally found a pair of bolt cutters they used to tear the seat free from its mount.

Ben had proven more difficult — he was unconscious, bleeding from multiple wounds, and Julie had at first nearly gone crazy trying to pull him out. Reggie and Sarah pulled her back, calming her, while Freddie was working the large man out of the seat.

She was watching now as Freddie carried Ben's limp form out of the aircraft. Reggie ran to help, and together the two men brought Ben toward Julie, where she was waiting with a massive parka. They had each found a parka and extra clothing, and Sarah and the other soldier — a kid named Sampson — were working on starting a fire on one of the streaks of oil.

It wasn't snowing, and Julie was offered a clear view of Sarah and Sampson as they worked. Sampson spread some pieces of a seat cushion they'd ripped apart — no doubt something that would give off plenty of poisonous fumes once lit — over the frozen oil slick, while Sarah held out a match and tried to light it.

They quickly found out that the seats were fireproof, so they scrounged around and found a broken piece of a crate and some articles of clothing. That lit and they soon had a small but raging fire brewing.

Julie glanced up at Freddie and Reggie as they carried Ben over to her. She felt her heart rising in her throat. She hadn't yet asked the question that had been nagging at her. Ben had been alive when they'd taken her and her seat out of the aircraft, but he'd quickly thereafter fallen asleep and ended up unconscious.

She wasn't sure what his injuries were, only that it looked like something had struck his head and that he was bleeding from his side.

Neither man met Julie's eyes. They set Ben down on top of a parka Julie had spread on the snow, slowly and carefully, then Freddie tucked another parka over his still body. His head was bare, but no one moved to cover it. They needed to examine him.

Julie sniffed, feeling her breath catch in her throat. It wasn't from the cold. She extracted herself from the snow and stood, then crouched next to Ben's body.

Still, no one spoke. Sarah and Sampson were preoccupied with the fire, neither daring to look up. Julie wanted to scream, but the cold suddenly found its way into her through every pore of bare skin. She shuddered, then reached a hand out.

Suddenly Ben coughed, a choking, pained sound.

Julie gasped, pulling her hand over her mouth.

Ben coughed again, and Reggie fell to his knees, placing his hands on Ben's chest, preparing to do chest compressions.

"Wait," Julie said. "I think — I think he's cleared it. He's breathing normally now."

She too placed a hand on her husband's chest and felt the gentle, rhythmic breaths. He inhaled a choppy, forced breath, but then as he released and inhaled again, the breaths became more normalized.

Finally, he blinked. His eyes were mere slits, but she could see the pupils sliding around beneath the eyelids.

He swallowed, breathed for a few more seconds, then finally spoke. His face was still staring straight up at the hazy white of the sky.

"So... this place is incredible. Which one of you is going to tell me I've died and gone to heaven?"

BEN'S HEAD was killing him. He wanted to shove his entire face and forehead into the snow to bury himself up to his neck. He couldn't imagine how it would feel if it *wasn't* below freezing out here.

He groaned in pain as Reggie and Sarah finished packing the makeshift wrap around his wound. The cut he'd suffered from the plane crash was deep, but the bleeding had slowed, and he was sure he'd be able to walk well enough in a day or so.

The problem was that they might not *have* a day or so — from what they could all tell, they were stranded in the middle of a massive plane of ice and snow, mountains in all directions but for one, and in that one direction was ocean.

There were no buildings anywhere in sight. No humans besides the ones directly around him.

The pilots had perished in the accident, as had the young soldier who'd been sucked out of the plane after the side of the plane had been ripped apart. Ben tried not to envision his face when he closed his eyes, but keeping them open against the wind seemed to hurt more.

"You okay?" Julie asked. "Your wound seems to be healing already."

"It's just because it's frozen solid," Ben said. "I bet if this were the desert, I'd have melted all the blood out by now."

"That's disgusting," Reggie said.

"That's scientifically *impossible*, too," Sarah said. She offered Ben a smile. "Glad you made it."

Ben nodded, his eyes inadvertently bouncing over to Freddie. The huge bear-shaped soldier was sitting next to his soldier friend. Neither man was talking much.

"How's he doing?" Ben asked.

Reggie shrugged. "Lost a good man today. Probably happened before, too, but never... like this."

"Yeah," Ben said. "No shit."

"So, what's next?" Julie asked. "We're... probably going to want a plan."

Ben's eyebrows rose. "You're not waiting for me to decide, are you? I mean, you could have been hauling my fat ass back to the nearest Applebee's all this time, and instead, you waited for me to —"

"Applebee's sucks, man," Reggie said, cutting him off. "Chili's, maybe. But if Applebee's is it, I'd probably rather stay out here and —"

"Don't finish that sentence, please," Sarah said. She turned back to Ben. "Well, now that you're awake, I guess it's time to fill you in on what's been happening here."

"What — what's been happening?" Ben asked. He looked around at their makeshift campsite. "I thought it was pretty simple. Plane died, we almost did, now we're stuck."

"Well..." Julie looked away.

"What?" he asked again. "All right, look. This ain't the time to be cryptic."

"Right," Reggie said. "So, look. You see the plane over there?"

Ben squinted through the haze of fresh-falling snow. The fuselage of the cargo plane was half-buried in fresh powder, but Ben could see the jagged lines of the blackened burn marks striping up from the ice and covering the back half of the object. *Where it slid,* he realized.

The plane was cracked in half around the mark where the side had been splintered open midflight, and the front of the fuselage, and no doubt the dead pilots inside, was lying about two hundred feet farther away. It was almost impossible to see.

"What about it?"

"Well, you said the plane 'died.' That's… not entirely accurate."

"What's that supposed to mean. Planes live in the sky; this one stopped flying. That's the problem."

"Ben," Julie said, her hand on his arm. "Ben, look again."

He squinted once more, trying to understand what had his team all riled up. It took him a moment, but then he noticed. "Oh," he said. "Oh, shit."

"Yeah."

The fuselage section he had been in, the one closest to them, had a massive round hole in the side of it. He'd seen it happen in real-time, so he hadn't noticed it until that moment. But now that they'd pointed it out, it was clear as day.

The hole hadn't been caused by a mechanical failure. It wasn't a failure of engineering, or simply a freak accident.

The hold had been *blasted* out of the airplane. By something monstrous. Something explosive.

"We were attacked, man," Reggie said, finally putting words to what Ben had just realized. "We were shot down."

"Yeah," Ben said, nodding along. "Yeah, I can see that. That means —"

Julie continued. "It means we probably don't have to wait long out here, and we might not have to even walk back to civilization if we could even find it."

"Because they'll be coming for us," Ben said. "But —"

"Right," she interrupted, "they're probably only coming to finish the job."

He felt a tug on his arm, and Freddie was there suddenly, hovering over him. "Hey, boss man," Freddie said. "Glad you're doing okay and all, but I wanted to mention that, uh, we see something."

"What?"

Reggie and Sarah shot up, focusing in the direction Freddie was now pointing. His soldier friend was rummaging through a case, probably looking for something to arm himself with.

Ben couldn't see anything at first, but a minute passed, and he suddenly recognized the flash of shadows against the ice. He watched them materialize over the course of another minute, finally realizing how quickly they were moving. He saw they weren't running on their own, but riding atop large, flat vehicles that plowed over the snow as if it wasn't there. There were also larger ATV-looking vehicles with glass-enclosed cabins and smaller traditional-style ice trawlers.

He watched them advance onto their position, seeing now the details. The uniforms were all matching. Perhaps six people in total, all of them bearing down on Ben's group.

All of them carrying guns.

CHAPTER 21
BEN

THE FIRST THING Ben noticed was the heat. Compared to the below-freezing temperature outside combined with a windchill factor that plummeted the effective temperature down into depths he couldn't even imagine, the heat inside felt almost stifling.

And if he wasn't already in severe pain from his injured side, he may have actually enjoyed the warmth.

The Tucker Sno-Cat they were riding in had split off with another vehicle, heading to a simple ice-encrusted doorway one man had swung open. They were all pushed along by four black-clad soldiers, roughly tossed down a staircase that led to a wider, dimly lit hallway. The door behind them swung shut, and the noise was sucked out of the space. He heard the telltale sound of a locking mechanism sealing the door shut from the outside.

He tried to make mental notes for conjuring later, but Ben was woozy and unstable. He knew he was bleeding, and he knew if it continued, he'd have far bigger problems.

The second thing he noticed was that at the bottom of this staircase, Julie and Sarah had been plucked away from the group and sent down the hall in a completely different direction. He, Reggie, and the two soldiers may have argued, but in the state they were in, and the fact that their captors were brandishing shining black subcompact machine guns, meant they couldn't do anything about it.

The third thing Ben noticed was that Julie and Sarah had, in fact, been sent down a *hallway*. Only then did he consider how strange this all was. They'd been corralled into a tiny space beneath the Antarctic ice, through a modern metal doorway, but then into an ancient-looking space that seemed to have been formed in stone.

He figured he was hallucinating, as it seemed odd there were any structures large enough on this continent to be big enough to house a true, actual hallway. Yet that was exactly what he was looking at. He winced as the soldier — a giant, generic Russian who hadn't had the common decency to introduce himself — yanked Ben's arm and pulled him to the side, sending him toward another doorway whose metal door stood open, leading to another space. He pushed Ben along, Reggie and the two American soldiers just behind.

The soldier holding Ben's arm barked something in Russian at another similar-looking man standing guard just inside this doorway. He couldn't understand what words were exchanged, but it didn't seem to have any effect whatsoever on the soldier's mishandling of Ben's injury. He felt blood oozing from his wound as the man forced him over the threshold.

The floor beneath him felt uneven. He looked down and realized again that it seemed to be lined in stone. The smooth surfaces of the rocks rubbed raw beneath his boots. He couldn't figure out what it was about the place that struck him as odder — that someone would build a building out here, or that they would do it using stone. As if these people had cut tunnels into the ice and then chosen to lay linoleum. He wondered if these Russian assholes had a secret affinity for interior design.

Yeah, I must be hallucinating, Ben thought.

The four male members of the CSO group were left in the room, the guard leaving. The space they were in was similarly decorated —

stone floors, walls, and ceiling. No other insignia or designs anywhere to be found.

Ben quickly saw that this space was not actually a singular space, but an antechamber that led to multiple open spaces, each separated by a narrow, deep inset doorway. Three in total, one against each wall, not including the doorway he had just been shoved through. As soon as all four of them were in the main space, the Russian soldier pushing Ben backpedaled and slammed the door.

"What the hell?" Reggie yelled. "Who the hell are you guys? And where the hell —"

"Hello," a new voice called out. It had come from the room to Ben's left. "Welcome to... ice base," the man said. The voice was heavily accented, also clearly Russian.

Ben turned to face the doorway, trying to brace himself for whatever might show. Rather than being met with another large, brooding Russian soldier, Ben suddenly saw a relatively small, thin man with glasses. He had a shaved head and looked to be about Ben's age. "Ice base?" Ben asked.

The man nodded. "Well, that's what we are calling it anyway since none of us knows its true name or purpose. Where did you come from?"

Ben wasn't entirely sure what he meant, so he stuck to the basics. "We are Americans. Plane crash. They came and grabbed us. About twenty in all, though we were split off from most of them."

The man frowned but didn't offer any feedback.

"And where the hell did *you* come from?" Reggie asked. Ben noticed that Freddie and his soldier friend were huddled close together against the wall nearest the doorway they had entered from. Neither of the younger men had spoken.

"We are scientists," the man answered. "Well, me and two of the others here, as well as two women who are in the women's chambers."

"Yeah, what's up with that?" Reggie asked. "We had two ladies with us as well who were *unceremoniously* removed from my group. I'd love to have a word with whatever assholes thought that was a smart move."

"They need to make sure you are not American soldiers," the man said, as if that explained everything. Freddie raised an eyebrow but said nothing.

"So, what if we are?" Ben asked. "Seems a little sexist to assume that only men can be soldiers, right?"

The man shrugged and motioned with his palms up. "I'm just a scientist. But they want to make sure we are who we say we are."

"We have told no one who we are yet," Reggie snapped. "I'd love to, but no one out there seems to speak English."

"They will come, and they will want to know everything. Best you tell them the truth."

Ben wanted to laugh. "And why is that? Let me guess, they're angry Russian soldiers thinking Americans are here to spy on their little operation and report back home to Uncle Sam?"

Ben could immediately see from the look in the man's eyes that he had gotten rather close to the truth. "Let me assure you," he said, "none of us are soldiers. None of us are here to hurt anyone."

He didn't glance at Reggie, Freddie, or the other man standing next to him. He tried to remember the kid's name but could only recall the name of the other young soldier, the one whom he'd watched get sucked out the side of the plane. *Scott, Scotty, something like that*. He made a mental note to do better with names.

As if on cue, the Russian man in front of him reached forward and shook Ben's hand. "Names Evgeni Volkov," the smaller man said. "We've been here for about three days. They feed us well, and we are mostly free to move around. I think they are trying to keep us safe as much as find out what we are doing here."

Ben had too many questions. He wasn't sure where to start, so he was glad Reggie stepped in to begin. "Speaking of a place to keep us safe, it *is* nice and warm in here. What the hell is this place?"

CHAPTER 22

BEN

BEN LOOKED AROUND AGAIN. There was some ice on the walls, but only in cracks that were farther down to the ground, on or near the floor. Anything above that glistened and dripped from contact with the heat. Did that mean they really were underground? And how was this place heated?

"We are not sure," the man said, answering his earlier question. "It seems to be some sort of Russian base, but not one I have heard of."

"Trust me, it's not one *anyone* in the world has heard of, either. The US was absolutely not informed there was any sort of Russian operations down here in this area."

The man nodded. "Yes, yes, we know. My team was sent down here on a research mission. We were picked up — not gently, I might add — by these Russian soldiers. My own countrymen. It seems their mission differs vastly from ours."

"And what was your mission, exactly?" Ben asked.

"Research, that is it. We were taking ice core samples there when we found something interesting and sent the results back home. Within a day of returning to our ship off the coast, we were picked up by these guys and brought here."

"Back to the first question," Reggie said. "Where is *here*?"

"We do not know," Evgeni said, shrugging. "Best we can gather, it is somewhere on the peninsula where our ship was docked. None of us have been upstairs to see if there are any recognizable landmarks nearby."

"So, that means we are underground?"

Evgeni nodded. "Yes, it seems to be so. And none of us have seen that door up there opened for any reason until you showed up. We believe it is a failsafe — an exit, for emergency only. You'll notice the door was twice as thick and insulated. That's probably how they are keeping this place warm. Deep geothermal vents, perhaps? We are not sure."

"Who's *we*?" Freddie asked, stepping forward. He reached a hand out, and it completely enveloped Evgeni's. "Name's Freddie, and I'm with these three. This is Scott Sampson, but we call him Gator."

That's it, Ben thought. *Gator.* He had been told the man's name and nickname but couldn't for the life of him remember either.

Freddie continued. "I'm not sure what the hell's going on here, but I don't like for a single second the fact that my buddies and I were plucked off the surface of the earth *after* someone shot our plane down, then forced to come here against our will. I do like the warm air, so I guess that's a good start, though."

It appeared Evgeni wasn't sure how to take the great bear of a man and his deep southern drawl. He shifted a bit on his feet, glancing at each of the four men. Gator was wearing a half-grin, leaning against the wall and chewing the inside of his lip.

"Well," Evgeni said. "Nice to meet you, Freddie and Mr.... Gator. I feel the same way you do about being brought here against your will."

"You keep saying *we*," Freddie said. "Are there more of you?"

Evgeni nodded. "My team of four is all here in these rooms some-where. Luka is in the mess hall getting food just down the hall. The two women in my group, Tatiana and Mia, are somewhere on the other side of the base. My best guess is that your two women have joined them in their quarters and are getting acquainted."

"Can we see them?" Reggie asked.

"Let me rephrase that for my friend here," Ben said. "We are *going* to see them, and we are going to see them *now*. Where are they?"

Evgeni looked shaken. "I — I'm not sure that's a good idea. The Russian soldiers here need to debrief everyone and make sure —"

"I didn't sign up to be interrogated by no Russian soldier," Freddie said, his chest expanding. "And by my count, I see one scrawny little Russian nerd and a couple of other Russian goons that probably won't take much work, if you know what I mean."

Ben placed a hand on Freddie's chest. "No reason to get worked up, bud," Ben said. "Let's play this by ear; see how things work out. If anyone here thinks we need to talk to one of these Russian knobs first, we will."

He wanted to believe this guy; he wanted to trust that he was being told the truth. That the Russians had merely brought them here to make sure they weren't American spies.

But there were two things wrong with that assumption: first, from the perspective of these Russians, Ben wondered if they might actually *be* spies. Their mission here was vague on purpose; they had been sent down here to investigate whatever it was these Russians were doing — to find out if there was any sort of foul play they needed to worry about, and whether they needed to call in the big guns from back home.

Ben had a sneaking suspicion that to anyone, that sort of thing would seem an awful lot like espionage.

The second problem he had with his assumption was that the reason for what they had just been through was still unanswered. He still had an injury, and he and his team had been brought here against their will, pushed and jostled around like cattle in a slaugh-terhouse.

And no one had yet answered the *real* questions on all their minds: why the hell had their plane been shot out of the sky?

And who had done it?

CHAPTER 23

JULIE

JULIE FELT her heart rate rising as soon as she had been separated from Ben. This was a foreign place, in the most inhospitable landscape on the planet, and their hosts had so far not been any less hostile after being separated from the men. Julie and Dr. Sarah Lindgren had been tossed into a small room, hewn from the same stone as the rest of the place they had walked through, and quickly found that they were not alone.

They had joined two other women, both Russian, who had greeted them with questioning and confused expressions.

It hadn't taken long for all four women to introduce themselves to one another and realize that neither of them was a threat to each other. They had been part of a Russian research team taking ice core samples for further environmental research, and Julie began to hit it off with one woman, Tatiana, who seemed to have taken a liking to her as well.

They swapped quick stories about how they all ended up here — both Russian women aghast that the two newcomers had survived a plane crash not two hours prior, but Julie was more concerned with figuring out what their next move should be.

"So, you are free to move around in here? Even though these soldiers are holding you hostage?" Julie asked.

"Oh, well, it is not like that," the woman replied. "They are asking us questions to find out whom we are really working for, to see if we are spying on the Russian government.

"Yeah, you mentioned that," Sarah said. "But doesn't this seem like an awful place to be spying on the Russian government? Who would send spies to Antarctica hoping to find Russian political strategists?"

The researcher seemed to not understand what Sarah was talking about. She turned to Julie and addressed her instead. "Truth be told, I am glad we are here, where it is warm and dry at least, compared to the boat. The *Rezak* was no warmer than the ice out on the expeditions, it seemed. And the food here is not bad, either."

"But how long will you be here?" Julie asked. "They can't just keep us all indefinitely."

The woman shook her head. "No, of course not. We think they are going to take us back to our boat in another day or so."

"Have they said that?"

The two Russian women exchanged a glance, then both shook their heads. "Not really..." she said. "But where else would we go? Why would they hold us here?"

"That's exactly the question I'm going to find an answer to," Sarah said. "First, though, I think we need to get reunited with the rest of the group. Why did they take all the men and separate them from the women?"

"They assume the men are soldiers. American or Russian spies."

Sarah frowned. "Women can't be soldiers?"

She shrugged. "I guess they are a little more traditional here."

"And if you are all Russian, and the soldiers are all Russian, shouldn't you all be on the same side?"

"Yes — assuming whatever this all is about has something to do with furthering the Russian goal. But it seems pretty obvious that they are not taking any chances, for whatever reason."

Julie could guess the reasons, but she didn't want to. They all ended with this brief stay becoming a much longer and more painful experience. She looked around once again, realizing for the hundredth time that this was not some simple humanitarian mission, and it certainly was not a vacation.

Wherever they were, it seemed to have been purpose-built for keeping people safely inside, away from the elements.

Or keeping people securely inside. Locked up, like a frozen underground prison.

She felt the chill and rubbed her upper arms with her hands. "This place gives me the creeps," Julie said. "Why would your country build such a place, especially way out here? These rooms, too — it seems like they were expecting a lot more people to show up."

Tatiana nodded. "Yes, that is what we assume as well. As of right now, we have only seen a handful of Russian soldiers, maybe five or six, as well as a few other countrymen who are wearing civilian clothes. Mostly the soldiers come here, but we believe there is another space somewhere we are not allowed to go, where the other people are."

"All those 'other people' were who brought us here," Sarah said. "They plucked us off the ice and brought us here."

"But there is a lot of food, and the infrastructure we have seen in the base suggests they are prepared for more."

"And you said we are free to move around?"

"Eventually, yes. But they will want to ask you some questions first to make sure you are not lying to them."

Just then, the door opened. It was a large metal thing, bolted into the stone and ice surrounding it. It was the only non-natural looking structure around besides the work lights hanging from the mounts on the ceiling. Julie had seen three just like this one on the way down here, not including the massive double-paned door that led down here.

A huge Russian man with a scar for a smile entered the room and looked Julie and Sarah up and down. Julie was almost impressed at his ability to simultaneously check them out and show disdain. "You — come with," he said, motioning two big, beefy fingers at Julie and Sarah. He flicked his hand toward the door and hallway behind, where Julie could see the shoulder of another similarly shaped soldier.

"I heard there was food," Julie said. "Any chance I can grab a burger and fries before we get interrogated?"

The man frowned, either not understanding or not caring to humanize the twisted conch shell he wore as a facial expression. "Now," he said. "Food later."

He stepped out of the room, waiting with his counterpart while Julie and Sarah decided what to do. Julie shrugged, then looked at Sarah. "I'm guessing we don't have much of a choice," she said.

"I'm guessing you're right," Sarah answered. "I don't like these guys, and I'm not sure what to think of these two nice ladies, but something tells me the only way we're going to get real answers is to follow this sack of meat. Besides, it sounds like the food's on the house if we just listen to the timeshare presentation first."

Julie smiled and nodded, then followed Sarah out of the room.

CHAPTER 24
REGGIE

"YOU ARE AMERICANS," the man said. It wasn't a question.

"*You* shot my plane down."

"You are Americans," he repeated.

"You shot my —" Reggie laughed. "You know what, asshole? I'm tired of this. It's a game — it always is. Who put you up to this? You got anything else? Maybe Scrabble, Monopoly? Both are great American classics. Oh, wait — did I just out myself? Shit, I think the jig is up." He raised his palms outward in mock surrender. "Now you know the truth, that I *am* an American."

"You are American spy."

"See, now that's where I feel like you're not really listening."

"You are American —"

"Save it, meatface," Reggie said, smacking his hands against the top of the metal table he was sitting behind. He stood up but immediately felt two vice grip-like hands on his shoulders, pushing him back down into the chair. He didn't resist. He clucked his tongue and smirked. "*Two* meatfaces, it is? You boys think I can't take on two of you rinky-dink Russian nesting dolls?"

"You are American —"

"Are you really going to ask the same question over and over? Is that your interrogation tactic? You hope that you'll, what — annoy the hell out of me, and I'll suddenly crack and reveal all my deep, dark secrets?" Reggie sighed. "Okay, I'll make this interesting for both of us, in that case. You asked the same stupid question, and I will give you a different answer each time. Each of them will be *truthful* answers, but none of them will be the answer you're looking for."

"You are American —"

"Apple pie. Favorite dessert, hands-down. Wait — cheesecake is probably up there, but I can never really — you know what, let's call it apple pie. That's the most American answer."

"You —"

"Nineteen, been dating her for a few months, but it was high school, you know? Even took her out to a nice spot outside of town, like my granddad would've done. You know, that's also somewhat of an American tradition. You guys have anything like that back in the Motherland?"

"You are —"

"Ex-Army. Sniper. Ranger, actually. Never great at the 'following orders' part, but pretty damn good at the 'shooting people in the head from really far away' part." Reggie leaned forward and smashed his elbows on the table. The metal top and legs shook and rattled, sending a shockwave into the stony, icy floor.

For a moment, both men stared at each other. Both of them had been trained for just this sort of occasion, both men likely wanting nothing more than to dispense with the pleasantries and start going to blows.

One could dream, Reggie thought. He wondered what Ben was doing in the next room over, or Freddie and Gator back in the space they had just left. He and Ben had been plucked from their new quarters and told to wait in these makeshift interrogation chambers while the other two men stayed behind.

It didn't give Reggie a lot of answers, but it gave him enough:

whatever this place was, it was understaffed. They only had enough crew to interrogate two men at a time.

It also told Reggie that they were, for the time being, out of direct danger. If either of these guys had any interest in *actually* trying to extract answers out of him or Ben, they long since would have resorted to some sort of physical punishment for insubordination.

As it stood, however, Reggie wasn't so sure this method was less effective than straight-up torture. He was getting past the point of being annoyed to the point of actively wanting to reach across the table and gouge the man's eyeballs out with his fingers.

He had asked the same question almost twenty-five times now. It didn't make the man come across as a very strong negotiator.

That led him to think the man standing behind him — the one who had pushed him down into the chair — was the *real* power in the room. The real boss.

Reggie swiveled in the chair and turned his head up to look at this guy. "You in charge here? Surely you can't be stupider than this guy, right? I mean, you've got to have more English in you besides just 'you are Americans,' right?"

The man looked down at Reggie, his eyes examining him, then his mouth broke into a tight-lipped smile. "Very well, you are correct. But that does not change the fact that we need to know the truth. Who are you, and why are you here?"

Exasperated, Reggie put his hands up again. "I was in an airplane, minding my own damned business when somebody shot a hole out of the side of it — sucking out one of my teammates, I might add — and now I'm here. Why don't *you* tell *me* why I'm here?"

"Planes do not fly this far south."

Reggie cocked an eyebrow. "Well, I've got the remains of an otherwise perfectly good airplane out there on the ice that might challenge that assessment."

"I fear you have misunderstood me," the giant Russian man said. "Planes *do not* fly this far south."

Reggie stuck his tongue into the inside of his cheek. *Okay, guy. Playing ball the smart way. It's going to be riddles and parables from here on out.* "Fine," Reggie said. "Thought we would do some sightseeing."

"And what sights have you seen?"

Now Reggie shrugged. "Didn't get to experience much of the scenery before the aforementioned explosion in the sky."

"What are you hoping to accomplish here?"

"What are *you* hoping to accomplish here?"

"I represent a party interested in secrecy."

"Let me guess: is it the Russian government? It's the Russian government, isn't it?"

The tight-lipped smile didn't waver. "This party has reason to believe the United States of America is sticking its nose into the operations of this project."

"Well, as far as *I* know, the United States has a perfectly good reason to be down here on this ice cube. I don't, however, think that *your* country does. So which one of us is supposed to be here?"

Reggie turned and faced the man seated across from him. "Let me guess: 'you are American,' right?" Reggie roared in laughter, wondering if it was the adrenaline still firing on overdrive that was making him delirious, or if some of the alcohol from four days ago had somehow not worked its way through his system.

"Speaking of alcohol," Reggie said, "I could use a beer right about now. You guys have a liquor store around here? I'll even take some vodka if that's all you've got."

CHAPTER 25

BEN

BEN LOOKED AT REGGIE. "They interrogate you as well?"

Reggie smirked. "If you can call asking the same question a hundred times in a row an interrogation, I guess."

"You tell them anything?" Ben asked.

"Yeah, sure," Reggie replied. "I told them everything: we were flying, then we weren't, then we ended up here. There's really not much else to tell."

Ben cocked an eyebrow and stared at Reggie quizzically.

"Come on, brother. You know I didn't spill the beans about any of the top-secret government CSO stuff." Ben just nodded and turned back to Freddie and Gator. "What about you guys?"

Gator shrugged. "Nothing, really. I think they've identified you two as the brains of the operation and us as the brawn. Only question they asked me was my name."

Reggie laughed. "What did you tell them?"

"They don't seem to get the idea of nicknames. Whatever, their loss. It's a sweet nickname."

Ben paced through the stone rooms once more. He and Reggie had returned at the same time, then Gator and Freddie had been questioned and then returned to the cell. The scientist, Evgeni, was lying on a cot in the room off to the left of the main chamber. Sometime while Ben and Reggie were gone, he had been joined by his teammate, Luka, who was asleep on his own cot in the other space.

Ben entered the chamber where Evgeni was lying down. "Wondered if I could bug you for a minute," Ben said.

Evgeni nodded, rubbed his eyes, and sat on the edge of the cot. "Of course."

"Well, seeing as how you and your guys haven't tried to kill us yet, I guess that means we are on the same side."

"I'm not sure we could kill any of you if we wanted to," Evgeni said, winking. He waited for Ben to react, then swallowed and straightened his back when he didn't. "Of course, you are correct. We have no reason to harm any of your team. I assume the feeling is mutual?"

"So far," Ben said. "These handlers of ours — obviously Russian soldiers — they seem to want to know the answer to only one question: are we American spies? We aren't, but I'm not sure there's anything we can do or say to convince them otherwise. Thing is, playing that game is a two-way street. I would be hard-pressed to believe these guys aren't the ones who shot our plane down."

Evgeni's eyes widened, then narrowed. "I assume you are correct, Mr. Bennett. They have shown us no harm so far, but they seem to believe everyone around them is a threat. If they had the means to shoot your plane out of the sky, I wholeheartedly believe they would have taken the opportunity."

"And do you think they have the means?" Ben asked.

"Who knows what is on the surface of this station? We have been cooped up in here for days, awaiting any news from the outside world. For all we know, we are prisoners of the Russian government and will all be forgotten down here. None of us have seen sunlight, which is a terrible pain for Antarctic researchers like us."

Ben nodded. "Yeah, I can see that. Here's the deal, though. I have no interest in being anyone's prisoner. Certainly not the Russian government and certainly not in this frozen hell. I'm getting out of here, and I'm getting my team out with me. I am more than happy to bring you and your guys along as well, but I need your word that you aren't playing both sides of this."

Evgeni seemed concerned and confused. "How — how would we be playing both sides of this?"

Ben shook his head. "You tell me, Evgeni. You don't seem to be a soldier, but that doesn't mean you're harmless. You are the only guy around who speaks fluent English *and* Russian, so it makes sense that you would be the one interacting with us the most."

"I can assure you, we have no interest in harming you or your team. We are just as confused as you are as to why we are all here, and we are just as eager to escape."

"Okay," Ben said. "It's not like we have much of an option either way. Trusting you helps both of us for the time being, so we'll leave it at that."

Evgeni nodded, then curled his lip to the side. "There is a question, though: where will we even go once we are out? We are in Antarctica, right? None of us were drugged when we were brought here, so we know we are still close to where we were when we were picked up. You have expressed to the same — that your plane went down a few miles from here, correct?"

Ben nodded. "Yes, definitely. We haven't gotten there yet, but we'll have an answer. These guys may play the dumb soldier act, but dumb soldiers have smart commanders, and smart commanders have brilliant generals. If this is all part of some political game, there's much more beneath the surface — or above, in this case — than just five or six guys walking around a sub-Antarctic base. They have support somewhere, even though we can't see it. That is our number one priority: find a way to communicate with the outside world or find a way to get away from this place and head toward one of the other American or British bases nearby."

CHAPTER 26

BEN

EVGENI NODDED. "Yes, yes. That is a good plan. My team will aid you in any way possible."

"And that leads me to one more question as well," Ben said, hoping to keep the small man talking. He knew that any information was good information. If they couldn't use it immediately, they might be able to use it later. "Is there anything you can provide us with now? Any information you think is necessary? About the guards, or who they're ultimately working for? You have been here longer than us, and you say it is a relatively free space to move about in. Some sort of mess hall? What about offices? Is there somewhere that seems to be a bridge or control tower?"

Evgeni shook his head. "Sadly, not much. The guards all stay in one of the rooms down the hall. My teammate Luka scoped it out earlier. It is like this one. There is another steel door bolted to the frame, just like every other space. We have been in all of these rooms except the guards' room, but they are seen entering and leaving multiple times a day, so that is our best guess as to what is beyond that door. They do not talk to us much, mostly to deliver orders or tell us to get back to our rooms. I overheard two of them whispering to each other about something called 'Gorod,' but it sounded like they were simply discussing off-topic trivialities."

Ben took mental notes, hoping to compare them with Reggie and the others later. For now, he wanted to keep Evgeni talking, to either hear the man slip up or to hear him give Ben more information he could try to put together with the other pieces of the puzzle.

"And it is not a mess hall, just another room like this one, but larger."

"Where does the food come from?" Ben asked.

"The guards have a kitchen in their space; we see two of them carrying it out multiple times a day."

Ben frowned. "That doesn't seem likely, Evgeni. They are sleeping and cooking in the room that is supposed to be no larger than these? And where are they storing all that food? For that matter, where is it all coming from in the first place? Are we talking nonperishable goods like canned food and chips?"

"No, not at all. The food is decent, obviously frozen and thawed before cooking. They have offered drinking water, also cola, and I've even seen one of the Russian soldiers with a can of beer."

"I see. And you have only seen five or six guards?"

And again, he nodded. "Yes, there are two or three on duty, while two or three more are in the guards' chambers. They have a rotation, but we have not paid close enough attention to understand the rhythm and timing of it all."

"That's okay. Our guys can figure that out pretty quickly. Most likely, just a standard security guard operation."

"We have overheard two names of the guards, but they rarely converse with one another when they are on duty, nor with us. We assume it is to keep up the ruse and prevent us from feeling comfortable here."

"Well, they are feeding you and staying out of your way, for the most part, right?"

"Yes, they are. But that is like saying we are free to move around a small condominium or apartment, but we can never step foot outside."

"Yeah, I understand that completely."

"So, what do we do now?" Evgeni asked. "I can introduce you to the female counterparts of our crew, and I would like to meet yours as well. We know the room they are in, and I am sure they are all getting along together just fine. After that, should we get something to eat and discuss your plans on getting out of here?"

Ben looked around one more time. The stone wall looked like a cobblestone path; the smooth rocks frozen in place because of the temperature of the ice behind them. It was a remarkably odd choice for building material, especially here. Ben knew Antarctica was an actual continent, with real earth and dirt beneath its masses of ice. Had they been taken that far down into the earth's crust? Were they underneath the entire ice shelf, and this facility had been erected from stones normally hidden beneath it?

If that were true, it would have been an absolutely massive under-taking. He could think of a dozen better ways to get a job like this done, and he wasn't even an architect.

No, what he was looking at was something more. It didn't fit — none of it fit. Why their plane had been blasted out of the sky, why they had all been taken and questioned immediately, and why this team of Russian researchers was also seemingly at odds with the Russians themselves.

"Food is always welcome," Ben said, finally addressing Evgeni's question. "And we can talk plans later." *After I figure one out,* he thought. "First, however, I think our teams should get together and start chatting about the real question that's been nagging at me."

"And what question is that, Mr. Bennett?"

"Please, call me Ben. And the question is simple: what type of research were you all doing down here? And what did you find that caused the Russians to freak out and throw you in this stone prison?"

THE WALK to the space they were calling the mess hall was just as short as Evgeni promised. They found Julie and the rest of the women already seated behind the two tables inside. Ben rushed over and hugged Julie, ignoring the pain in his side until she began poking and prodding at it, questioning if he was okay and if he needed more bandages.

He waved her away, eyeing the meager display of food on the table. A plate of hot dogs and a bowl of mashed potatoes sat huddled on one side of the food table, near a yellow paste in a jar that he had to assume was mustard. Plastic plates and forks sat on the other side, and in-between them all in the center of the table was a pyramid of sodas and water.

"They built a little pyramid," Evgeni said, smiling. "They never built a pyramid for us."

Reggie shrugged. "I guess we are VIPs. Maybe we'll even get a room upgrade. Luxury-class instead of stone floors."

Julie followed Ben to the food table, and he began picking out two room temperature hotdogs and placing them on his plate. There were no buns, no napkins, and besides the yellow paste, nothing to put on the dog. He typically ate his with ketchup, mustard, and relish, and he often even spread some mayo between the split bun, but today he would have to adapt. Food was fuel, and he needed fuel.

"Everything going okay?" Julie asked. Her voice was low, no doubt trying to keep out of earshot of the others in case Ben wanted to alert her to something important.

Ben nodded. "About as well as it can be, being held captive in an underground stone building by cryptic Russians after your plane gets shot out of the sky," he answered.

"Do you think they're the ones who did it?"

"I do, though it seems a little far-fetched that they were working alone. A handful of dudes? Doesn't seem likely they'd have a state-of-the-art surface-to-air missile defense system just parked upstairs. Whatever did the job requires some pretty serious tech, and I have seen nothing like that around here yet."

"One woman in our room said there is a guards' area. Maybe there's something in there?"

"Yeah, I got the spiel as well. I'm not convinced they're guards' quarters, though. Apparently, all the food comes out of there. Seems like there's more to this place than just these little stone rooms, and I'd bet my life the secret is behind those doors."

Julie nodded. "Oh yeah, without a doubt. There's something else here, but they are keeping us at arms' distance away until they know exactly who we are."

"Did you tell them?"

"Not even our names," Julie said. "They didn't ask for them, though, strangely enough. Just asked if you guys were spies and told us to prove that you weren't. We all just said we were here for research, though I'm pretty sure that story broke down." She laughed. "I told them I was here to study penguins."

Ben rolled his eyes. "Really? Penguins?"

"What? They caught me off guard! How was I supposed to know we would have to have a cover story? That should have been in the general's brief, don't you think?"

"I think a lot of things, but I try not to. Anyway, what did Sarah tell him?"

"You know her — she's too smart for her own good. She told them we were here to get ice core samples, which I guess is a pretty common thing to do in Antarctica."

"It's sort of like the mini golf of the south," Ben said. "They don't have a lot of movie theaters around here, I suspect, so ice core sampling must be the thing to do on the weekends."

Julie chuckled. They walked over and found a chair at one of the folding tables, where Reggie and Sarah and the two American soldiers were seated already. Evgeni's group had melded together once again and were seated at their own table.

"You told them what we were supposed to be drilling for, right?" Julie asked, addressing Sarah.

Dr. Lindgren nodded and smiled. "I just said we are measuring historic weather patterns."

"Yeah, that's almost generic enough to be believable," Reggie said. "Trouble is, we might have to work on the details of it. Evgeni's research team is also here for ice core samples."

"Yep, we heard that," Julie said. "Did they say what they were looking for, specifically?"

Ben shrugged. "Evgeni started telling me a bit on the way over here, but I told him we should all talk about it together."

Ben called his name and motioned for him to join their conversation. Evgeni turned his chair around as the others at his table watched on. They had all been introduced to one another, though Evgeni was the only one doing the talking.

Just then, the metal door opened a bit wider, and one of the Russian guards stepped in. He gave them all a curt nod, walked over to the hot dog tray, and shoved a tube of meat down his throat. He swallowed, then nodded once more and walked over to the doorway and stood next to it. He didn't say a word, and after a minute, Ben understood he was only here to listen in on their conversation.

"Evgeni, you were telling us what it was you were studying. My team would love to hear the details as well."

"Sure," he said. He threw a thumb over his shoulder. "We already told these guys, so none of it will be new information to the soldiers."

Ben raised his voice slightly, directing it so that the Russian soldier near the door would hear it. "If anything, it should only help prove that none of us are here to steal Russian secrets." He didn't know if this man even understood English, but it was worth a shot.

Evgeni nodded and began with his explanation. "We were brought here as part of the ground crew for a ship called the *Rezak*, which is a research vessel based out of Vostok Station. We were hoping to come to this site to drill for core samples that might tell us a bit about what the earth was like thousands of years ago."

"You mean the weather?" Sarah asked.

"Yes, but also more. The weather patterns, frozen into place beneath the ice surface, can tell us so much about what the actual *planet* was like in the past."

"Is there anything in particular you were hoping to find?" Julie asked.

"No," Evgeni said. "We were just here to get the samples and return to the *Rezak*, where they would be studied under better laboratory environments."

"I see," Ben said. "Do you have any idea why these Russian goons picked you up, then? It seems like they shouldn't have bothered with you, especially since you are all Russian citizens, unless you found something very interesting."

Ben immediately felt a shift in tension in the room. Eyes glanced at one another; a couple of Russian voices whispered. Evgeni bit his lip, glanced back at the guard, then back at Ben and the others. Finally, he lowered his chin and asked a question.

"Ben, what do you all know about the Minoan civilization?"

CHAPTER 28
EVGENI

EVGENI LOOKED AROUND THE ROOM. He felt the chill, the rush of excitement and dopamine as the revelation of their project was once again brought up. He and his team had sat with the truth of it for four days now.

They had gotten no sense of excitement or intrigue from the Russian soldiers when they'd explained it to them. The soldiers had just seemed completely disinterested, still working under the assumption that all of Evgeni's team were liars, trying to pull the wool over Russia's eyes.

But now, with a literally captive audience — an audience that may also understand some of the meaning and impact of this discovery — Evgeni felt like a kid once again.

It was all so exciting; it was all too much. He had wanted to tell them immediately, the moment they had been brought into the base. But he didn't know who they were, and he didn't know why they were here. As much as they wanted to feel him out and make sure they weren't liars, his team wanted to do the same with them. As Ben had said, trust was a two-way street.

This conversation would be a test of that trust. If this American group reacted negatively or positively to this revelation, it would mean they are most likely who they say they were. Yet if they balked, or didn't seem interested at all, it only meant one thing: they *already* knew about it, and they were here under some sort of guise.

"The Minoans were one of the early Greek peoples, right?" Julie asked.

"Not Greek, but certainly one of their predecessors," Sarah said. She reached out a hand and shook Evgeni's hand. "I know we met earlier, but I wasn't able to give you the full introduction. Dr. Sarah Lindgren, anthropologist."

Evgeni's eyes widened. "Anthropologist? That is... remarkable. How does an anthropologist find her way to a place like Antarctica?"

"There is definitely a bit of irony there," she said, flicking her eyes toward the guard at the door. Evgeni watched his face but didn't see any sign of recognition or acknowledgment. "I'm with these guys," she said, finishing her thought in the most abrupt and nondescript way.

"Well, perhaps *you* will be able to help *us* in that case. We are research scientists brought out here to collect weather data, so having someone like you will only make things go faster."

"I'll do whatever I can," Sarah said, smiling. "But yes, I'm familiar with the Minoans. They were a Cretan civilization, one of the earliest in that area. Remarkably advanced, too. Especially for their time."

Reggie jumped in. "In fact, we realized a while back that the people in that area were probably *far* more advanced than we ever thought, especially with the technologies they used."

Evgeni noticed Ben shooting Reggie a glance. The others did not seem to pick up on it, but Reggie did not continue along this train of thought.

"Well," Evgeni said. "We have been trying to do more research into the Minoan people, but there is really no way to do that here. We know they certainly were remarkable, and they certainly were ahead of their time. For one, we now think their language was not an exclusivity — one created solely by them — but one that was adopted from an even earlier language system."

Sarah frowned. "That's interesting. I thought that the Minoan writing system we know of today *is* exclusive to them? There are some languages based upon it, but for all we know the original language was essentially created in a vacuum."

"Of course," Evgeni said. "And we only know that because of the few remaining artifacts of that time we have found. We think — at least, it is our working hypothesis — that stone and bronze were later developments. That the Minoans reached a height and pinnacle that far overshadowed their later achievements, and most of that work was done with organic materials. Wood, stone, etcetera."

"That is an interesting theory," Sarah said. Evgeni could hear the disbelief in her voice. "I am certainly no expert in the Minoan civilization specifically," she continued, "but for a claim like that to be made, it must be backed by some sort of discovery that at least upholds the underlying premise."

Evgeni could hear the question behind her words, and he nodded before she finished the sentence. "Of course, of course." He turned to the woman named Tatiana, who cleared her throat and then spoke up.

"When we were trekking into a valley off the coast," she said, "we saw something quite remarkable: a massive section of ice that had sheared off and left a scar, revealing the original valley's contours. In addition, it revealed some of the actual stone beneath the ice."

"Wow," Julie said. "That is absolutely astonishing. I don't think we've ever seen that, have we?"

The woman shook her head. "Not that I am aware of, no. Not at that low of an elevation. This could be related to changing climates around the globe, but nevertheless, it happened. We could see the original valley — at least the general shape of it — hidden beneath what was only a shallow layer of ice."

Evgeni watched Ben's face as the man's eyebrow rose. He was

intelligent, a common-sense sort of man. Evgeni liked him already. He may not have been a scientist, but he was not an idiot, either.

"You found something else as well, didn't you?" Ben asked. "Beneath all that ice, something was hidden that you guys found."

"And it would have to have been hidden for a very long time," Sarah said. "What is that much ice? It had to be, what — a thousand? Two-thousand years old?"

Evgeni's smile grew. "No, you are mistaken. The ice in this region, at least at the depth that was sheared away from the stone — was well over four-thousand years old."

Dr. Lindgren and the others shifted in their seats and looked at one another.

Tatiana continued. "We know this not only because of the samples we could obtain from a nearby undisturbed section of ice, but from exactly what you said, Mr. Bennett. We *did* find something in the ice."

Evgeni felt the intensity of the room ratchet up a notch once again. Everyone leaned forward a bit, Evgeni in his chair facing the other table and the others on his team and Ben's team leaning over their own tables. Everyone hanging on her next words.

"We asked you what you knew about the Minoans because we found an artifact from the same civilization."

"That's — that's impossible," Sarah said. "It *has* to be. To find a *Minoan* artifact, even if it were made of stone and could withstand all that time and pressure, it would have to have been brought here from their island. That's — I don't even know how far — but that's too great a distance. Their boats would never have made a journey that far."

"We can assure you; their boats could make it here just fine. We are not sure how they could do it, but it is possible, because that is exactly what we found. A boat."

Ben let out a puff of air from his cheeks. "Really? You're serious? A boat? Like, a whole... boat?"

"Indeed, yes," Evgeni said. "A boat that looked to be quite seaworthy, even after having been stored beneath the ice for thousands of years. We were able to get a sample from the wood that had been exposed, and we can confirm its age. This is what we took back to the Rezak for further investigation before we were brought here.

"We are no experts, however. It doesn't seem likely that anyone would have been able to sail this far, that long ago, but based on the style of the ship and the age, we are left with no other better alternative than that: we believe this is a Minoan vessel."

CHAPTER 29

BEN

BEN LOOKED at the other members of the CSO team. There were signs of confusion, intrigue, and disbelief, but he thought he sensed something else: hope. If these Russian scientists were telling the truth — that there truly was an ancient artifact buried beneath the ice somewhere nearby — it could mean all of this was nothing but a misunderstanding.

Perhaps the Russian soldiers were here to simply guard the treasure, to keep it safe while their country sent a specific research team to study it.

But as Ben locked eyes with the Russian soldier who'd entered the room and was standing sentinel at the doorway, he sensed that he already knew the truth.

These guys were here to keep the CSO team and the Russian scientists away from something else. Perhaps it was the Minoan boat the Russians had claimed to find, but there was no mistaking that they were intent on keeping them locked away in this subantarctic station.

They were serious about security, for whatever reason. Ben had a feeling they would not be able to waltz around the space unchecked, that the Russian soldiers would keep track of their every move.

Ben looked away and saw Evgeni staring at him.

"It's true?" Ben asked. "A *Minoan* ship?"

Evgeni nodded excitedly. "Indeed, Ben. We saw it with our own eyes. Locked in the ice."

"Where?"

"We were picked up from our ship, the *Rezak*, and taken here. We are not sure exactly where 'here' is, so I do not know where the ship is now."

"I see. But there's more to this base — these rooms and the single hallway, it's just a piece of a larger facility."

"You mean through the guards' rooms?"

Ben nodded, then lowered his voice. "It has to be. The food comes from there, the guards come from there, and you've never been in there. If there's anything to be found in this place, it'll be through there."

Ben noticed Reggie talking quietly with Freddie at the other end of the table. They were whispering, but they kept glancing up at the guard. *Must have the same idea as me,* Ben thought.

Evgeni seemed troubled. "What is it you are thinking of doing, Ben?" he asked. "These soldiers are not messing around, and I would bet they are —"

"They'll kill us," Ben said. "I've got no doubt. *Someone* shot our plane out of the sky, and this isn't exactly a populated place. My money's on these assholes."

"So why ruffle their feathers? If they can just believe that we are not here to steal secrets, they may let us go."

"Go to where?" Ben asked. "No, they're waiting for orders from your country's military. They want to kill us and be done with it, or — if they think we're lying about something — torture us."

Evgeni gulped. "Why — why would they think that?"

Ben didn't respond, but Julie redirected the conversation. "Ben's right," she said. "Something needs to change the status quo before it's too late. There's little chance they let us walk out of here alive, so we need to make sure that happens. If there's more of an answer in the guards' rooms, then that's where we need to go."

Evgeni nodded, then conversed with one scientist in Russian, keeping his voice low so the guard couldn't hear him. When he turned back to Ben, Ben could see that the man was excited, a slight twinkle in his eye.

"There is a way, perhaps," Evgeni said. "These doors, you will have noticed, all lock from the outside."

Ben nodded. "I noticed." It was just one more reason he was of the belief that these Russian soldiers were here to keep them where they wanted them — the facade of freedom as they moved throughout the space was just that: a facade.

"Well, we also know their schedules. Two of them eat dinner at a time, after we have eaten. The second guard joins the first here, and then they both sit and eat together. There are usually two others inside their rooms during this time."

"Okay," Reggie said, suddenly leaning over the table on Ben's left. "That's great. That could work. Freddie, Ben, and I could rush the guards' room, while Sarah and Julie can lock the other two in here."

Evgeni nodded excitedly, but Ben saw that the other Russian scientists didn't seem to share his enthusiasm. They were a wild card to some extent — the language barrier notwithstanding. None were soldiers, and if he had to guess, he assumed none of them would be particularly interested in pissing off their captors.

"Great," Ben said. "Let's make a plan, but let's do it back in our room. No need to spill the beans and have this guard ruin the surprise."

They agreed, then one by one finished eating and returned to their cells. Ben waited with Julie until everyone else was gone. After Reggie and Freddie left, the Russian soldier exited the room, and Ben watched him walk down the hallway and turn left at the end, back into the guards' room.

He shifted in the chair, the wound on his side suddenly lancing out in pain. He needed to stand up slowly, to stretch and readjust without reopening the laceration. He grunted, pressing a hand over the top of the bandage beneath his shirt.

He turned to Julie. "Something about this is... weird."

Julie smiled and raised an eyebrow. "You mean like how we were shot out of the sky by a *missile* on a continent that is legally bound by treaty to not have a military presence?"

"Yeah," Ben said. "And how we're now being and interrogated and surveilled 24/7 by Russian soldiers."

"It doesn't add up."

He shrugged. "Not if the part after the equal sign is 'innocent research.' But if the equation results in, 'top-secret Russian project worth killing over,' than I think it adds up just fine."

She nodded. "You think it's smart to rush their room tonight? To get the jump on them? They have to know we'll try something, and they're armed, Ben."

He looked over at her. "A United States Army General asked us to come here. Sent his special forces-trained nephew along for the ride. He *had* to know this wasn't just a sightseeing journey, and that means *we* had to know that, too."

"But four armed soldiers, all equally well-trained."

"What, you don't like the odds?"

"You do?"

Ben chuckled. "No, certainly don't think they're in our favor. And that's part of the reason I know it's the right thing to do. Seems like the CSO has a way of getting itself into jams that are nearly impossible odds."

CHAPTER 30

BEN

SHOWTIME. Ben rolled off the cot in the corner of his stone-walled room and looked for Reggie. They had eaten dinner an hour before, and Ben had decided to get some rest before their upcoming exhibition against the Russian guards.

He saw that Reggie and Freddie were already standing near the door, watching the hallway and chatting with Evgeni. When Reggie noticed Ben, he walked over.

"Morning, sleepyhead. Thought you were going to be catching z's through our little excursion."

"Wouldn't miss it for the world," Ben said. He pulled himself up, but it was too quick. He groaned in agony, his side splitting with a shot of electricity.

"Easy there, big guy. No need to crack open the wound any more than it already is. Maybe you should just —"

"Don't even finish that sentence," Ben said. "I just need to stand up and loosen it up a bit. I'll be fine."

"Good, cause I'm tired of carrying your ass over the finish line," Reggie said with a smirk. "Plan is to move out in five. We'll wait for the ladies to get the mess hall door closed, then we'll rush the guards' room. Hopefully two-by-two, so we can spread out in the hallway as much as possible and take them two-to-one."

Ben nodded along. It was a decent plan, but he had to wonder how it would go wrong. *No plan survives first contact with the enemy.*

He hoped Julie and Sarah were ready, but he knew they had the easy role — closing and locking a door should be no trouble.

As if on cue, he saw the two women appear at the other end of the hallway, heading toward the open mess-room door. He nodded once as they looked down at him, and he saw two other Russian women peeking out from around the corner.

Hopefully, they'll be smart about this, he thought. He didn't want the Russian scientists to interfere or get in the way, and he certainly didn't want them inadvertently messing up the mission by distracting anyone.

He watched as Julie stood to the side as Sarah walked through the door. He couldn't see inside, couldn't tell if there were, as Evgeni had promised, two guards eating their grub. But the instructions had been clear: if there were, in fact, two Russians inside, the mission was a go. Otherwise, Sarah would grab a piece of toast or something and then head back to the room.

His question was answered a second later. Sarah backpedaled quickly and slammed the door closed. Ben heard a shout from inside the mess room, but Julie was already at the door, rolling the deadbolt closed and locking the men inside.

Easy, Ben thought. *Nothing to it.*

Perhaps too easy.

"Go!" Reggie said. He and Freddie took off down the hallway, toward the guards' room.

Ben followed along with Gator at his side. He had barely spoken a word to the man, but there was a calm, defiant confidence about the man that Ben enjoyed. On top of that, the guy was nearly as tall as Freddie and had the biceps of a grizzly. He'd pair the kid up with any of the Russian soldiers he'd seen so far.

Reggie and Freddie reached the doorway just as one of the Russians spilled out. Freddie reacted swiftly, catching the guard under the chin with a meaty fist. He fell to the side, and Reggie caught him and pulled him down to the hallway floor.

Another man, one Ben hadn't seen before, appeared at the door, eyes wide. He was holding a straight razor and had shaving cream on half of his face.

Ben raced up to the man just as he dropped one hand into a fist and held the razor up in front of him, preparing for a fight. As Ben rushed toward him, the Russian lashed out with the razor in a graceful, lightning-quick lunge.

The razor clipped a small chunk off of Ben's forearm. *Great*, Ben thought. *Death by a thousand cuts.*

But Gator didn't stop moving, even when he'd connected with the soldier. There was a grunt as a thousand pounds of human muscle collided together, and the two simply disappeared.

Ben recovered and jumped through the doorway to find the men tangled in a heap on the floor. The tussle didn't last long, with Gator ending up straddling the man's sides, raising a fist.

He pummeled the Russian's head once, and it was over. The fist came down like a drill press, punching the smaller man's head straight back into the stone floor, and it was lights-out for the guy. Ben almost felt sorry for how quickly it was over.

Reggie was there. "I see you got a boo-boo," he said, snickering.

Ben narrowed his eyes. "I loosened him up a bit. My distraction worked."

Freddie and Gator laughed as Gator stood once again. "Thanks, Ben. Couldn't have done it without you." He winked.

Julie and the other women walked up behind them, and together they examined the new space they'd found. The two teams were combined, the CSO group and the Russian scientists intermingling as if everyone sensed their fates were now inextricably linked. As they all milled about, Ben took in the details of the newly discovered addition to their prison.

It was the standard set of three rooms, just like the two spaces they had been corralled into, and it did seem to be nothing but quarters for the Russian guards. Cots on the floors, duffle bags by their feet, and a folding table with a pair of laptops opened and plugged into a massive battery bank.

The battery bank was a large cube with individual charging devices plugged into it — the type of power blocks Ben had used for traveling. There were also two long extension cords that traveled up onto the ceiling, then around the corner of the room, and out into the hallway. The power for the lights Ben had seen strung up throughout the facility.

"Seems like just another room," Reggie said. "Damn, I was hoping for —"

"Another door?" Julie asked.

They turned and followed her pointing finger. In the third space, farthest from the hallway door, Ben saw it. Tucked away in the corner, next to another folding table, stood a thick stone doorframe. This doorway had no actual door in it.

Reggie slid over and shut the door they'd entered from, locking the mechanism. Ben noticed it was the only door that had a lock on the *inside*, and it meant that this space had, in fact, been designed and purpose-built to be a prison. The security was nothing impressive, but considering where they were, it still seemed like overkill.

Were we the targets all along? Ben thought. *Did they build this for us, knowing that we'd be coming?*

Or had the Russians erected this subterranean jail for the scientists they were holding inside?

There were too many questions, but before they could start answering them, they needed more information.

"What should we do?" Sarah asked. The Russian scientists were gathered near the laptops, Evgeni examining the devices and the

Cyrillic that filled the screens. Ben hoped they'd be able to extract some useful data from them, but it was just as likely he was looking at the Russian version of Facebook, and that these low-level guards they'd overtaken had no sensitive data on their computers.

Ben looked around. "I don't know about you, but I've had enough of this place. I'd like to see what's behind that door — if the food's coming from back there, I'd love to see if they have a burger place."

He walked toward the opening in the wall, just as a noise emanated from that direction, around a corner.

Then a light flickered on, and Ben stepped over the stone threshold. He turned to the right, toward where the light had come from, and stopped. His mouth fell open.

My God.

He waited until the others were there, standing behind him, but couldn't think of the right words. Instead, Julie's hand found his and gripped it tightly.

What the hell have we gotten ourselves into now?

CHAPTER 31

BEN

BEN GRIPPED Julie's hand tighter and pulled her close, a natural instinct even though there was no threat of immediate danger in front of him.

Truth be told, he wasn't sure what exactly *was* in front of him.

"Dear God," Reggie said. "What the hell is this place?"

The Russian scientists all piled into the new space, the door closing behind them. Ben wasn't sure if it would automatically lock, but it didn't matter. He had no interest in heading back that way.

The space in front of them was similarly subterranean. Stone lined walls, floors, and ceilings as far as he could see — a short hallway directly in front of them but widening about twenty feet away and morphing into an open atrium.

It was this atrium that had him transfixed. The space was massive — another three or four levels, at least, of descending stone staircases fell into the abyss, the depth of it impossible to comprehend. Around this circular arena were cells much like the ones they'd just left, all single-room spaces cut into the ice and earth behind it.

And it was colder here. He hadn't seen a generator in the soldiers' room, but he knew there had to be one somewhere. However, this space was at least twenty or thirty degrees chillier, and he was already feeling the effects of the cold on his ears and fingers.

Julie pulled in closer, and he involuntarily put his arm up and over her shoulder. Reggie and Sarah repeated the same motions, and together all six of the remaining CSO team, as well as all four of the Russian scientists, stepped forward and toward the atrium. There was light from somewhere up above the atrium, but Ben wasn't close enough to see the ceiling to examine its source.

"This is... incredible," Julie whispered.

"This is *impossible*," Dr. Lindgren added.

Ben nodded but didn't speak. He couldn't. He knew what Sarah was talking about, but he didn't want to believe it. Not yet. He wanted more proof. He reached out and touched the walls, feeling the stones, noticing their smoothness, their perfectly spaced mortaring, the well-planned sizing of each stone.

And he noticed, for the first time, their age.

The stones were rubbed smooth, some of them even shining in the dim light.

He hadn't allowed himself to notice it before when the Russians had brought them here. He had believed his conscious mind, told himself it was an elaborate, well-constructed prison. That for whatever reason, the Russians had dug this space out of the ice, moving thousands of tons of frozen seawater to erect an underground Antarctic base with thick metal doors.

He had known it made little sense, but the truth of it seemed even more impossible to believe.

"We're standing in it," Reggie said. "So it's not impossible."

"But... it just doesn't make sense."

Evgeni spoke from behind Ben and Julie. "I cannot believe my eyes, he said. This place — it is not Russian."

"It's not?" Gator asked.

"Well, it's Russian *now*," Ben said. "I'd bet there are more guards here, so keep your eyes and ears peeled. But it definitely didn't *start* Russian."

"No?" Gator asked again. "Then... who built it? And why? All this ice, in a place where no one else lives, no animals, nothing. It's a hell of an undertaking for something that would never be useful to anyone."

Ben came to the edge of the precipice, leaning over the steep opening of the atrium. He peered below, seeing the ground about five stories deeper. The lights on the ceiling had been added later, the same shop lights that were hanging around the earlier space, but this time collected into bundles of three lights each that together were powerful enough to cast illumination throughout the whole space.

He waited for the others to arrive and spill out on the ledge pathway that encircled the open area. Steps led down on his left side, then circled around a quarter-turn, then more steps descended before another quarter-turn. The entire complex was built in a corkscrew-type shape, each progressive circle slightly smaller and one level beneath the last. The circle at the bottom of the pit was about a quarter of the size of the stone ceiling above their heads.

"It was certainly used," Ben said. "And it was used for a long time, by many people."

"Or it was *built* for many people," Reggie added. "Hard to say if anyone ever lived here."

"That's a fair assessment," Sarah said. "But I'd bet we can find a definitive answer. Want to look around? The stairs go up on our right side and head down on our left. Either way will probably reveal some new hallways like this one, leading to even more spaces that we can explore."

"We'll definitely explore," Ben said, turning to address everyone on the pathway. "But let's not forget that we're in a hostile space. Those lights up there, the metal doors that have been installed — it all tells me that none of this is new to them, none of this is a surprise anymore. And since the food we've all been eating had to come from somewhere, my guess is that there are plenty more Russians around here somewhere."

"And they will not be too happy about us knocking out their friends," Reggie said.

"Right. So, we need to move together move slowly. Let's head up first, since if we have to get caught with our backs against the wall, I'd rather it not be in that tiny pit down there."

Reggie and Gator nodded, but Ben noticed a confused expression on the young man's face. "Even so," he said. "I don't understand. If the Russians didn't build this place, then who did?"

Ben smiled and shared a glance with Julie as Sarah answered the question. "I think the Russian soldiers were intrigued by what Evgeni and his team discovered. But then they started digging around some more and realized the artifact, the ancient ship, wasn't the *only* neat discovery to be had here."

"The Minoan boat?" Gator asked.

"Gorod," Evgeni whispered.

Ben frowned. "Is that Russian for 'ship' or something?"

He shook his head profusely, his eyes lighting up in the way he'd seen from the man a few times already. "No, no. It is not 'boat.' It's 'city.' They were talking about *this* place — the city."

"Yes," Sarah said. "I think it wasn't just a *boat* hidden under the ice. I think we're looking at the last remains of a Minoan *city.*"

Ben was about to ask more questions when somewhere far away, a massive metal door opened, the echo sailing outward and pinging into each of the stone chambers.

"Hear that?" Reggie asked.

The sound was underscored by shouting, all in Russian.

"Sounds like someone knows we're here," Ben whispered.

"What do we do?" Evgeni asked.

Ben looked the man in the eyes. "Stay alive. That's the mission now, Evgeni."

EVGENI HAD NEVER BEEN under attack, not like this. He had never had his physical livelihood challenged more than a schoolyard brawl or a coordinated, friendly exhibition during his brief stint with athletics in high school.

He had been a terrible soccer player, but it was something he'd enjoyed. Still, all the games he'd played as a kid were friendly. Any of the minor spats between players quickly fended off and diffused by the parents and coaches.

So he was surprised to feel a rush of adrenaline and excitement as he heard Ben's words. Something about the way the larger man spoke, the authority and confidence with their situation, gave Evgeni strength.

What was even more interesting was that Tatiana was looking at him with a quizzical expression. The smaller, petite blonde woman wore an expression somewhere between intrigue and confusion, and possibly a bit of fear.

He stepped closer to her, away from Ben and his team. "Are you okay?" he asked her.

She nodded. "Yes," she answered in Russian. "I am scared, but we are going to be okay."

"These people are good," Evgeni replied. "I trust them, and you should, too."

She nodded once again, but Evgeni saw she wasn't watching him anymore. She'd turned her attention to Ben and the others but addressed Evgeni, anyway. "I trust *you*, Evgeni."

He felt the blush start deep from beneath his cheeks, and he tried to hide in the dim light, pushing both closer to the shadows. He laughed. "We will be okay as long as we stay with them. As long as we stay together."

He was about to leave and return to Ben to ask about a plan when he felt her hand brush his. His heart immediately raced, the blood heating within him.

Stop it, Evgeni, he told himself. *Now is not the time, and certainly not the place.*

Still... he wondered if it had been an accident. He looked into Tatiana's eyes, and the answer he saw there told him immediately that it was not.

He grabbed her hand quickly, gave it a squeeze, then released it. He cleared his throat and gave her a slight nod. *Not now,* he tried to tell her with his eyes. *But later. We will talk later.*

It gave him even more of a boost, and he felt stronger. Felt as though there was something he could now do to help, even if the muscle and experience of their fight would be provided by Ben and his team.

"What should we do?" he asked Ben. "How can we beat them?"

"The Russians?" the man named Reggie asked. "Not much, not like this. They know this place — whatever it is — far better, and they're armed. They can just shoot us like fish in a barrel."

"Which is why we will not get stuck in the barrel," Ben said. "We'll head up, toward the top level."

"And how will we fight them if they are armed?" he asked. "Even if we are not, as you say, 'fish in a barrel?'"

"We need to isolate," Julie said. "Pick them off one at a time, or as few as possible. Get them surprised, catch them on their own. It'll take time, but it's the only thing we can do to stay alive."

"Not the only thing," Ben added.

Evgeni and the others looked at the leader of the group. "What do you have in mind?" he asked.

Ben shrugged. "It's rule number one for engagement. If you don't want to die, don't join the fight."

"What do you mean?" Reggie asked.

"I mean, Julie's plan is good," Ben said. "But it requires us to move slowly, stealthily. We need to stay out of their way until it's a damn-near guarantee we can split off one or two and take them down. No chances, no missed opportunities. One gunshot and they'll be bearing down on us. All of them. Not to mention any communications they'll have set up. One of them sees us, it's over — we'll have twenty pissed-off Russians running after us."

Evgeni nodded. "Yes, this makes sense. My team can move quietly, Ben. We can do this."

Ben smiled. "Thank you, Evgeni. Let's move up the path, see if we can't stay ahead of these guys. We'll keep our eyes open for anything useful, including any information about where we are. But the number-one priority is to stay out of the way of the Russian soldiers."

"Got it."

"Yessir, boss."

"Okay," Ben said. "First things first. No one speaks unless we absolutely have to. Noise carries, and it'll bounce off this stone forever. Quick way to give up our exact location."

"Second thing," Reggie said. "Never get lost. Stay together, I'll hold up the rear, Ben takes point."

Evgeni nodded and spoke a quick string of explanation to Mia, Luka, and Tatiana. They seemed scared, but they were breathing normally, controlling their heart rate. They were a good team, and Evgeni knew they would prove him correct.

They just needed to not get killed.

It was a tall order, but Evgeni felt confident.

Just then, the unmistakable sound of bullets pinging off a surface reached his ears, almost at the same time the sound of shots being fired hit him. It was deafening, and he felt himself off-balance, suddenly tripping and not sure which way was up.

"Get down!" someone shouted. "Get to the ground!"

He fell, seeing the three other Russian scientists following suit. Reggie and Ben were shouting at their group, shouting something he couldn't understand.

And then they were on their feet, pulling the others up.

"Come on, Evgeni!" Ben yelled. "Let's go!"

He didn't know how to react, so he simply followed the order blindly. The gunshots were ricocheting everywhere. Had they been spotted? Was it just the sound of a single gun shooting in their direction? Perhaps the echoing made the single stream sound like cacophonous warfare.

Another burst landing on the rock near his head gave him his answer. He dove forward, nearly tackling Tatiana, and both crashed to the side wall as chips of stone splashed out and cut his ear.

He screamed, then felt himself falling forward, toward the central atrium. Something yanked at his sleeve, jerked his arm sideways.

He heard Tatiana gasping for air, calling his name. He tried responding, but only felt the sensation of falling. No words came out.

This is how it ends, he thought, squeezing his eyes shut. *This is how I die.*

CHAPTER 33

SARAH

THE RUSSIAN SCIENTIST seemed to have had completely lost his mind. Sarah had heard the gunshots, seen the ricochets as they impacted and bounced off the stone walls and floors, and she'd seen everyone around her react.

She and Reggie, along with Freddie, Gator, and three of the Russian scientists, had immediately fallen to the stone floor and pulled their hands over their heads. Ben had tried to do the same, but it seemed as though he wanted to be sure the Russian scientist was safe. He ran toward the scientist and yanked him up and toward the wall, narrowly missing a three-round burst of gunfire from across the chasm.

She watched as Ben pulled the man down to safety, noticing that his face had gone completely slack. He had been stunned into a stupor; no doubt having never been in a situation as terrifying as this.

Julie had dived forward, toward them, then crawled closer to the edge of their hallway, near the atrium's opening. Sarah had been concerned she was getting too close to where the shots had been from, but as it turned out, Julie's gut had proven correct once again.

The hallway ended in the open, circular corkscrew, and the shots had, in fact, been raining down from somewhere higher and opposite their location, but Julie had also found that there was a simple solution to their dilemma.

Sarah followed behind Ben and Evgeni and Julie as they rounded the corner of the hallway they were in and entered another space, moving back against the opposite side of the same wall and into a space far enough back to be out of the way. Even better, Sarah saw that this space jutted up against another opening — a dim light hanging above an alcove near a stone doorway.

They ran toward it, the other Russian scientists following, and Gator and Freddie bringing up the rear. The gunfire from the Russian soldiers across the corkscrew fell into the background, and then ultimately fell silent.

They had escaped, but Sarah now realized the truth: they were trapped inside an ancient Minoan city, beneath the ice of Antarctica, being chased by Russian gunmen. There were a few situations she'd been in that could compare, but for the life of her, she couldn't figure out how they would get out of this one.

"...rock and a hard place," she heard Ben telling Julie. Both were sitting against the back wall, near the doorway. Evgeni was next to Ben, his head cradled in his hands with his elbows on his knees.

"What's that?" Reggie asked, entering the room and looking around. He had a surprised expression on his face as if he were shocked they were all stopped and waiting around.

"Just telling Jules it seems that we always find ourselves in positions that are, uh, unpleasant."

Reggie smiled. "Yeah, and we always find a way out of them as well."

Ben's eyebrows rose, and Sarah stepped forward. "Are you saying you've got a way out of this?"

Reggie backed up a foot. "Me? Hell, no. I was just trying to put everyone's mind at ease."

Evgeni let out a small gasp and collapsed even further into himself.

"Hey," she said, addressing the leader of the Russian scientists with as calm a voice as she could muster. "Hey, it's going to be okay."

"You know this?"

She nodded, then pointed to Ben, sitting next to him. "Yeah, I do. This guy — Harvey Bennett — you may not have heard of him back home, but he's a pretty big deal. He's been through *way* worse and brought us all out of it."

"Well —" Ben started.

"Hey now," Reggie said. "*I've* been pretty helpful in these situations, too, and —"

"Would you two knock it off?" Julie said. "She's trying to help."

"I am," Sarah said. "Evgeni, you and your team are still alive, and we plan to keep it that way."

"H — how?" he asked. "They have guns. We have no weapons."

"Weapons are overrated," Ben said.

"Weapons are *awesome*," Reggie said. "But he means we won't need them. Everyone will have a hard enough time shooting accurately down here anyway, and I don't plan on being anywhere near the end of their guns at any point. That brings us back to the point from earlier: we need to stay ahead of these guys, no matter what. See if we can't split them off one at a time, get behind a couple at once, that sort of thing."

"But they know this place better than we ever could," Julie said.

"Not necessarily," Sarah said, jumping in. Everyone's eyes turned to her. She cleared her throat and continued. "We're pretty sure this is an old Minoan city. Somehow, that seems to be true, right? In that case, the Russians didn't build it. Sure, they strung up some lights and dumped cots in some of the rooms, but from what we've seen so far, this place is *huge*. And it's empty, for the most part."

"Which means they're only using a small portion of it," Ben said. "The space we were just in, and quite likely another space similar to it somewhere else."

"Right," Sarah said. "Because they're exploring down here, too.

They've been here longer, sure, but they're still learning the ins and outs of this place." She paused, turning to address Evgeni. "How long have you guys been here?" she asked the man.

He thought for a moment. "Three — four — days? It is hard to keep track."

"That's what I thought. We can't know for sure when the Russians first got here, but I'd imagine it wasn't a long time ago. A week, maybe two tops? You said there was plenty of food, and I'd bet that's because they're still working through the beginning of their stock. They brought a lot of stuff with, and we thought it's because they're preparing for *more* people to get here."

Ben stood up, pacing the room. "Yeah, that makes sense. They sent the grunts here to set things up, to clear the way for whoever'll come next. That means this place is new to everyone involved, and it also means we should do our best to get out of here before our unknowing patrons show up."

"But that could be two minutes or two days from now," Evgeni said. "It is impossible to know."

Suddenly, the other male scientist, Luka, raised his hand. Sarah smiled. Everyone looked at him as he spoke. His English was broken, but clear enough. "I — I actually think I know the answer to this," he said. "I overheard a communication after lunch today between two of them. They said something about more people arriving. I assumed they were talking about you — the Americans."

"Why weren't they?" Reggie asked.

He nodded. "Yes, well, because I heard one of them say 'about ten hours,' but at that time, you all had not been here for ten hours. I was confused, but maybe it meant your plane was brought down ten hours ago?"

Reggie sighed. "*Or* maybe it meant their benefactors are arriving ten hours from now."

Sarah swallowed. She knew that had to be it. "I have to agree with

Reggie," she said. "We need to assume that there will be more Russian soldiers or another component of their team arriving soon."

"Good assumption," Ben said. "Okay, we need to move. Same plan — pick these guys off, one by one. Can we try to nail down a timeline? If Luka here says it was lunchtime, what's the best guess for how many hours we have left? Two?"

Luka swallowed. "I am afraid I ate early today," he said. "That was around 10:30."

"You're shitting me," Reggie. "Dammit, man, can't we get some good luck?"

Sarah looked at Luka, whose eyes were wide. Evgeni's were still on the floor. "Luka, by your best estimate, we've got less than two hours before reinforcements show up?"

Luka paused, as if waiting would change the answer. Finally, after a precious few seconds ticked off, he looked around and nodded. "Yes," he said, apologetically. "Yes, I believe that means we have less than two hours."

"LESS THAN AN HOUR before we're trapped in a locked-down ancient city," Ben muttered. "Great."

"And don't forget that even if we can get free," Reggie added, "we're underneath a sheet of ice a continent wide."

"But we get to kill some Russians," Gator said. "Sounds like fun."

Everyone turned to stare at the young soldier, who finally seemed to notice that he was sharing the room with four Russian-born scientists, all of whom were huddled against the wall.

He raised his hands up. "Whoa," he said. "Sorry. I mean — you know what I mean."

"Yeah, let's just figure out where we are. We can start talking as we go," Ben said. He approached the door on the other side of the room. "Keep your voices down and let's try to talk only if there's new information we need. Judging by the sounds of the gunshots, I don't think voices will carry terribly far, but we can't be too careful."

He walked through the stone doorway to leave the room, Julie and Sarah behind him. The Russians all stood up and reluctantly fell into line.

Ben's goal was twofold: explore the city, try to find unique points of interest, and anything of value that might have brought the Russians here, as well as try to find anything they could use to defend themselves.

"Let's start with this place," Ben whispered. "Why are the Russians even here? Are they trying to turn it into a museum or something?"

"Not going to have great attendance for that, my man," Reggie said. "Probably trying to get something out of it. Oil, maybe?"

"Why send soldiers, then?" Julie asked. "Not a geologist or climatologist? No petroleum engineers?"

"We don't know that they didn't," Ben answered. "Remember, there are more guys on the other side of this place, somewhere."

"Still, why keep a few soldiers all the way back here, guarding prisoners? And why make it so hush-hush? Questioning us?"

"*Interrogating* us is what you mean," Sarah said.

"Right — seems like a bit much if you're just looking for oil."

"But that would be *very* frowned upon in the international community," Reggie said. "Remember the general's brief? No oil extraction allowed, period, at least until 2048 when the treaty ends, and even then only if a third of the signatory parties agree *and* there's a regulatory system in place."

"That doesn't mean they couldn't still be extracting secretly — it's not exactly easy to police down here."

"True," Reggie said. "They could be planning to do it all underground, using this old city as a cover. That way no satellites would be able to see them."

"But unless they're *also* shipping it out by submarine," Julie said, "which is probably impossible, those satellites would see all the oil tankers lining up to be filled, right?"

Reggie nodded. "And I don't think there's a lot of oil here, anyway. At least not stuff that's cheap enough to extract and haul away for refinement and still sell at a profit."

"So not oil," Ben said. "But I have to believe it's *some* sort of resource. The Russians — and no offense to our new friends here — have historically used any excuse they could find to advance their cause."

"Well, they're no different from any other country in that regard," Julie said. "They want to be powerful, and natural resources are a great way to get there. Since it's on this continent, they'd almost *have* to do it secretly. No way they'd get away with it otherwise."

"And somehow we found out about it and got our plane shot out of the sky for snooping around."

"So you are spies," Evgeni whispered.

Ben had almost forgotten about the man walking right behind him. He stopped, turning slowly. "Spies? No. But we were sent here to find out what your countrymen are doing. Those soldiers are clearly doing something they don't want the world to find out about."

"So you are like police officers."

Ben sighed. He felt tired, mentally and emotionally drained. Not to mention the pain in his side had only subsided into a dull throbbing ache. Added to all of that, he didn't appreciate the implication Evgeni was making. It wasn't the first time Ben had heard it in reference to the organization he led. The press and media had an uncanny ability to take everything good in the world and twist it into something people could get upset about. "You know what?" he began. "Sure. We're police. We're not the boss of everyone, nor are we the world's saviors, but we're here to make sure no one's doing something they shouldn't be."

"And you decide what is good?"

Ben swallowed, trying not to let the pain get the best of him and delve into an argument with this small man. Instead, he gritted his teeth. "Yeah. Yeah, we decide what's good."

"But —"

Evgeni's voice was silenced by a Russian woman's. Tatiana, one of the other scientists, began speaking excitedly in Russian.

"What is it?" Freddie asked.

Ben pushed back toward her and saw where she was pointing. He had to squint to see it, but once he did, his eyes revealed more.

Symbols, hieroglyphics, covered the wall.

"Anyone have a light?"

Heads around the room shook. Their phones had been taken, and nowhere had Ben seen a flashlight. The bulbs strung up to the ceiling were bright enough to navigate through the structure comfortably, but they weren't nearly strong enough to provide ample light on the walls.

Still, Sarah walked forward and felt them with an outstretched hand. She frowned, then stepped back.

"Egyptian?" Ben asked.

She shook her head. "No, these are different. Older, and I only recognize a few symbols. Even then, I'm not confident they're Linear A."

"Linear what?" Reggie asked.

"The Minoans — at least the later civilization that we know lived on the island of Crete in the Mediterranean — used a written language we call Linear A, which is still undeciphered."

"Is there a Linear B?"

She nodded. "It's actually the early form of what became Mycenaean Greek. It predates the Greek alphabet by a few centuries, and it's the only early Aegean language to have been deciphered."

"So we're looking at a wall of gibberish that's impossible to read?" Reggie asked.

"Well, sort of. I can't stand here and just speak the text like in movies."

Freddie snickered. "That's good, because that *always* leads to someone accidentally invoking some ancient rites that summon a reincarnated mummy or something."

"Thankfully," Sarah continued, "we have no record that the Minoans mummified their remains."

"We have no record that they *didn't*," Reggie added.

She flicked him a glance that made Ben smile.

"Okay, here's the deal though: these types of things are always simpler to decipher than, say, a stone tablet found in a field somewhere. That's usually for two reasons: first, a mundane tablet like that would have been used for calculating prices at market, or it would host a simple letter to someone far away. In a word, it was unimportant. Second, those would have been written in a vernacular that would have existed at the time, whereas something like this — a wall of text found inside a clearly important location — would use the highest form of the language. The most specific, impossible to misinterpret vernacular and up-to-date understandings."

"So... can you read it?"

"Still no. But I recognize symbols that are from Linear A, even though I doubt it is that language. There was a prior written language the Minoans used, which we call Cretan hieroglyphics. That's even more rare, and we've only got a handful of sources for it. Thing is, most of them are tablets that are dated to about 2,000 B.C."

"That's not old enough," Ben said. "Evgeni said the ship they found was at least 6,000 years old, with a tiny margin of error. If we believe that, then that means this language — and this place —"

Sarah cut him off. "It means this place is not *Minoan*."

CHAPTER 35

BEN

"THEN... WHAT IS IT?" Ben asked. "Is there any way to know?"

She shook her head. "Unfortunately, no. Not without more information. This text, though, is not Minoan — at least not any form of Minoan I've ever seen."

Freddie jostled closer to the wall. "But I thought you said you couldn't read Minoan, anyway?"

"I can't," she said, sighing. "But... okay, think about it like this: you know how you can hear someone speak an unfamiliar language and know, for the most part, what language it is? Or at least what area of the world it's from?"

He nodded.

"Or, even better, you can see something written and just know it's Asian, Western, Eastern, whatever — even modern or old."

"Sure, with exposure, it gets easier," he said.

"That's exactly what's going on here," she said. "I've been *exposed* to so much of this stuff — I've got a doctoral degree in it, after all — that I can see it and just *know*, generally, where it's from. This tells me it's hieroglyphics, which makes complete sense as one of the earliest forms of language — writing through pictures and symbols that represent whole ideas rather than sounds — but it's not Egyptian. And the Minoan that I've been exposed to, like Linear A and Cretan hieroglyphics, is… different. Compared to this, it's modern. There's simply no way it's Minoan, not way out here."

"Not without crustal displacement or something of the like," Evgeni said. Ben watched the man as he spoke, but the scientist offered no more information. Ben filed the statement away as something that must have crossed the small man's mind but was still in the 'half-baked idea' phase.

Interesting. No one else made a comment or asked for more clarification.

"Okay, that all makes sense," Freddie said. "But it doesn't help us *now*. Those Russians don't care about history. I'd bet they'd blast this place without even —"

His voice was cut off by the sound of voices approaching from somewhere nearby. Ben still didn't have his bearings, but he knew they wanted to proceed *up*, toward the roof of the stone building they were in.

"Come on," he whispered. The entire group fell in silently without argument.

Ben led them around two more corners, then into another short hallway. The voices were getting louder. Two men, laughing and joking in Russian.

So they're not as on-edge as we are, he thought. *Maybe we can use that to our advantage.*

He noticed the hallway was pockmarked with smaller, cave-like openings. Rounded instead of squared doorways, shorter, sat closer together. Inside each one seemed to be a small single space cut out of the stone.

He wondered if it was an ancient caste system — every one of the inhabitants had a place to live, but society's more elite persons and families had larger rooms and spaces like the ones Ben and the others had been corralled into. These were mere holes in the wall, space enough to sleep and eat but barely anything else.

He shuddered as he passed by — he was glad once again to be living in the modern age.

Reggie grabbed his arm and pulled him to a stop. "Hey, let's wait to the side, in these little hidey-holes. Those guys are probably right around the corner, and it sounds like they're not paying attention. Freddie and Gator and I can ambush them from up front."

Ben nodded. He stepped down and to the side, entering one of the holes. His head barely fit beneath the top of the stone doorway, even in a crouch. The others followed suit, the Russian scientists splitting into two groups of two and entering the holes on the opposite side of the hallway.

Ben immediately felt constrained, claustrophobic. He hated small spaces nearly as much as he hated planes, and the irony was not lost on him that in his travels, he *always* seemed to find himself on a plane and entering tight, cave-like spaces.

He watched and waited. Julie was across from him, Sarah to his right. Freddie and Gator were tucked into the spaces to Ben's left and across from him to Julie's left. Reggie waited in the hallway, crouched down and out of sight.

The two Russian soldiers appeared from around the corner. It was another hallway, at a perpendicular intersection with their own. They were still chatting, focusing on one another rather than the space in front of them. Each man was carrying a subcompact machine gun, the Vityaz-SN, a closed-bolt Kalashnikov variant. They were small but deadly, firing the 9x19mm Parabellum rounds many overseas manufacturers were producing.

Ben had no interest in having one pointed in his direction. He felt the pang of fire in his side as he shifted. It was already getting better — the pain ebbed and flowed now instead of being a constant — and he wasn't bleeding. Still, it was a specifically annoying feature to be carrying around right now.

The two young Russians turned up their hallway, and Reggie was there immediately. Ben had seen the man perform amazing feats —

he'd seen him kill an enemy with nothing but his wristwatch, he'd seen him take out an enemy from an impossible distance, and he'd seen the stealth and power overwhelm plenty more.

But he'd never seen what he saw now: instead of *fighting*, Reggie was *surrendering*.

"H — hey," Reggie said shakily, his hands up. "I think — I think I'm lost. Do you speak English?"

The soldiers' eyes widened, both weapons now trained on the taller man. One of them barked something in Russian, but neither moved forward.

"English?" Reggie asked again. He took a step toward them.

Ben realized what he was doing. It was a great tactic — to invisibly urge them to come his direction; he pressed *toward* them. He'd guessed correctly that the young soldiers wouldn't want to just shoot him on site. They could get a far bigger reward by bringing this American, alive, back to their leader.

As soon as he did, the soldier on the left began speaking rapidly. He grabbed Reggie's arm and twisted him around, then pressed the end of his gun into his back, pushing him forward.

Reggie was now walking *toward* Ben and the others, silently watching and waiting in the hallway. The two guards moved swiftly, their new prize in front.

Reggie looked down and winked at Ben just as he passed Gator's and Freddie's holes.

And both American soldiers *exploded* into action, simultaneously moving up and toward the Russian soldiers, their motions completely silent.

It was incredible, and Ben was stunned speechless. Though he had been in situations like this, and he'd seen Reggie and others operate with the training and skill sets they had gained over a lifetime of military and special forces service, he had never seen two working so *flawlessly* together. Their motions mirrored one another; their movements were like a perfectly synchronized dance.

And the Russians never had a chance.

The one closest to Ben gave him a perfect view of the attack — Freddie lunged upward and swiftly drew a hand around the Russian's waist, pulling out a KA-BAR knife sheathed on the man's side that Ben hadn't even noticed.

Without slowing, the knife came up and slid in front of the man's face, then pulled around the cusp of his neck. The carotid was lacerated, and blood began pouring from his neck immediately, the soldier himself gasping and sputtering as he tried to protest.

Freddie held him tightly until he was down to the ground, then released and allowed him to fall face-first on the stone.

Every second Gator replicated the movements, his own soldier falling into a heap next to his partner.

Ben's mouth dropped open.

CHAPTER 36

BEN

"THAT WAS INCREDIBLE," Ben said, coming out of his hole. Julie and Sarah were standing nearby, but the Russian scientists were still hiding inside their own stone cutouts.

"Don't get all hot and bothered," Reggie said, smiling. "Julie might get jealous."

"Actually," Julie said, "as smooth as that was, I wouldn't mind having another guy around the house — I'll bet they dance as well as they fight."

Ben shook his head and chuckled, and Gator and Freddie smiled. "Well, uh," Gator began, "I don't think, I, uh —"

"Save it, idiot," Freddie said, hitting his friend on the shoulder. "She's just messing around." He faced Julie, tilted his head, and addressed her. "Right?"

"All right, all right," Ben said. "I may not be able to dance, but I wouldn't go down as easily as those two. I know a thing or two about fighting off would-be pursuers."

Julie laughed. "I didn't peg *you* as the jealous type, Ben."

He ignored her and listened for any more movement from the hallway the Russian soldiers had come down. Hearing nothing, he turned to the group. "Okay, let's get these bodies out of the way.

Stuff them in some of these holes, toward the back. Nothing we can do about the blood, but we'll have to just take our chances."

They got to work, but then Ben felt a tugging on his arm. He turned to find Evgeni frowning up at him.

"Ben," he said. "There is a problem."

"A *problem?* As in, we're inside an ancient Minoan city in Antarctica with a bunch of Russians chasing after us?"

Evgeni paused for a moment, then spoke up. "It is Mia, the other woman with our group."

"What about her?"

"She's gone."

Ben froze. "Gone? How? Where did she go *to?*"

"I — I do not know, Ben. I just walked out to check on them and Tatiana said she had turned away and she was not there. Luka was next to me in the crawlspace, but after the soldiers were killed..." his voice trailed off. "We must find her, Ben."

Ben sighed. *Of course we must.* He knew it was the right answer, but that didn't mean he loved the idea of backtracking, of losing even more time. "Evgeni, I —"

"We can't," Reggie said, abruptly. "Sorry, bud. It's too dangerous."

"We *must,*" Tatiana suddenly said, her tiny frame appearing beside Evgeni's. "She is our friend,"

"I've lost friends before," Reggie said. "It sucks, but you get through it."

Sarah scoffed and walked to the group that was congregating in the stone hallway, joined by the last of the Russian scientists, Luka, who was breathing heavily. "Look, Tatiana, it's just — what Reggie's trying to say is that we are under a serious time crunch here, and we can't afford to split up. We don't know if —"

"She may be *alive,*" Tatiana pleaded. "Please."

"I'll go back," Ben said. "You keep this area under watch for a bit. Fifteen minutes, max. It won't take us long to get back to the main guards' quarters, and then we'll *carefully* make our way back here."

"They're going to be watching the guards' quarters," Reggie said. "What about 'sticking together no matter what?' Come on, man, this is a risk we can't afford to take. You know that."

Ben *did* know that. He knew it all too well. He tried to think back to the times he'd made this same call, done the very thing he was proposing, chosen to backtrack and try to save one of their teammates.

And he couldn't help but be reminded of those teammates' fates, just about every single one of them.

Still, though he knew the odds, and even though he understood the risks and had the data to prove it, he knew what he would decide.

Reggie and the others did as well. Finally, Reggie sighed and stepped forward. He reached out and tapped Ben on the shoulder. "Freddie and Gator alone will be enough to keep the Russians at bay — and now they've got weapons. Add in Sarah and Julie and they can easily hold the fort for fifteen minutes."

"So you're coming with?" Ben asked.

He nodded. "I'm always saving your ass; better not stop now, right?"

"I'm not sure that's entirely accurate."

"Fifteen minutes, not a minute more. If we're not back in fifteen *on the dot*, Julie and Sarah are in charge, and they will order Gator and Freddie to get everyone out of here. Got it?"

Ben nodded. "That was my plan, too."

"Great," Reggie said. "Let's roll."

Ben took a step back toward the open-air atrium around the corner when he noticed Luka matching his steps. He stopped and turned to the scientist. "You, uh, probably should stay here."

"I will go with you. She is my team, my friend."

"I know that man, but —"

"I will go with you."

Reggie started to argue, but Luka held up a hand. "We will not negotiate. I am going with —"

"Christ," Reggie said, cutting him off. "You Russians really are bulldozers sometimes, aren't you?" He looked at Ben, waiting for a response.

Ben shrugged. "Whatever, as long as he stays out of the way."

Ben didn't mind a third pair of eyes looking over their previous steps. They could use him as well if they *did* find Mia, and she was injured. His own side was holding up, but that was because he was only carrying his own weight.

"Fine," Reggie said. "I'll take point. Luka, you're in the middle. Stay out of the way and don't make any noise."

The trio set off, heading back in the direction they'd come from. Ben knew they could move more quickly now that they were retracing steps they'd already traveled, and he wondered if they could get to the guards' quarters and back in less than ten minutes.

Besides, how far could Mia have gone?

CHAPTER 37

BEN

BEN FOLLOWED Reggie and Luka around the path that drew near to the larger atrium, walked over the spot where he'd been when the Russians had fired from high above. He tracked the area with his eyes, trying to pick out anything that didn't fit.

So far, he had seen no Russian soldiers, nor had he seen any sign of Mia or other human life. He wondered where the Russians had gone — had they spread out through the space, or were the two they'd already encountered the only ones currently on patrol? He had to imagine that the larger group of Russians that had been firing down on them was still here somewhere, hunting for them.

Reggie turned right, heading back toward the guards' quarters, but Ben veered left and came up to the sheer edge of the drop. It had to be three-hundred feet straight down, onto the small circular rock floor they'd seen earlier. The lights were still dim, shining down from above them, but it was just enough to reveal a bit of the swirling, irregular stones that made up the floor, as well as —

Ben pulled back; not sure his eyes were telling him the truth. He crept forward one more step and tried looking again, focusing on the spot where he thought he'd seen it.

A shadow, but of what? Smaller than the stones down there on the floor, but somehow not part of the floor or structure around it.

And then, impossibly, it *moved*.

Ben gasped. It wasn't just a shadow. Not just an inanimate shape. It was Mia.

She had somehow fallen over the edge, all the way to the circular floor of the corkscrew-like interior atrium.

Ben squinted, looking again. It was her arm, bent slightly and at an odd angle, but it moved. There was no doubt about it.

"Reggie," he said. He wanted to shout, to yell at Reggie and the others and at Mia, to see if she was okay. But she obviously wasn't, and he obviously couldn't just start yelling — it would attract too much unwanted attention.

"So, what is it?" Reggie's voice returned. Ben didn't turn around — he wanted to keep his eyes on her, to make sure he wouldn't lose her in the drifting shadows of the stone far below.

"I — I found her," he said.

"You what? Really? Where is —" Reggie's voice trailed off. He must have seen where Ben was, what he was looking at. "Shit, are you serious? How'd she fall? I mean, she was with us back there with the two soldiers, right? In one of those little stone cubbies?"

Ben nodded. "I don't know. Come here, make sure I'm not going crazy."

He heard footsteps, then Reggie's voice again. "Hey, where's —"

His voice fell again as he heard an impact. A hollow *thud*, like the sound of —

Ben whirled around. "What the hell?"

There was a shadowy ball of limbs and extremities rolling toward him. He noticed Reggie's larger, taller body, and...

Luka?

"Hey!" Ben shouted, focusing his voice on the two men. "Hey — knock it off. What the hell?"

Reggie pulled back to land a blow on Luka's face, but it went wide. Luka took advantage and kneed the man out of the way. Both slid closer to Ben, and he prepared to pull the smaller scientist off of Reggie if need be.

What the hell is wrong with him? he thought. *Why would he —*

Luka pulled back from the brawl and turned to Ben, and Ben's throat tightened. He suddenly had all the answers he needed about this man.

Even in the dim light, it was clear. The Russian had been acting, playing him. There was no doubt about it. Luka's face was pock-marked, full of scars, and now it was pulled back in a tight, evil sneer.

He whispered something in Russian. *Gorod.* Ben didn't know what it meant. Did it mean he'd killed Mia? Had he thrown her off this cliff? Why? He shook his head, trying to push it all away; it was too unbelievable.

Reggie had separated from the fight as well and was backing a step away. Ben knew what was coming next. Reggie would lurch forward, launch his entire frame at the man, and knock him out.

Reggie crouched and prepared for the attack. Luka was looking at Ben, but Ben could see that his eyes were focused on Reggie. *Was he waiting? Prepared for it?*

Ben knew he needed to do something. He stepped to the side, getting ready to jump forward if Reggie's own attack failed.

Reggie moved on Luka, springing up in a blaze of speed, aiming right for Luka's center of mass.

Then, just at the last moment, Luka stepped *toward* Ben, dropped a leg to the side, and tripped Reggie, who sailed into the stone wall behind the Russian.

Shit.

But that wasn't all — Luka's attack was not finished. With the same leg he's used to sweep Reggie's legs, he used the momentum and swung it up and around his body.

Toward Ben.

Ben saw it coming, but he was helpless. The boot was rising fast, and there was nothing Ben could do to stop it. He held his forearms up, at least to stop the direct hit.

It would have worked fine, had Ben been on solid ground. As it happened, Ben was not on solid ground.

The kick landed — harder and stronger than Ben had imagined. Clearly, Luka had experience and training in hand-to-hand combat. Ben made a mental note to beg Mrs. E to train him and the team a bit in her preferred style of fighting, Krav Maga.

But there was no time for that now. Ben defended himself as best he could, taking the blow with his forearms and pushing against the boot to parry the momentum. The physics were not in his favor — he felt his upper body falling backward, keeling over the edge.

No, no. He felt the feeling of weightlessness just as he saw Reggie running toward him.

"Ben!" Reggie shouted.

Ben's arms were now flailing wildly, grasping at nothing but air, nothing that could keep him steady. Nothing that could keep him alive.

He felt the absolute terror of what was about to happen coming over him, but still, he fought it. *No,* he told himself once again. *No, I will not —*

Reggie was there, reaching for his arms. Ben couldn't stop them, couldn't latch onto Reggie's hands. He screamed, the thought of this being his last chance at survival finally getting the better of him.

Luka was gone now, disappeared back into the dark shadows.

Reggie tried once more, but Ben was already at his waist and still falling. His left foot left the edge, then his right.

Reggie's eyes were wide, screaming at him. Begging him to grab him.

Ben tried, and he couldn't. He was parallel with the floor now, about the same height as well. His backside and lower body were pulling him down, and his upper body and arms couldn't do a damned thing about it.

As Reggie watched down at him, Ben saw him get smaller. He was falling.

He was falling, and he was going to die.

He screamed again, and then Reggie and everything else around him faded to black as the light fell away.

CHAPTER 38

JULIE

IT HAD BEEN TEN MINUTES, and while the team had waited patiently for the return of Ben, Reggie, and Luka, hopefully along with Mia, Julie couldn't help but worry. Ben was capable, but he was injured. He was qualified, but he was also trying to make the best decision for the group at large, not just for himself.

Julie knew he could be rash, especially as a younger man, so she hoped he could maintain a bit of selfishness and protect himself. She needed him more than the others did.

She sighed, looking around. The lights were still on, which told her that the Russians chasing them needed them as much as they did. That was good — if they turned off, Julie had no doubt it would be impossibly dark here, and they may as well give up. None of them had a flashlight or even a phone.

The two Russian scientists remaining, Evgeni and Tatiana, were huddled together across from her in the small hallway, near one of the tiny cubby holes that had been carved from the stone. The two dead Russian soldiers had been stuffed into the cubby next to Julie, but she didn't turn to look at them. One man's eyes were still open, pointed up and out of his grave, directly at her.

She shuddered. Death was not something she'd ever considered, at least not seriously. She'd seen plenty of it — some of it even death by her hand — but she'd never truly stopped to think about the finality of it. It was absolute, finite. Everyone died, and almost everyone who had ever lived had already died. She and all the others here would eventually be a part of that.

A never-ending cycle, one that — so far — humans had never broken free of. And while she believed that there was a reason behind all of it, a higher design that had allowed her being here for a tempo- rary amount of time, she also figured that there was supposed to be a reason *why*.

A reason she had been put here, in this place and time. A reason she was alive.

It was a strange thing to reckon with, and only recently had she started considering it from this perspective. She wanted to know what her purpose was; why it was she had found Ben and the CSO and all that it had accomplished.

She wanted to know why *she* was here in Antarctica, inside an ancient city built by a long-dead civilization, trying to stop Russian soldiers from killing them.

It all seemed so strange and unnatural, and yet somehow it fit. As if the strangeness *was* natural to her. As if she had been put here to do this job — whatever it may be.

She let out the sigh and stood up, hoping to catch some time with Evgeni and Sarah — in her mind, the two most likely candidates for figuring all of this out. They both seemed to have come at the Minoan problem from different sides, from opposing viewpoints, and yet could still discuss and learn from one another.

Ultimately, she wanted to know why the Russians were here — what this particular place contained that the Russians had deemed important and interesting. They had already ruled out oil, but could there be another natural resource, so valuable that the nation had to subvert a trusted treaty and keep their plans tightly under wraps, to the tune of even shooting down a plane in the sky because of it?

Dr. Lindgren was standing to the side, talking with Gator and Freddie. Both men seemed completely unfazed by the fact that they'd just taken the lives of two young soldiers and stuffed them unceremoniously into a crack in the wall.

When she approached, Gator and Freddie peeled off and continued their conversation in the hallway.

"Hey," Julie said to Sarah.

"Hey."

"Holding up?"

Sarah looked around. "Yeah… I guess I'm okay, considering."

Julie laughed. "Hey, you should know by now what hanging with all of us is really like."

"Yeah, I guess that's true. You know, a few days ago I was preparing a lecture and trying to keep Reggie and Ben from drinking all the whiskey in the state."

Julie smiled. "Been down that road — there's a *lot* of whiskey in every state, and it turns out there are a lot of states."

Sarah nodded. "Ain't that the truth. Now here I am, waiting for my boyfriend to return with a long-lost Russian scientist so we can continue walking around in an old Minoan maze."

"Yep," Julie said. "Sounds like a CSO mission. By the way — I wanted to get your take on all of this. Where we are, *why* we are, that sort of thing."

"I'm still chewing on it, really," she said. "You know most of it."

Julie threw a thumb over her shoulder toward where Evgeni and Tatiana were chatting quietly. "You think he knows anything else?"

"Who knows?" Sarah said. "He's smart, I'll give him that. But he's not an anthropologist, and he already admitted that any Minoan history knowledge he's got came from Wikipedia and Google searches."

"Right."

"Besides, he seems to be working on… *another* problem at the moment."

Julie turned and followed Sarah's gaze. Evgeni was leaning back against the stone wall inside the cubby-sized room, but he had shifted over slightly, getting closer to Tatiana.

Julie's head fell back a bit. "Ah, I see. You think our little Russian friend's smitten?"

Sarah grinned. "Seems like it. Shared trauma is really supposed to be good for long-term compatibility."

"That sounds like the kind of thing a psychologist would say to make their trauma-victim patients feel better about themselves."

Sarah shrugged. "Hey, take it or leave it. Just going by what the textbook told me."

"Also, you mentioned that this place is *not* Minoan. And just now you said it was."

"Well, it's complicated. I mean, it's not the Minoan that I learned about — the Minoan civilization we've all heard of. But that civilization likely didn't just spring up from out of nowhere. It was based on something. Something older, something with different language and writing features, and probably from a slightly different area. We just know of the Minoans from what they've left behind."

"So there could be an even *older* civilization we don't even know about?"

CHAPTER 39

SARAH

"IT'S ACTUALLY LIKELY," Sarah said, clearing her throat and feeling the lecturer in her awakening. "People have to come from somewhere, all the way back from when the Homo sapiens split off and became its own species. That was probably sometime around 70,000 years ago."

Julie was standing in front of her, but both women turned around and stared down the hallway when a strange sound echoed around them.

"You hear that?" Julie asked. Sarah noticed the others had taken an interest in the sound as well, though no one offered an answer for what it was. It sounded like a muffled crash in slow motion, but it was faint. If it hadn't been for the fact that this area of the ancient city was incredibly quiet to begin with, Sarah might not have noticed it at all.

"Want me to go look?" Freddie asked.

Julie shook her head. "No, let's give them the rest of their agreed-upon time. Without knowing what it is for sure, we can't risk getting ambushed while you're off checking."

He nodded and dropped back into conversation with Gator. Sarah saw both men were standing in the hallway on either side and flicking their eyes around regularly. *Standing guard*, she thought. *They probably can't even help it and don't realize they're doing it.* Still, she was glad for them — they were enormous assets to the team, even for just moral support.

And they had proven to be assets in the *physical* support arena as well.

"Anyway," she continued, "after humans became humans, there was probably some time early on that we were, effectively, still just apes. Living in caves, eating raw meat, foraging for food, that sort of thing."

"But we adapted."

"But we adapted," Sarah confirmed. "We — at some point — became tired of raw meat, learned that staying in one place could offer a different sort of prosperity, and realized that our larger brains and the intuitiveness of hand tools could give us a leg up."

"And then we got the internet."

Sarah laughed. "Exactly! I mean, you're joking, but if you really think about it, we obviously know humans are capable of creating things like that, because we *have* them. We also know where we came *from*, so filling in the gap just becomes a game of cat-and-mouse with a timeline."

"From what I remember, the story of humanity really only reaches back 10,000 years or so, right?"

"Precisely," Sarah said. "What we *know* — at least, what we *think* we know — only goes back that far. But things get dicey after about 4,000 or 5,000 years. We've got a rough estimate of what we did, where we were, that sort of thing, but there's not much to go off besides that."

"Because it didn't last?"

"That, and the fact that it's probably buried far deeper than our research can go."

"How is that possible?"

"Well, remember the Younger Dryas that Evgeni mentioned?"

Evgeni stirred at the mention of his name, but he didn't get up. Sarah saw that his hand was suspiciously close to Tatiana's now, and she couldn't help but smile. *Love always finds a way,* she thought. *Even in a cave beneath Antarctic ice, with the threat of imminent danger present.*

Julie nodded. "Yeah, the cataclysmic event that wiped out a bunch of animals in North America?"

"Yes," Sarah said. "But not just 'a bunch of stuff' — it was a big enough even that it could have wiped out *civilizations*. Like, completely wiped them off the map. Their structures, especially if they were built from wood or earth, would have just ceased to exist, and then any materials left over would have disintegrated. My colleagues hate to admit it, but we've got no idea, for the most part, who was there before us."

Sarah had given this lecture before, and she always found it fascinating. The fact that modern archeology was fascinated by this idea of a 'Clovis civilization always bothered her. Sure, it had been all but proven wrong, but the way her peers clung to long-held beliefs was a statement that proved their insecurity with their careers and thinking outside the box instead of being willing to challenge and try out new ideas.

Freddie ambled over and interrupted Sarah's train of thought. "Hey, uh, I'm thinking it's getting close to the time..." his voice trailed off.

Sarah nodded, finishing his statement in her head. *...when they should have been back. If they're not...*

Julie turned to face him. "They'll be back. I know it."

Sarah looked at Julie strangely, realizing for the first time that day that she hadn't been paying attention to this woman's emotional state. Was she okay? She had been sitting quietly by herself for the first half of Reggie and Ben's absence, and Sarah had assumed it was simply to clear her thoughts, to take a breather.

Now she considered it might be due to something else — was

there something deep in Julie's eyes that was begging for recognition? Was she trying to hold it together, when inside she was simply a wreck?

Sarah knew the feeling — she'd felt it before. She knew the physical tightness in her chest, the strange euphoria based on anxiety, a general calm nervousness. Was Julie feeling this right now?

She reached out and grabbed Julie's hand, then squeezed it. Julie's eyes flicked toward her, shocked.

"It's okay," Sarah said. "You're right. They're going to —"

There were footsteps approaching, and Sarah whirled around, Julie and Freddie already looking toward the end of the hallway. The two soldiers' guns had found their way into Freddie's and Gator's hands, and both men were stepping gently toward the edge of the hallway, holding the weapons ready.

Sarah felt tense, but then she let out a deep breath. Reggie's body appeared from around the corner. He was running, only now slowing.

And then she saw his face, and the fear returned.

No.

Julie ran forward. Gator was there, grabbing Reggie's arm and holding him up. "Everything okay, boss?" Gator asked him.

"Ben," Julie whispered. "Ben — where's Ben?"

Reggie was panting, breathing heavily, his eyes flicking around. "— Bastard. Where — Luka?"

"What?"

He grabbed the weapon out of Gator's hands and whipped it around, suddenly pointing it back at the rest of them. Gator and Freddie took a step back.

"*Where is* Luka?" Reggie asked again. "Is he here?"

Sarah saw he was shaking. His eyes were wild, red and bleary from — *tears?*

She swallowed. *Oh, my God. No, this can't be —*

"*Reggie!*" Julie shrieked. "Reggie, *where is —*"

"He's *gone*, Jules!" Reggie said, spitting out the words. "He's —
Luka..."

Gator was chewing his lip; Freddie's face a mask of confusion and
dark energy. Evgeni and Tatiana were standing next to Sarah, both
wide-eyed.

"Show me," Julie said softly.

Reggie looked at the floor. He shook his head. "Julie, I —"

"*Show me.*"

He sighed, then lifted his head. Tears streaked down his face. He
didn't wipe them, but he cleared his vision with a thumb and fore-
finger in his eyes. "Fine," he said. "Let's go. We've got less than half
an hour before... oh, for Christ's sake, I don't even give a shit."

He turned around and started walking down the hall.

CHAPTER 40

PETROKOV

"I NEED AN UPDATE," Mikhail's voice rang into Petrokov's ear.

"I — sir?"

"An update, Petrokov."

Petrokov couldn't help it. He panicked. He was not sure what his boss was hoping for; he had not heard from his contact in Antarctica in over two days, since they'd last spoken on the phone.

He rolled over, finding the bed empty. The woman he had hired for the evening last night had apparently left during the night. He felt slightly betrayed, even though he knew the drill. These days, the business was all about apps and digital currency, not cash. Not like it used to be.

Now, an escort had his credit card number online and accessible the moment the 'fun' was over, the moment she felt their transaction was complete. It was like the new ridesharing apps — the driver did not even have to speak with the rider; it was all handled magically and silently.

He sat up, groaning. He had had a lot to drink last night — *they* had had a lot to drink. First, it had been hors d'oeuvre at a nearby tapas restaurant, then dinner at a five-star that his brother had recommended, and finally a room-service dessert.

His brother was gone now, dead. He had wanted to celebrate the man's life, his contribution to the Motherland, but it had felt more like a cheap trick. Petrokov had been the one who'd gotten to enjoy the night, not his brother. He had been the one to take the woman back to his hotel room to continue the celebration long after the lights had gone off.

He sniffed, cracked his neck, and rubbed his eyes. "I am sorry, sir. I am not feeling well this morning. You would like an update?"

"I would, Petrokov. And the longer you delay, the worse it will look on your record."

He swallowed. "Okay, right. Well, the last contact I had with —"

"Bullshit, Petrokov," Mikhail's whiny voice called out. *"I already know you must have spoken with him; I need to know what about."*

Petrokov frowned. He legitimately had no idea what Mikhail was going on about; his last interaction with Luka had been two days prior. *Had something happened?*

Petrokov needed to get out in front of this. As the project's ambassador — the person listed as the point of contact between both the mission lead and the head of defense for the Russian government, Petrokov was supposed to know *everything*. Worse, he was supposed to be able to predict the next steps each side would ask about.

And he knew nothing.

Something had happened. He needed to know, but he needed to ensure Mikhail didn't *know* he didn't know.

He let out a breath. *Politics.*

"Okay, I will tell you," he stammered. "I received a transmission from Luka last night —"

"Not a phone call?"

"No, not through usual channels. Therefore, I did not call it in."

"What about?"

"The mission has taken a turn," he lied. "Luka seemed distressed. Therefore, I did not file it through the official communications channels."

"I see," Mikhail said.

"This is unfortunate, yes?"

"Unfortunate? You think the Americans infiltrating the main Gorod installation is 'unfortunate?'"

Petrokov smiled. His ruse had worked — this is what Mikhail was calling about.

"Yes, it is unfortunate, Mik—"

"It is inconceivable, *Petrokov. I knew that allowing Luka to play scientist and pretend he was part of the Rezak crew was a stupid, elementary error. Something that should be relegated to the schoolyard, not be used on a mission of this sort of importance."*

"My thoughts exactly, sir," Petrokov said. He rubbed his eyes again, now standing in front of the hotel room's mirror, stark naked, examining his aging body. There was an outline of a soldier there, but that outline had aged, grown weak. He almost chuckled. He had not paid the woman nearly enough.

"What else do you know?"

"I am afraid that is about it, sir," Petrokov said. "As you can imagine, receiving communications of this sort, so unexpectedly, they were kept brief. I was alerted that the Americans had escaped their quarters, along with the *Rezak* crew —"

"No doubt all a part of Luka's ruse," Mikhail interrupted. *"Some plot he cooked up to convince them of his innocence."*

"Right," Petrokov said. "Yes, exactly. They entered the main Gorod base at some point in the past day."

"Strange. I thought it was only hours ago."

Petrokov cleared his throat. "Yes, well, I was not thinking in terms of the time difference. It is difficult to say. Sir," he said, trying to change the focus from the less granular details to those which were easier to fake. "What are my next steps?"

There was a long pause. He knew his boss would have wanted Petrokov to be more involved, so he could cast some of the blame in his direction if things got hairy, but he also knew Mikhail had to keep him at arm's length, so Petrokov was in no danger of stealing the glamour if things went well.

"I need you to stay put," he finally said. *"There are going to be updates coming more quickly, now."*

"Yes, sir." *More all-expenses-paid time at this lovely Washington, D.C. hotel, I guess,* he thought. *I think I can work that into my schedule.*

He looked at his other phone — his private, personal cell — and wondered if the same woman would be working two nights in a row. Surely, she had had a good enough time with him? She seemed to have been happy with him, and she had certainly enjoyed the free booze and food.

"We need to be kept abreast of the changing situation in Antarctica. The rest of my team is playing defense against the ever-invasive UN board of reviewers, and they are fielding questions that seem an awful lot like interrogation. You know Russia, Petrokov. She does not like to be interrogated."

"Yes, indeed. That is fine, sir. I will forward along any further communique I receive from Luka."

"Very good."

Mikhail mentioned something about another meeting, but Petrokov jumped in. "Is there... is there a plan in place, just in case..."

"In contingency?"

"Yes."

"Of course, Petrokov. You know how these things go. There is always a contingency."

"Will there be anything I can do to help?"

He hoped the question came out as he'd intended — that he was eager for more, to please his superiors — not as a way to get an answer to his real question: he wanted to know what was going to happen to Luka.

He didn't care for the weaselly man; the man was nothing to

him. But professionally, Luka's failure could mean good things for Petrokov's own career. If there was any way to leverage that...

"There will, Petrokov," Mikhail said. *"There will, indeed. But we are still in the early stages of enacting that plan. There is still time for Luka to succeed, and it is of the utmost importance that we allow him the time to find that success."*

Petrokov's heart sank. He was hoping for something more definitive.

"However, we are currently working to send an expeditionary force to Antarctica. A small extraction team, one we will use to penetrate the Gorod facility and remove any last threat from the Americans, including their own team."

"I see," Petrokov said. He couldn't hide the excitement in his voice. "And... may I ask — what of Luka and his team?"

"The mission is the victory, Petrokov. The players on the board are simply that — players. Once the mission is complete, we will eradicate the board of all players. No one can know what happened there."

Petrokov couldn't help himself. He pumped his clenched fist. *This is good,* he thought.

He never enjoyed his countrymen being killed, especially by their own government. But, in this case, he allowed himself a bit of leeway. This would play nicely on his resume. He would survive and thrive, and he would use Luka's work down in Antarctica as his own.

This is very good.

He hung up on his boss and then immediately flicked over to the app he'd used the previous night. *I believe another celebration is in order.*

CHAPTER 41

BEN

PAIN WAS a feeling he assumed most people had never experienced. Most people knew what a simple laceration — a cut — felt like, as well as a burn or rash. Perhaps they had known as well the pain of a cut or burn deep enough or bold enough to cause lasting damage — a scar.

And most people understand the lifetime feeling of loss, of losing someone loved enough, that having the physical sensation of a searing knife turned over and over inside their heart for the rest of time was but a small reprieve from the mental and emotional state.

But he assumed that not many in the world — at least not those alive today, with all of life's luxuries and accouterments and simplicities — had felt *both*.

He, at that moment, was feeling both.

The pain of loss was compounded by the fact that he was, in every worldly sense, in severe physical pain.

And all of that was strange, since he had no recollection of ever leaving the worldly state. From what he could remember, he was still on earth.

Yet Ben knew there was something unworldly about his specific location. He was traveling across a universe of bright pain receptors, both emotional and physical, and there was no sign that he was slowing down.

He smiled — or at least attempted the best virtual version of it — drifting onward and upward, toward that thing they all called 'the light.' It was unbelievable. Ironic, even. He had never imagined it would be like this — pain all the way home. Pain from the beginning, pain until the end.

Maybe that was the game? Perhaps the design of his life had included a very human truth that *pain* would guide his progress, even through the pearly gates. He wasn't particularly religious, but he had beliefs. None of those beliefs had prepared him for this.

The pain was extreme, even as he got closer to that thing he had called 'the light at the end of the tunnel.' 'The End.' The goal of his life's work; the destination at the end of his travels.

He had no question that this was the end of his earthly life, but he was surprised that the beginning of his heavenly one was so damned painful. In his dreams, in the fleeting moments between lucidity and opacity, when his mind was trying to orient itself against reality, he had considered that death might be a far more onerous burden to bear than just 'letting go.'

In fact, he had experienced firsthand this phenomenon with his own mother's passing. Her last words to him had been garbled and confused, her own reality spinning out of control as she fought with the fear of losing what she knew and the recognition of the fear of what she didn't. Ben had, at the time, simply watched on in horrendous wonder.

Now he had a front-row seat. Death may be only the beginning, but it was a beginning he wasn't entirely sure was worth the effort.

The wound on his side cried out with a shaky, groaning creak, like his torso was a tree trunk that had been nearly split by the ax of a seasoned lumberjack. He was being split — pulled, even — into two halves, ripped apart by the pressures between his left and right side, and his injury was bearing the brunt.

But it wasn't the only thing screaming for his attention. His mind was racing, trying to assuage the individual complaints of many parts of his body. His legs felt numb, helpless, in that annoyingly common pins-and-needles way, but with an elevated purpose — each pin and needle were attached now to an electric current of a million volts.

His arms were butter, but only after having been crushed between two grinding plates, churned into mere liquified solids, unable to offer him any help.

And his chest — his entire body's supply of breathable air — was punctured or compressed or restricted or something he couldn't even understand. The oxygen simply could not reach his lungs. He wanted to gasp, to scream out loud, to cry for help, but his chest had assumed control of his entire being and was now guiding him directly toward that cursed light.

Even as he sank — as the feeling was generally a feeling of sinking, he realized — he prayed. He prayed for his own salvation as an afterthought, focusing his awareness and attention on Julie and Reggie and the other members of the team — *his* team — and the ones he couldn't even remember but knew he had encountered and wanted the best for. There were scores of people he needed to mention, right? Scores of people he must call out by name, or this — whatever it was — wouldn't work.

Even as he sank, the prayer morphed into a pleading sob of realization that his time on the planet was nearing its end, and that realization led to another that caused him to realize something else entirely: that his time here was *not*, somehow, *complete.*

He was not *dead.*

He was dying, but not dead.

The end was near, but he had not reached the transitory point between *the end* and the *new beginning.*

The planes of existence he believed in were not as separate as he might have imagined, and that was something he could grasp onto.

He didn't know how, but he grasped it. He reached out, visually, mentally, emotionally, virtually — however — and grasped it. He grasped that plane, the one he had come from, and allowed his broken mind one last attempt at making sense of all of this. He allowed it one last puzzle to solve, one final recognition that it did, in fact, have a purpose on this plane.

And that puzzle became clearer. The pieces were aligned, the peaks and valleys of each perfectly in line with each other, providing a bit of clarity.

The picture was fuzzy, but the edges of the pieces were not.

He knew now that there was an inkling of hope. He was not dead — not yet. His predicament was real, his struggle only beginning, but he could fight.

He could fight for one or the other — death or life. Or, really, *life* or life, whichever version of it — whichever *plane* of it — he wanted. Life *here* or life *there*. Both providing attractive potential outcomes, both providing attractive variables.

He needed to decide. *Life or life.* There was no other option.

Death on one plane meant life on another, or life on one plane meant death — or the postponement thereof — of another.

He knew which one he would choose before it had coagulated in his mind as a viable option. His smile grew wider.

Yes. This is the way.

He looked up, the light above dimmer than the light below. It was madness, the feeling of euphoria and confusion and chaos and fear and anger and elatedness all in one — but it was *his* madness.

It was *his* decision, at least for now, and he knew which version of reality he needed to accept.

He ignored the brighter light below him and swam upward.

Toward the dim light. Toward fear. Toward chaos.

Toward death.

CHAPTER 42

JULIE

JULIE FOLLOWED BLINDLY. She watched without seeing, listened without hearing. Everything she knew was upside-down, swirling around in the thick soup that was her mind. She was trying to hold together what little emotional steadiness she had left.

It would not last.

She reached out for the stone wall, hoping for its cool rigidity as a means to prop herself up. Instead, she found Sarah. Her hand fell to the taller woman's shoulder, but Sarah was steadfast. She didn't speak, and both women walked side-by-side behind Reggie, Julie's hand on Sarah's shoulder.

Freddie followed behind them, and the Russian scientists behind him, flanked by Gator. None of them spoke.

Everyone was in a daze, a palpable current of disbelief and shock flowing through them all. They turned back up the hallway where they'd found the writing, then back again toward the wide, circular opening. Near the first hallway they'd found themselves in after leaving the guards' quarters, Reggie stopped. He was standing near the edge of the chasm.

Julie dropped her hand and ran up to his side.

"Here?" she asked.

Reggie sniffed. "Here."

She looked down. It was dark, the bottom of the chasm obscured from view.

"How?"

Reggie didn't speak. He swallowed, a small stuttering gasp escaping his lips between breaths. Finally, he shook his head. "I — I'm not sure. It was Luka, and we were fighting. Wrestling. Ben was standing... he was standing..."

Reggie collapsed. He hit his knees so hard Julie was worried the crack would either break his kneecaps or at least alert the Russian soldiers, but they seemed to have gone elsewhere for now.

She placed an arm on his shoulder. She didn't squeeze it. She wasn't ready to dole out support — hell, she wasn't even ready to *accept* the fact that Ben was...

She couldn't even finish the thought. She looked down once again, trying to make out any movement, any sign of life.

But there was none. It was too dark, anyway.

"I could have — if I would have just —"

"Stop," Sarah said. "Reggie, you couldn't. It — it was a freak accident."

It seemed as though Reggie was about to accept this when suddenly he leaped up and spun around. He was shaking uncontrollably now, and Julie was trying to understand what the target of his rage was going to be when she saw them standing nearby.

Between Gator and Freddie, the two small Russian scientists, Evgeni and Tatiana.

"*You...*" Reggie grunted. His voice was horse, deep and cut. "*You bastard Russian mother—*"

"Reggie, no!" Sarah said. She tried to intercept, but Julie knew she'd not get there in time.

Sure enough, Reggie closed the distance with two massive leaps and was right in front of Evgeni in two seconds flat. His hand was rising, his palm opening.

He wrapped it around Evgeni's neck. Tatiana gasped and fell to the side. Reggie continued lifting, pulling Evgeni's body *completely* off the ground and up to Reggie's eye-level.

He backed him up against the stone wall, pressing hard against the man's jugular. *"You* did this. *You* set us up. For what? To pick us off, one at a —"

"Reggie!" Sarah said, louder this time.

He paused, but he didn't release his grip.

"Reggie, it's *not* his fault."

Evgeni's mouth moved, his lips working on a word that wouldn't come out. Reggie didn't relent.

Julie watched, unable to turn away. She didn't even care. Reggie could kill the man — throw him into the circular chasm — and she wouldn't feel a thing. Hell, she could watch all of them, including herself, jump into the pit, and she wouldn't bat an eye.

It didn't matter anymore. There was a mission, but it wasn't her problem. There was a CSO, but she was no longer interested in being a part of it.

Sarah was pleading, screaming at Reggie, and Gator and Freddie were trying to decide what to do. Finally, the soldiers wrested the small man from Reggie's grip, and he dropped him to the floor. Evgeni coughed, wheezed, and got on his hands and knees as he tried to recover.

He sucked in a deep breath of air while Tatiana sat nearby, sobbing. "I — I did..." Evgeni's voice cracked. "I did no... such thing."

"You *lie!"* Reggie screamed.

"I do *not!* I am not... I did not know..."

"Luka's a plant, asshole. On your own team. You mean to tell me you didn't *know* that? That you're *not* working with all the other Russians trying to kill us?"

Evgeni nodded, then shook his head. "I — I cannot — I am sorry, Reggie, but I —"

To his left, Tatiana spoke. "He is telling the truth," she whimpered. "I can assure you. It is not a lie. We did not know Luka was capable of this. We thought... we knew he was a part of our team, in good standing."

"I'd say throwing teammates off the edges of cliffs ain't much of a 'good standing' thing to do," Freddie muttered.

"Let him talk," Sarah said. She helped Evgeni to his feet.

"I cannot... I cannot express my grief over your loss," he began. "But please, understand. We — Mia, Tatiana, myself — we are just scientists, as we have explained. Luka, we thought he was one as well. We had no reason to believe he is not."

"How did you end up here?" Sarah asked. "In Antarctica. You were sent here to collect samples? Core samples?"

Evgeni nodded profusely. "Yes, yes. That is the truth, I assure you."

"And how did you come to find this project?" Freddie asked. "Or did it somehow find *you*?"

Evgeni swallowed, and his eyes fell as he realized the truth. He didn't speak for many seconds, but Tatiana finally did. "We were called here by an organization we had never heard of before. They claimed to be interested in researching ancient core samples, and we would be compensated generously."

"I see," Sarah said. "And this organization had no connection to the Russian soldiers running around?"

Her eyes widened, and Julie watched on, uninterested.

"No, of course not," Tatiana said. "If there was a connection, we did not know about it. It was not revealed to us."

"I'm sure that was on purpose."

She nodded. Evgeni was breathing slowly, trying to gain his composure. Reggie was standing over him, the subcompact gun sitting next to his feet on the stone floor.

"And who brought you onto the project?"

Both Evgeni and Tatiana looked up at Sarah.

Slowly, feebly, Evgeni let out a sigh. "I was asked to take part before the others. I invited Mia and Tatiana onto the team, as they were close colleagues I had worked with before. I was told I would lead the project, and the research findings would be split four ways — between me, Tatiana and Mia, and the person who brought me onboard."

Julie didn't need to hear it, but he said it anyway.

"By Luka."

BEN

BEN REACHED up and toward the dim light. Every muscle ached with the exertion, but he pushed on anyway. He wasn't sure why; it felt far better to ignore the light and drift further into the warmth of unconsciousness.

He realized he was swimming, moving upwards slowly. Yet it wasn't water or even pure liquid he was swimming through — it was something denser, something almost solid. It felt like he had been dropped into a vat of ketchup.

Dropped.

He remembered now. He remembered the feeling of weightlessness, the feeling of losing all control, the feeling of —

Betrayal.

Luka, the Russian scientist, had kicked him off the ledge. He had fallen through the air in the wide-open expanse of the main city's atrium, the corkscrewing design of the hallways and pathways twisting around him until he landed.

But he *had* landed, and he *had* somehow stayed alive. But then he'd been sucked beneath whatever viscous fluid this was, pulled down into an impossible vacuum of pressure and unconsciousness and nothingness.

And he now had his bearings. He was pushing back up, back through the thick wall of semi-liquid mass surrounding him. It had no taste, no smell, or his senses weren't working enough to clue him in. It was semi-opaque, clear enough to see through, to see his destination.

He was about to break through the surface and gasp for a breath of air when his hand brushed against something. It was cold, stiff, but not completely hard. He kicked upward once again and crowned up and into real air and only then realized what it was he had hit.

Mia.

Her lifeless body was dangling there, where he'd seen it before, halfway above and halfway below the surface. Her lower half was stuck in the goop, but her face and one of her hands were floating freely. She had slid to the side, out of sight and near the stone wall. He looked up, noticing that anyone looking down on them would not be able to see them from this angle.

Ben wondered if she had died here, stuck in a terrifying, unknown place. If the fall had killed her or if something else — or *someone* else — had. He thought of Luka, the bastard who'd tried to kill him. Perhaps he had done the same to Mia and succeeded?

Even if he hadn't, even if Mia had accidentally stumbled and tripped over the edge in the darkness, it didn't matter. Ben would make sure Luka paid for her death. It wasn't an 'eye for an eye' situation.

To Ben, it was far simpler: Luka had tried to kill him. That meant the man would die.

Hopefully, he could make that happen before he got back to the others. If Luka had somehow overtaken Reggie as well, there would be nothing stopping Luka from sulking back to the group and pretending the Russian soldiers had interfered. From there, he could maneuver around and pick them off one by one.

Ben needed to get out, but the problem was that the sides of the stone vat of goop were too far above his head. He wasn't sure if he could even pull himself out of the heavy liquid-like mess, but if so, it would be impossible to scale the steep walls and get to the first level.

Unless...

He looked at Mia's lifeless body, half in and half out of the goop. Her eyes were closed, a peaceful expression on her face. At least there was that. From his perspective, it seemed that she had simply died in her sleep. He assumed Luka had injured or shot her, but if so, the wound was beneath the surface, hidden from sight. The fall alone should not have killed her, but whatever had was still an unknown.

He didn't like the idea of using her corpse for his gain, but he simply couldn't come up with a better solution. He hadn't known her well, but he thought she might have wanted him to get out, to avenge her death, and try to help save her friends.

He sighed, then took a deep breath. *Sorry about this, Mia. You were a good person. Hate that it has to end this way.*

Ben took a bit of comfort knowing that she would at least be pushed beneath the surface, hidden from sight. It wasn't much — certainly not a real burial — but it would be better than nothing. It would have to do.

He grabbed her arm, pulling her toward him as best he could, trying to get her legs and lower body pulled up as well. He tried to imagine her as a human, not just as a tool he was putting to use. Her body was stiff, hard as a board, and the thickness compounded by the awkward angle made moving anything difficult.

Finally, after ten minutes of working and reworking the body, taking a few steps forward and a couple back every minute, it was as good as it was going to get.

He rose, pulling his body gently onto hers, making sure to not move too rapidly. The harder he tried, the harder the gunk would work to pull him back in. It was like quicksand, but only moving when he did. As though it were alive, laughing at his progress and offering an opposite reaction to each of his actions.

But he prevailed, and eventually, he found himself mostly out of the goop, thick chunks of it dripping off his frame and splatting to the surface, or on Mia's body. He shook his head, hoping he had been correct in his assumptions about the physics at play here, and then tried to stand.

Mia's body was sucked down into the goop as he put his full weight on her chest. He balanced, his feet and legs shaking as he stretched up. The edge of the first level was right above him. His hands grasped at the wall. The slick stones turned into oily bars of soap as soon as the messy gunk touched them.

He could do it — he *had* to. There was no other option. No other alternative. He had been dead, resurrected by a strange twist of fate. Whether it had been God or luck or something else entirely did not matter to him. He was *alive,* and he would not waste it. He had survived a plane crash and ended up here, dead once again.

Twice in as many days. It was impossible to imagine, yet here he was.

And yet, he couldn't get a handle on the edge of the wall. There was no way he was getting up and over the lip on his own. He scratched and peeled off the goop in massive chunks, the slippery liquid leaving an oily residue that only made things more difficult. His palms slapped the wall, pushed upward and over, and yet unable to offer him any support.

He pushed and pulled and stretched for another ten minutes.

And, through it all, Mia's body was slowly sinking. Where before he could get a couple of knuckles up and over the edge, now he could reach it only with his fingertips. He was losing the battle, and every time he tried to stretch and hop onto her body, the corpse would just sink further.

It was a sick, cruel game, and he was losing it.

He watched the top of his cage float away, floating higher with every passing second.

And then a hand appeared at the edge.

His heart leaped. He smiled. *Yes. God, thank you. Yes.* He was going to get free.

The hand was joined by another, and then two more.

He frowned. These hands were connected to arms wearing sleeves, a dark color to them that was almost black. Almost like...

Shit.

He heard voices. Russian. Speaking with one another and speaking to him. He swallowed, waiting. The hands found him, started grabbing at him. Pulled him up.

He saw their faces. Rough, scarred heaps of flesh zigzagging across one of them, pockmarks and swollen burn marks on the other. These weren't the faces of his team, nor were they the faces of the Russian scientists.

They *were* Russian, however, and he knew immediately that they were the faces of soldiers.

One of the men mumbled something quietly, something Ben didn't understand. The other man grinned a wicked smile, then laughed.

This is not good, Ben thought. *Not good at all.*

They pulled him up and over the edge, then let him gasp for air and recover while they reached for the weapons they had cast aside. They lifted them up, slung the straps over their shoulders, then pointed the ends down at him.

The man who had spoken addressed Ben in broken English. "You are American," he said. "And you have killed my men. You will answer for their deaths."

CHAPTER 44

SARAH

DR. SARAH LINDGREN watched the floor as they rounded the hallway. She had found it the most reliable way to determine whether there would be anyone waiting for them around the next corner — their shadows would often give them away, even if they weren't moving.

What she hadn't expected, however, was for the first attack to come from behind.

She whirled around when she heard the muffled grunt of Gator going down, saw the flash of light from his wide eyes as the knife plunged into his neck, felt the cold terror of dopamine hitting her system as she realized the Russian soldiers had been silently tracking them all along.

And just like that, Gator was dead.

"No!" she heard Freddie roar. He was near the front of the line, walking just behind her and Reggie, standing next to Julie, but he quickly blew past Evgeni and Tatiana to reach the back of it. The two Russians who had snuck up on Gator and taken him out were ready.

Freddie launched his huge body into the first of the Russians, who was trying to dislodge the knife from Gator's neck and prepare for the next attack. Freddie beat him there, and together both men crashed to the stone floor and began rolling around, each trying to gain purchase on the other.

The second Russian soldier ignored the battle for the moment, focusing his attention instead on Reggie, who had turned the submachine gun he'd picked up toward the back of the line. Sarah knew he wouldn't fire until it was abundantly clear they were all out of the way, so she backed up and pressed herself up against the side wall.

Evgeni and Tatiana, for their part, hit the ground and ducked out of the way. Julie watched on with the detached expression on her face. If the Russian thought she may be a threat, he didn't show it. He sprinted up the hallway toward the main atrium opening on that level where they had been heading, aiming for Reggie.

The two soldiers collided in midair, neither even attempting to juke or feint. They simply *slammed* into one another, only a grunt from the Russian man telling Sarah that they were human enough to feel it.

She knew how Reggie was feeling — he had hardly said a word to her and based on his rapid pace through the maze of corridors in this place, she knew he was out for blood. She had felt it herself when she'd believed her father to be dead. He had ended up alive and well, but it didn't change the days of despair and turmoil in the unknown. For Reggie, however, there was no unknown — he had seen his best friend die firsthand. He had explained it to the group in simple, blunt terms, giving them only enough information to understand the plight of their voyage and what it meant for their survival.

Luka was working with the Russian soldiers.

All the Russian soldiers wanted them dead.

They were still trapped inside an ancient city, beneath the ice in Antarctica.

It was an impossible situation that Sarah herself couldn't even believe, yet here she was, smacked against a stone wall, watching two superhuman soldiers battle it out for their lives.

Reggie punched the Russian with the butt of his gun, but the

Russian man didn't even feel it. He righted his head, ejected a few teeth with a brutal, bloody swatch of saliva, and then returned the favor with a huge, meaty fist.

Only then did Sarah realize it was the guard who had been watching them earlier. The one who had been eyeing her out of the corner of his eye and had even tried copping a feel shortly after their arrival.

She'd wanted Reggie to win the fight, but now she wanted to *join* it. She screamed in anger and launched herself toward the two men in the hallway. Still, Julie watched on, her face a mask of blank nothingness.

Sarah landed atop the Russian soldier's head, immediately going for his hair. She pulled it out in chunks. The man shouted something obscene in Russian but continued pressing Reggie. Reggie was slugging him in the sides, stomach, and groin, but none of the blows seemed to do much harm.

Sarah doubled her efforts, pulling herself up higher and then jamming her thumbs as far into the man's eyes as possible. She felt flesh tear, the watery sinews of the skin inside the man's sockets peeling away and intermingling with blood, which had dripped out and down his face.

That did the trick. The Russian wailed and dropped to his knees. It was gruesome, and she was repulsed even by the thought of it, but she was thankful the dim light of the connecting hallway's single bulb made it difficult to see.

Reggie took advantage of the moment and brought an elbow up and back, then smashed it *through* the man's nose. Blood exploded up and onto Sarah's face, and she frantically grasped through the slime to keep her thumb in place.

He stopped moving forward once he had hit his knees, and the Russian was now swaying gently, rocking back and forth. Sarah found purchase and applied more pressure, felt more squishy things popping inside his head.

She couldn't believe she was actually doing this, but she couldn't will herself to stop. She remembered his groping looks, his cold heavy claw on her backside, the disgusting grin as he saw her blush...

She pressed again and groaned with the exertion, and he groaned beneath her as he gave way and fell forward. Still, she held on.

"Sarah..."

Reggie's voice didn't register at first.

"Sarah, hey —"

"No," she said. "I've *had* it. This bastard, this *mother* —"

"*Sarah*," Reggie said again. His arm was there, his hand motioning. She looked up, saw his face. The concerned expression on it. He reached down and pulled her up, his steady grip easing her shaking.

She allowed herself to release the dead Russian, finally. She stood, only then noticing what had gotten Reggie so concerned.

It wasn't her — it wasn't the repulsive murder she'd just committed.

No, it was something else.

They weren't alone.

The two Russians who'd attacked them and killed Gator were no longer only two. Now there were more.

A lot more.

All of them waiting patiently for the Americans' attention.

All holding guns and pointing them at her.

CHAPTER 45

BEN

BEN'S BODY was still dripping with goop, and his feet slid down every step. Still, his Russian captors didn't slow — they kept him moving, guiding him upward around the corkscrew first level onto the second. Here, there were larger caverns drilled from the stone, each the size of a warehouse. Lights dotted the walls on strings of extension cords, and folding tables had been set up in rows on the floor.

Men — not soldiers, but civilian-looking — worked behind laptops, seated at the tables on folding chairs. A few soldiers milled about; their weapons slung over their shoulders. He thought he recognized one of them, a guard from the place they had been held earlier, one man who had interrogated him and Reggie. No one gave him more than a cursory glance as he entered, all of them busy with some other secret important tasks.

It was a large operation, whatever it was, and Ben was impressed and surprised by the scope of it.

"What is this?" he asked. Not surprisingly, neither of the soldiers who had brought him in answered. Instead, they brusquely pushed him toward a table near the side of the room, gave him a folding chair, and then stood behind him. He was facing the wall, the entire operation of Russians and their computers, and submachine guns behind him. He hated having his back to all of that, but they hadn't given him a choice.

He knew it was a power play, meant to keep him off-balance, and it was working. He was getting chilly, what with being covered by a thick, gloppy mess of some alien substance.

Ben waited there with the guards for a few minutes until another man walked through a gap in the stone to his right, entered the great space, and looked directly at Ben.

Ben felt his stomach rise to his throat.

Luka.

"You bastard," he muttered through gritted teeth. "You killed —
"

"Mia?" he said, walking over and taking a seat directly across from him. His English was impeccable, the broken stuttering from before clearly an act. "Yes, I did. And I will kill each of the other scientists as well, as they are losing their usefulness. After that, your own team. What did you call it? CSO?"

Ben shifted in his seat but didn't answer. He glared at the smaller man.

"I needed to know who you were, Harvey Bennett," Luka said. "I apologize for the dramatic reveal, but there really is no better way to monitor your mission than to actually be a part of it."

"The others — Evgeni — they all think you're a scientist."

"I *am* a scientist, Ben," Luka said. "A damned good one, actually. Studied in America, believe it or not, but my work has always been for the greater good of my home country."

"And what 'greater good' is that?"

"All in good time, Ben. I'm afraid it's not time you have."

"Then why am I here?"

"I told you — I need to know what you know. Two years ago, I hired Evgeni to put together a team to run some ice core samples here, to prepare for what you see now, but I wanted to monitor him, so I joined the team myself. I did not expect you and your group to arrive, though we were expecting a bit of US interest in the project."

Ben thought back to the initial encounter with the Russian soldiers in the ancient city. They had been shot at, but none of the shots had landed, even though their attackers had the higher ground, had the numbers, and had weapons with more than enough range.

He remembered Luka's expressionless face as they were attacked, too. *He had known about it all along. He had probably ordered it.* Ben had to admit that as sick as it was to order an attack on his own team, on himself, it was a solid way to convince everyone else you were on their side.

To what end, though? he thought. *Why go through all this trouble?*

"I can assure you, none of us has any idea what the hell you're doing here. Or what this place even is."

"I'm not sure you *can* assure me of that," Luka said. "I've been doing research on you — all of you. You're capable, smart, and quick. You have plenty of successes stacked up, lining your pockets. You take cases you believe to be in the best interest of your own version of the 'greater good,' do you not? It's nice. It's all very humble, very appropriate. Very American."

Ben didn't speak, waiting for Luka to get to his point.

"But when that mission interferes with the mission of the greatest nation on Earth, it is something that must be dealt with." He leaned forward in his chair, his elbows on the table, his eyes examining Ben's. "I *must* know what you know. What you would — if you could — tell your superiors back home."

"Did you shoot down our plane?" Ben asked.

Luka blinked, but otherwise didn't seem at all fazed by the question. "Yes. Testing a new missile defense system — a small-scale surface-to-air launch apparatus I had the military ship over. I'd say it works well, wouldn't you?"

"We lost a good kid from that. And pilots. They were innocent."

Luka smacked the table. "They were flying you here to *stop* us, weren't they? Is that innocent? They were nothing but chauffeurs, showing you around the area?"

"Fine," Ben said. "We came here to see what you were up to."

"To spy."

"Do I look like a spy?"

"This isn't Hollywood, Ben," Luka snapped. "*No* spy looks like a spy."

"Whatever. I'm not a spy."

"But you were sent here to spy."

"We *came* here to see what you were doing. That's it. And, for the record, I still do not know."

"I like that you protect your superiors, even when it is pointless. Who sent you?"

Ben shrugged. "Just thought we'd check out the area, like you said. Call it a fluke we found you."

Luka chuckled. "We have ways of —"

"Making me talk? Really?"

"It works. Without fail, really. It's just a matter of time with the stronger ones. I suspect you'd crack later, but you'd crack, I assure you."

"I told you already — we know nothing about your plans here. What is this place, anyway? You obviously found it, but whose was it before? Is it really Minoan?"

Luka shook his head. "Older. We found the ship, and while it is in perfect condition, it is difficult to classify the civilization it was built by. It closely matches the Minoan or Cretan region, but we think it is even older than that."

"That's incredible."

"It really is," Luka said. "Almost as incredible as this place. Built by the same hands that crafted the ship, over the course of many decades, most likely."

"Why? Why live here?"

"We are not sure they ever did, aside from while they were building it. We have seen no signs that they spent much time here. We are not entirely sure why."

"You are not sure, or you just don't want to tell me?"

"A little of both. But no, we do not have all the answers here. That is why your team is still alive. We were hoping there could be some sort of... how would you put it? Camaraderie?"

"You thought we'd *help* you here?" Ben asked.

"We hoped you would be interested enough in finding the answers you would lend a hand."

"That's why you stayed with our group," Ben said. "You were trying to glean information from us. From Dr. Lindgren."

"She is an intelligent researcher, for a woman."

"For a woman? You know, you guys are all a bunch of ass-backwards old-school sexists. I mean, really — women can't be soldiers in Russia?"

Luka grinned. "Yes, of course they can. But this is my project. Although I work for my homeland, I do not agree with all of their modernized regulations."

Ben chewed his lip. "Hmm, yeah. I've known some dudes who weren't really into women. I have no problem with —"

"I am not —" Luka stopped himself, and Ben smiled. He was finally getting to the man; he'd obviously found a sore spot.

"What is it about them? Their looks? Can't get any work done when you've got women around? Or is it that you actually believe they're inferior, and you can't stomach the fact that one might know something you don't?"

Luka looked as though he were about to pound the table or flip it over, but he remained outwardly calm. "That — that is enough."

"Or is it that —"

Before he could slide in another slight, Ben was interrupted by the sound of footsteps approaching behind him.

The soldier appeared in Ben's peripheral and leaned down, then spoke into Luka's ear. After a few seconds, Ben saw Luka relax and shift in his seat. He thanked the man in Russian and turned back to Ben.

"It seems as though my team has performed their job admirably," he began. "And *your* team will join us soon."

CHAPTER 46

BEN

BEN WATCHED in horror as his entire team was marched into the room. He saw Reggie first, the man's head low and facing the stone floor. He was unarmed, and his arms were being held tightly by two Russian soldiers. Julie was next, and she was looking straight at Ben.

It took a moment, but she cocked her head to the side, disbelief on her face. Finally, she opened her mouth, closed it again, and then her jaw dropped.

"B — Ben?"

He grinned, rising from the chair. He looked over at Luka, who nodded. Apparently, Luka was trying to play the role of gracious host, allowing his captives to embrace and forget the fact that they were still about to die.

Ben didn't care. He raced over and grabbed Julie, lifting her off the ground. Every bone in his body ached, and his side reminded him that he still had an open wound there, but he ignored it and kissed her.

"How are you alive?" she asked. "And what's all over your body?"

"Magic goop."

"Magic what? And again, how are you alive?"

"Magic goop — it's what's all over me, and it's how I'm alive. I fell into… a vat or something. It's full of this ketchup-thick semi-opaque liquid."

"That's disgusting."

He shrugged, then grinned. "At least I'm alive."

Reggie was there too, and he grabbed around Ben's waist and picked up *both* him and Julie. Ben groaned in agony and nearly gasped in pain before Reggie finally released him.

He laughed as he stepped back from Ben. "And yeah, she's right — whatever was in that hole you fell into, it's all over you."

"Wasn't aware," Ben said. "Thanks for the head's up."

"Just being helpful," Reggie said. "Good to see you again, bud."

"You too. Oh, and thanks for leaving me hanging back there."

Reggie looked shocked. "Leaving you — what? You weren't hanging on anything but *air*, brother. Even I couldn't save your ass from that one. How'd you even make it out?"

"'Magic goop,' apparently," Julie said. "The stuff that's all over him. Would love to see what that's all about."

"Trust me, you don't."

Ben looked back at the door and saw Freddie standing there with Sarah and the two Russian scientists. All looked haggard, solemn. He made eye contact with Freddie, who just shook his head.

In a flash, it all came back. Ben remembered what Luka had done; he remembered the plane crash and the injuries and the death. He remembered his vow.

He turned back to Luka and addressed him loudly enough for the others to hear. "Okay, time we all caught up, wouldn't you say?"

Luka spread his arms wide before responding. "Indeed," he said. He was facing Evgeni and Tatiana. "I do apologize for my secrecy, but it was the only way to determine whether the project's full mission remained a secret."

Evgeni looked like he wanted to cry, but Tatiana stood there, resolved and resolute. Neither spoke.

"If you will all follow me, I would like to show you something."

He turned on a heel and walked toward the small doorway Ben had seen him come out of. Ben wasn't sure what to do, but Sarah and Reggie didn't hesitate. They followed Luka. The Russian soldiers who had brought them in were in tow, their guns pointed toward the floor but only a second away from being ready to fire into their backs.

Freddie approached Ben's side. "Hey man," he said.

"Hey. Sorry about —"

"It's fine. Listen, we're running out of time."

Ben tried to understand. "We don't even know what that's all about, remember? And Luka was the one who overheard it, and now we find out he's been the one behind all of this?"

"Still, I'm thinking there's something we don't know."

"There's a lot we don't know."

"I mean..." his voice died away as they walked. Julie grabbed Ben's hand and walked next to them.

"What are you trying to say, Freddie?" Ben asked. "Just spit it out. You think there's still a game clock? Something happening soon?"

"It's just... I don't know. Something doesn't feel right."

Ben looked straight ahead, trying to put it together. Luka was going to show them something. Or kill them. Ben wasn't sure which — potentially both. Still, he had kept them alive thus far. Why? What was the point if he knew he was going to kill them, anyway?

They rounded a corner after moving through the doorway, and Ben saw another room, similar in size to the large one they'd just exited. Inside this one, however, were machines.

Lots of machines.

Ben had no idea what any of them did, but they were absolutely massive. Each was on a track, like a military tank, but instead of facing a certain direction parallel to the ground, they were vertical. A stout tube shot upwards from the top of each machine, about a foot in diameter and launching into the air about eight feet above the ground.

"What the —"

"This is the heart of our project here," Luka said, walking them around two of the massive mechanical beasts and stopping in the center. The eight machines were arranged in a semi-circle around Luka, facing the side wall. "We have three more rooms exactly like this one. All brand-new machines, built to replace the stone-age versions we found down here. These will be far more efficient."

"Thirty-two of these bad boys," Reggie said. He whistled. "And just what, exactly, are they?"

Luka smiled. "They are jackhammers, essentially. But instead of smacking the *ground*, they simply create a massive pressure wave, repeatedly, inside their pressurized tubes. Those are amplified inside each of the hollow bodies of the fuselage, which then reverberates the wave throughout the space. Each has been tuned to a particular frequency that we have discovered to be the optimal movement pitch."

Ben pinched the bridge of his nose. *They found an ancient version of these down here?* he thought. *Ancient noisemakers? Why?*

"Optimal movement pitch — what the hell?" Reggie asked. "All this cloak and dagger, sneaking around like you're some innocent Russian scientist, blowing planes out of the sky? Why? Just to hide your super weird mechanical orchestra?"

"I like that," Luka said, laughing. "'Mechanical orchestra.' I may use that." He paused, then addressed Reggie directly. "And no, it is not just for musical enjoyment. There is a very particular reason for their being arranged in this way. And all of it is for something *far* more important to the Motherland."

"I'm sure it is," Ben said. "But I don't really care about that right now. Right now, I just want to get out of here. Thing is, you mentioned something about 'killing us all anyway,' and I'm *really* curious to know why you haven't done that yet."

Luka swallowed, then approached Ben. He stopped a foot away, and Ben felt Julie's hand tightening around his. "Yes," Luka said. "It is regrettable that you all came here just to die. Unfortunately, there is nothing we can do about that. I told you earlier that each of you can serve a purpose to this mission before you are removed, or you can choose to go to your grave unwillingly."

"Not sure you're going to get the cooperation you're after, Luka," Reggie said.

"Actually, I am sure I will."

One of the Russian soldiers moved in behind Tatiana and raised his gun. He lifted it to the back of her head, then fired.

Luka didn't even turn around.

CHAPTER 47

BEN

TATIANA'S HEAD simply ceased to exist, and the rest of her crumpled into itself and dropped to the floor.

Evgeni put his hands over his ears, screaming in silence as he reacted to the deafening gunshot that had gone off less than a foot away from his head when he realized what had just happened.

"No!" he screamed. "No, no — what — what have you —" he dropped to his knees and pulled at Tatiana's lifeless arm. Blood slicked over his hands, pooling around his knees.

Ben felt the adrenaline once again return to his system, surprising himself that he had more to give. He lunged forward and was about to punch Luka when he felt a heavy hand pushing him to the ground. He fell, then felt a *smack* on the back of his head.

He wasn't knocked out, but he was immediately disoriented and dazed. He looked up, seeing two forms of Julie standing over him as well as two matching Russian soldiers, both retracting their weapon from the back of his head.

He turned the other way, rolling over onto his back, and saw two Lukas. The man seemed concerned, like he'd just watch a baby bird fall from its nest.

"Now, let us continue," he heard Luka say.

Julie reached down and tried to help him up. He made it to a seated position before realizing he needed a few more minutes on the floor. He took slow, steady breaths.

"I hope you realize that I do not *prefer* doing things this way," he said. "But I need you to understand the depths of my concern for completing this project *on time,* without interference. It is our belief that *interference* is exactly what we are going to encounter, and it is my belief that *you* — someone here, if not all of you — *know* about that interference."

"What the hell is he talking about?" Ben asked. Julie shook her head. He looked around. Reggie seemed just as confused. Evgeni was crying, the man lying on the ground next to Tatiana's body. Sarah was standing next to Freddie, but her face was emotionless.

Luka waited a few seconds. "Let us move on," he said. "Next."

The Russian soldier who had killed Tatiana slid sideways and pointed his weapon down at Evgeni. Evgeni didn't seem to notice, but Reggie did.

"Wait!" he said. "Hold on, hold on."

Luka smiled. "There we go. Mr. Reggie, yes. I am not surprised. What is it you would like to tell us?"

Reggie swallowed, and Ben watched his best friend. Had he been holding out on him? Did he know something no one else did?

"I, uh, think you're making a mistake."

Luka nodded, thinking for a second. "That is disappointing, Reggie. I thought you were actually going to tell me something *useful.*" Luka turned and addressed Ben. "This is exactly what I was talking about, Harvey. Your team is proving its *uselessness,* one member at a time."

He motioned for the Russian soldier behind Reggie to step up, and the man lifted his gun and positioned it behind Reggie's head.

Ben felt his stomach drop. He had nothing to offer, nothing to give. He had no plan, no way to fight off a room full of armed Russian soldiers.

He looked over at his friend, who was staring directly at Luka. He saw the Russian's finger sliding over the trigger, pulling it back toward him with his fingertip.

Reggie's head fell. Sarah screamed.

"Wait!"

The Russian soldier paused, the trigger half-pulled. Ben took in a deep breath and looked over at Freddie.

"Wait," Freddie said again. "I — I know what you need to know."

Luka looked at him strangely, then addressed him. "I will allow you one last chance. Prove your usefulness to me, Mr. Freddie, or we are done here."

Freddie nodded, gritting his teeth. "I know what's going to happen. I know about this 'interference' you're worried about."

"You do? And why is that?"

"I know about it because my uncle is the guy who's calling it in. I was given a very specific set of instructions."

Ben snapped his head over to Freddie. *No*, he thought. *Whatever it is, don't tell him.* He wondered if Freddie was still trying to play Luka, to buy them time, or if there was in fact something he knew.

"You overheard about it back in the rooms you were holding us in," Freddie said. "That's why you think it's going to happen soon."

"In thirty-seven minutes, I believe," Luka said.

"Actually, it's scheduled to happen in about twenty-three."

Ben's heart sank. *So it is true.*

"And what, *exactly*, is it? And how do you know about it?"

Freddie swallowed. "I know about it because it was my uncle who set it up. I'm the only one who can cancel it, and I'm the only one who knows. He gave me a very specific set of instructions. A command to call in and alert him that the mission here was accomplished."

"And if the mission is *not* accomplished?" Luka asked. "Like, for example, you are all being held at gunpoint inside this room and have no other option, no way to get the word out to your uncle?"

Freddie nodded. "Right, well, in that case, we're all dead. You're dead, we're dead, your puppet soldiers — all dead."

Luka's eyebrows rose. "I see — that is a very interesting theory, my friend."

"Not a theory," Freddie answered, shaking his head. "See, my uncle isn't just some regular 'ol guy. He's a pretty important guy as far as the U.S. government's concerned, and he's got a plane circling over our heads as we speak. A plane that's one-hundred percent under his command, and a plane with a payload."

Ben's head dropped, and he stared at the floor. Even though he hadn't heard this before, he knew Freddie was not lying.

"And it's ready to drop it on us as soon as the time runs out."

CHAPTER 48

JULIE

TWENTY-THREE MINUTES.

Julie watched and listened on in horror. Her mind had not been right for the past hour, what with hearing of Ben's death and then seeing with her own eyes his resurrection. She knew the man to be resilient, but this was something above and beyond.

And yet they weren't out of the woods. Not even close. Freddie had been withholding information from them all, information that had just changed the game. The event they had all been waiting for had nothing to do with the Russians; it had nothing to do with whatever Luka was planning here.

No, it was the general. Freddie's own uncle was sitting on a kill switch, a last-chance protocol that would decimate the area and kill them all.

She wanted to be upset, but she couldn't. It wasn't Freddie's fault. He was just following orders, acting according to his training. And he *was* a professional. He'd proven himself time and time again, even losing his close friends while doing it. There was nothing about the man that said to Julie he was capable of sabotage.

But it was maddening that they had come so close — *she* had come this close. Ben was alive, finally. And they were together once again. Only to find out that the madman who could kill them all wasn't even the madman who *would* kill them all.

"Can you stop it?" Reggie suddenly asked.

They were still standing in the large room full of tank-like machines, each of the massive things quietly waiting for their moment to come alive and start pumping sound into the space. For whatever reason, they hadn't determined yet.

Julie tried to understand it — why Luka's men were so adamant about creating a bunch of *noise*. Why they needed to fill the chasm out there with sound waves.

It was all confusing and strange, and more than a bit unnerving.

Freddie's response brought her back to the present. "No," he said.

Ben was on the ground next to her, breathing and trying to regulate his heart rate after the blow to his head. Thankfully, he seemed okay, but she wanted him to rest as much as possible.

"There's nothing we can do — nothing *any* of us can do," he said again, this time directing his words toward Luka.

Luka snickered. "The American way. I love it. Take charge, and if you can't take charge, take it. And if you can't *take* it, just blow it up."

"There's got to be *something* we can do," Sarah pleaded. "Can we call him? Somehow get a communication out to him that we're okay?"

"It needs to be me," Freddie answered, "and it needs to be my voice. Live. There is a validation question only I have the answer to."

"What if you had died in the plane crash?" Reggie asked. "We'd all be here for nothing — waiting to get blasted to hell?"

Freddie looked pained. "Look, man, I didn't... you know how this goes, right? I didn't have a choice."

"We always have a choice, son."

"Don't 'son' me," Freddie replied.

Julie felt the tension ratcheting up in the room but was surprised to see that Luka was simply smiling.

"You don't seem concerned, Luka," Ben said, taking the words right out of her mouth. "Got something to share?"

"Certainly not," he said. "What I *do* have is my answer. Mr. Freddie here has proven himself quite useful — you all, not so much."

He stuck a hand in the air and waved it around, and Julie winced. *This is it,* she thought. *He's going to kill us all.*

Instead, the soldiers began circling the room, approaching each of the machines. A few of them placed their weapons to the side and began fiddling with controls on an outward-facing panel on them. Two of the soldiers left the room and quickly returned with a gaggle of plainclothes-wearing men from the other room.

"You aren't going to kill us?"

"I will not waste the time on it, no," Luka said. "But you *will* die, that is certain. I wish I could be here to see it, but — as you've said — twelve minutes remaining. That should be just enough time to get away from this gift from on high your uncle will be delivering."

"It won't be," Freddie said. "It'll blast you off the face of the —"

"All the more reason to get a head start, my friend," Luka said. "I wish you all the best. This has been quite enjoyable."

He started to leave, but Julie stood up and whirled around. "Luka!" she yelled. He turned around, an impatient look on his face. "All of this — your work here, these machines, whatever it is you've been working toward — it'll be gone. Destroyed. And you're just... okay with that?"

He contemplated the question for a moment and then began to laugh. It started slowly, then rose a bit until he cut it off. "Actually, you might be quite surprised to learn that your friend here, Mr. Freddie, has made my job even *easier*. This will play into my plans quite well, I suspect."

Without more explanation, he turned once again and left the room, moving quickly and flanked by two Russian soldiers.

Julie spun around, taking it all in. The remaining soldiers worked on the machines, a few of them still standing by with their weapons drawn, their eyes on her and the group. Evgeni was sobbing on the floor, rocking back and forth. Sarah and Reggie were hand-in-hand like she and Ben, and Freddie seemed shellshocked.

"All right," Reggie finally said. "Twenty minutes left until the end of the world. Gonna be a lot of water around here in a bit — what say we, uh, figure out how to make that *not* happen?"

Freddie looked like a kid who'd just been bullied. "It's impossible," he said. "We will not hack a computer or even get a remote connection set up on an open one in time. The validation alone will take me thirty seconds, and then —"

Ben pulled himself to his feet with Julie's help, then turned to Freddie. "We're not doing anything with your uncle's help, actually. It's not possible, so it's not an option to waste time on."

"You got a better idea?"

"Nope," Ben said. "But I've been through a few of these 'no idea what the hell we're supposed to do' situations, and the answer always seems to scream at us, staring us right in the face."

"So... what do we do first?" Freddie asked.

Ben smiled, then pointed to Evgeni. "First, we need to ask this guy a bit more about something he told us about earlier."

CHAPTER 49

BEN

BEN CLEARED his throat as Evgeni and the others looked at him. "First, though, let's walk and talk."

"You think they'll let us?" Reggie asked.

"Only one way to find out." Ben took a step toward the exit doorway, away from the machines. The guards holding weapons shifted but didn't move toward him. None of the others in the room seemed to even notice.

"They're too busy with these machines," Reggie said. "Whatever magical noise they're trying to make with these things, they're pretty hellbent on finishing it."

"Why would a noise be that important?" Julie asked as they left the room. The next room over, the larger one, featured men behind their computer screens, rapidly tapping away and focusing on nothing but the text directly in front of their eyes.

Ben wondered if they even knew what their fate would be in twenty minutes. If Luka had filled them in, or if he was too preoccupied trying to save his own skin. And they were all men, which struck Ben as odd. He knew Luka had mentioned something about it, but he wondered if it was like a sort of cult, a group so willing to blindly follow orders and worked toward a common goal they didn't even care about their impending deaths.

"Must be a nice sound," Reggie said.

Without warning, a massive *crack* sounded throughout the room. A few of the men behind computers looked around, but no one moved from their chairs.

Ben and Julie had their hands over their ears, while Reggie was working his jaw, trying to pop his.

Freddie spoke, but his voice was far louder than normal, no doubt an aftereffect from the noise. "What in tarnal damnation was *that*?"

Another *boom* shook the walls, and some dust began falling from high above. A third cracking sound echoed around the room.

"I believe that's the wonderful sound we were so interested to hear," Reggie said.

Three more booms echoed, each one getting louder, and each coming from the room next to theirs. The fourth crack after that seemed to come from all around them, filling the space with cacophony.

"They're starting the machines in all the rooms," Ben said. "They're on a synced scheduled. One every five seconds or so."

"Great," Reggie said. "Sounds like our last twenty minutes on earth is going to be a real headache."

Freddie was now holding hands over his ears and screaming to be heard. "Do you always joke around like this on a mission?"

Reggie shrugged. "I never took well to falling in line and taking orders from a ringdinger you can out-shoot."

"Let's stay focused," Julie said. "We need to know what the *point* of all of this is, right?"

Ben looked over at Evgeni, who didn't have his hands over his ears but was still hunched over, cowering slightly. He seemed broken, beat down. "We need to talk to him. He mentioned something earlier, something that might be helpful."

"Crustal displacement," Sarah said. "It's a geologic theory, but it's half-baked and most of its core tenets have been disproven."

"The possibility of building a stone city in Antarctica thousands of years ago was also disproven," Reggie said.

"Fair enough," she said. "Evgeni? Want to tell us more about it?"

He looked left and right, then shuddered when the booming sound grew even louder.

"Shit," Reggie said. "I can't even hear myself *think*. Can we get somewhere else a bit *quieter?*"

Ben nodded. "We should keep moving, anyway. Anything to get us farther away from these weirdos and their crazy noisemakers."

They walked toward the exit of this room, the one that led out to the main corkscrew-shaped atrium that connected all the pathways and hallways to the central artery and found the noise there even louder. Ben's jaw was rattling, his ears ready to explode. The pressure every five seconds seemed to be too great, building and building until finally it released and withdrew. Any longer, and he was worried he'd bust an eardrum, or worse.

He led the group to a hallway that curved away from the lower level they were on, and immediately the noise subsided. It was still clearly audible, and the walls of the city still shook and rattled with each drumbeat, but it was far better than where they'd been.

"Okay," Ben said, checking his watch. "How much time do we have? Maybe fifteen minutes?"

"I'd say fourteen," Freddie said.

"Fine," Ben replied. "We'll make it work. We have to know what this is all about first, though. There isn't a vehicle on the planet fast enough to get us far enough away from here when that bomb goes off, so —"

"So we're hosed," Reggie said. "We're hunkering down in here, no matter what."

"Pretty much," Ben said. "That means if there's any way to save ourselves, it'll have to be here."

"Inside an impossible city that can't possibly be here and can't possibly be Minoan."

Ben cocked his head sideways, looking at Evgeni. "Actually, I think this place *is* Minoan, or whoever they were before. We were on the right track, and I think Evgeni and Sarah can fill us in on the details."

CHAPTER 50

JULIE

"BUT THIS IS IMPOSSIBLE," Julie said. "Right? The Minoans — or whoever they were — were not known to have ever traveled this far."

"But they were known to have *traveled*," Sarah said. "Our research from when we were on the island of Santorini proved that the Cretans were able to travel via ship much farther out from what we previously believed. It completely overturns the known history of the civilization."

Evgeni stirred, then straightened up. It seemed his scientific nature had gotten the best of him, and he couldn't help but get involved in the conversation. "And our research verifies that," Evgeni said. "It is not complete, and it is certainly not thorough, but examining the history of the known Minoan civilization and knowing that they were, somehow, able to get a boat all the way here seems to be more and more likely."

Julie nodded, taking it all in. She still couldn't believe her eyes. No matter what it was — no matter who had built this place — it was utterly amazing. "But it's *stone*, not ice. That means they would have had to bring all of it here, right?"

There was a pause, and then Evgeni spoke up. "Not necessarily," he said. "That's what Ben was referring to. It is a theory that I tend to believe, though I am in the minority in my community."

"What is it?" Julie asked.

"My team has been studying ice cores. We know, generally, the geologic history of this area, and much of the entire continent. From an epochal standpoint, my team and I hypothesize that Antarctica has been swayed much by recent Ice Age-type events."

"Which means what, exactly?" Ben asked.

"It means Antarctica, like every other continent, has been pushed and pulled by changing temperatures. Because of its current location on the globe, those temperatures seem to be consistently *low*, obviously below freezing for the entire year."

"What does *that* mean?" Ben asked.

"And what do you mean by '*current* location?'" Reggie added.

Evgeni nodded quickly. "Yes, yes, I will get to that, I assure you. First, though. Consider that the ending of the last Ice Age, when the earth slowly started heating — a phase we are still in today — took a complete break somewhere in the realm of 8-12,000 years ago. It is referred to as the 'Younger Dryas' period. It was a time of *rapid* cooling, like a return to ice age-levels in the span of *decades* instead of millennia. I spent my graduate fieldwork studying this period specifically, so I am especially well-equipped to debate its veracity."

He looked around as if waiting for someone to argue with him, but no one did. Even Sarah seemed content with his mini lecture so far.

Evgeni continued by clearing his throat. "Right. Well. That timeline lines up with the *supposed* end of the Minoan civilization, yes?"

Julie nodded, noticing that once again Sarah was nodding along, agreeing.

"And this place is built in stone in a place that is known to have very little of that hardy earth material." He chuckled at his own joke, but apparently no one else got it. "Very little, but not *none*."

Julie's eyes widened. "Oh, my God," she said. "I get it. I understand where you're going with this. Antarctica isn't *all* ice, is it?"

Evgeni's eyes twinkled.

"It's an ice *cap*, covering an actual landmass."

"Two or more major landmasses, actually."

"That's right," Reggie added. "There's some river that flows between them, right?"

"It is really just the ocean, narrowed into a strait between the two main Antarctic landmasses, which sets them both apart as massive islands. There is a lower one with fewer mountains, and a taller, more mountainous island. Now, ice covers the entirety of *both* islands, forming the much larger Antarctica as we know it today."

"You're saying the Minoans came here and built this city from stone found *in* Antarctica?" Reggie asked.

"I don't think there's any other way," Sarah said. "It's what I have been considering — that this place is actually from ancient stone that existed *here*, in Antarctica."

"Correct," Evgeni added. "The Minoans must have come here, built their city, either lived in it or prepared to live in it, before this was all covered in ice."

Ben chewed his lip for a moment, then asked the question Julie knew they were all thinking. "How is that even possible? You said the ice age *ended* when the Minoans would have done it, so why would Antarctica be uncovered, and *then* cover with ice when the ice age was over?"

Evgeni held a finger in the air. "Ah, yes. That is the ultimate question, indeed."

"One you have an answer to, I hope?" Sarah asked. "We're still running out of time, you know."

Evgeni looked sidelong at her. "That is what we were brought here to find out. The mission, if you will, of my team. It is what Luka wanted us to find. We were on the *Rezak* for ice-core sampling that would tell us, hopefully, where Antarctica was located during the Younger Dryas period, and prior."

"Where it was *located*?" Reggie asked. "Give me a break. You mean to tell me we're standing on a continent that's been floating around the ocean? I thought it's been in the same spot since, well... I don't know, the dinosaurs or whatever. How does that work?"

"It's like that Panera thing," Freddie added.

Everyone stopped and stared at the hulking man. Finally, after many seconds of dumbfounded confusion, Sarah burst out laughing. "You mean *Pangea?*"

Freddie snapped his fingers and pointed at her. "Ah, yep. That's the one. I knew it sounded weird."

"Pangea, indeed," Evgeni said. "Good observation, Mr. Freddie. Yes, the machinations of Pangea, however, were a slightly different geologic technology. What I believe — what we came here to prove — is that a machination of another sort has been at work over the course of millennia. One that turns a place like the Amazon basin into one resembling the Sahara. Or one that turns a lush, inhabitable continent into something that is a desolate, frozen wasteland."

"Like Antarctica."

"And *if* these machinations were truly taking place," Evgeni continued, "it would mean a civilization like the Minoans, known for their intelligence, intuitiveness, and general technological prowess, it would not be out of the question for their society to have discovered this geological countdown timer, so to speak."

Ben picked up the thread. "Meaning they figured out the earth's ticking time bomb, predicted the next one, and got to Antarctica to build an infrastructure to keep their civilization alive."

"Perhaps," Evgeni said. "But they calculated wrong, I'm afraid. Judging by this incredible find, the Minoans built their future in a place that was always doomed to be covered in ice."

"But why?" Sarah asked. "If they were smart enough to figure out this 'machination,' or whatever it is, and then smart enough to actually *calculate* the next one, where did they go wrong? What mistake did they make that caused them to lose a foothold on their home island *and* down here?"

"Well, we have a working hypothesis for that," Evgeni said. "It may be helpful to understand the theory a bit more."

"Sure," she said. "Doesn't look like we've got anywhere else to go for the moment, but may I remind us —"

"Time's running out," Ben said. "We're down to less than ten minutes. Problem is I'm not sure where we can go to get away from this bomb."

"Down," Reggie said suddenly. "Down, down, down."

"AS YOU SAID EARLIER," Reggie replied. "Walk and talk. We need to head down."

"Why down?" Ben asked. He was following both men as they hustled back down to the second level, where the Russian conference room and machine rooms had been set up. The banging and rhythmic pulsing sounds of the machines rose in volume, and Ben wondered if they were making the right decision.

As he wondered and waited for an answer to his question, another noise — new to his ears — joined the fray. A high-pitched whine, like a drone flying nearby, reverberated through the room. It got louder over the next minute.

"Wait a minute. Anyone else hear that?" Ben asked.

"It's like the machines are vibrating," Julie said. "Sounds like a vacuum cleaner motor or something."

"Great," Ben said. "Heading down *toward* the weird machines that are now whirring up out of control."

Freddie stepped over to Ben and Reggie. "Yeah, why down?" he asked. "We don't know what kind of —"

"We can assume," Reggie answered. "We *have* to assume."

"Assume what?" Ben asked,

"Assume that the general's not using a bunker-buster," he said. "Payload capacity's really twofold: either the blast takes out a huge geographic area on the *surface,* or it's a smaller, more surgical explosive that can dig down a bit and detonate after impact."

"And why do you assume it's the first type?" Julie asked.

"Well, for one, we're in Antarctica. All the fun stuff happens on the surface. There really isn't supposed to be an 'underground,' as far as this continent is concerned."

"And yet here we are," Sarah said.

"So," Julie asked, "you think that by getting as deep as we can in this place, we are actually *safer* from the explosion?"

Reggie shrugged. "Well, that's the idea. But..."

Ben looked at Reggie, then Julie, then finally at Freddie, who was shaking his head. "Yeah, that's what I'm worried about, too," the large man said.

"Worried about what?" Ben asked. "Seriously, guys — tell us everything. What are we dealing with here?"

"Oh, it's the same thing it was before," Reggie replied. "Giant bomb about to fall on our heads and all that. But it's not really the *explosion* that worries me. I'm assuming that the explosion will be a surface detonation, which means we should be safe from it down here."

"But any explosion up *there* is going to cause instability down *here.*"

Ben looked at Julie, whose eyes were wide. Sarah seemed to be beside herself in fear, grasping onto Reggie's arm for support. Evgeni, for his part, didn't seem at all to care. Ben knew he must be confused and still a bit off-kilter from Tatiana's death, so he wasn't terribly surprised.

"So," Ben began. "Let me get this straight: bomb goes off up there. We die if we are close to it. Alternatively, bomb goes off up there. We die because this entire place caves in on itself."

"Yeah, pretty much," Freddie said. "Either a landslide shuts us in and we die of asphyxiation from a lack of oxygen, or it's death from lack of food or water,"

"Or we just die because a massive rock falls on our heads."

Reggie and Freddie nodded.

"Okay," Ben said. "Then why are we still heading *down*? If it's going to be over for us either way, why not get it done quickly? What are we even doing messing around with the idea that we can escape the blast? I mean, whatever is going to happen, these massive machines are only going to add to the —"

Ben stopped himself. He couldn't believe he hadn't considered it until now. *Yes, it had to be,* he thought.

The others could tell he was considering something new. "What is it?" Julie asked. "Is everything okay?"

Ben nodded. "I don't have it all figured out yet," he said, "but I just realized something. The way Luka dodged out of here and tried to get as far away from this place as possible, all while completely ignoring us, it all seemed a bit... strange."

"Well, to be fair, that man *was* a bit strange," Reggie said. "And besides, he told us that he thinks we're all going to be dead, anyway. Because of the bomb."

Ben shook his head. "No, *not* because of the bomb — that's just it. I was under that assumption as well until just now. Remember how he reacted? When he found out about Freddie's uncle's plan, he almost seemed pleasantly surprised. He seemed to actually *appreciate* the fact that there was a bomb about to drop on all our heads. Why is that? These machines going off, all in sequence, all rhythmically staggering their bursts so that the effect is one giant, massive *noise* throughout the entire city, spaced five seconds apart."

Julie's eyes widened. "It's because the bomb, if nothing else, will *help* them."

"Help who?" Freddie asked.

"Help the machines," Ben said. "That bomb is going to send out a massive pressure wave. A *sound* wave. Just like the ones these machines are pulsating outward. The bomb will only help finish whatever these machines are trying to start."

"That's... terrifying," Reggie said. "Why the hell could so much noise be necessary? What's he trying to do? Cause a cave-in?"

Evgeni stopped in the middle of the pathway, causing Reggie to bump into him. "Hey man, what gives?" Reggie asked.

Evgeni turned slowly, looking up at Reggie. "That is... *exactly* what he's trying to do. I cannot believe it, but it has to be the truth."

"Okay, he's trying to cause a cave-in?"

"Almost. Essentially, but in a controlled way. Have you ever heard of acoustic levitation?"

Ben turned and faced the people behind him. "Look, Evgeni, I've had enough weird and arcane scientific theories thrown at me over the past few days. I'm covered in a gunk that's drying on my body with every step, and no, it's not comfortable. So if you're going to tell me you think Luka and his Russian minions were down here trying to build some miraculous thing that's strong enough to levitate giant rocks or something, I don't want to hear it."

"Well," Evgeni said. "I do not think that."

"Good."

"I believe the *Minoans* did, though."

CHAPTER 52

BEN

THEY HAD REACHED the lowest level of the city; the level Ben had reached by falling into the vat of goop. He was standing right near the same edge of that same vat now, the circular space directly to his left.

The cavernous corkscrew-shaped city above him, with the bowl of liquid next to him, gave off the impression that he was standing in an old Mayan cenote in Mexico. A roof far above his head, too dim to see, and a hollowed-out swimming hole below that stretched down to unimaginable depths. He remembered the research he'd done on them — the ancient Mayan civilization, believing the cenotes to be entrances to the underworld, used them for everything from common swimming pools to more ceremonious things like flinging children into their open maws as a cruel sacrifice.

Ben knew he hadn't enjoyed swimming in this cenote, and he certainly hadn't enjoyed being Luka's sacrificial lamb. He wondered if there were more bodies besides Mia's inside the thick goop. He was tempted to look over the edge and see if her corpse was still stationary just below the surface or if it had started sinking.

"Okay," he said, feeling the rhythmic pounding of the machines as he peered over the edge. "Let's see if there's anything —"

He stopped.

"What?"

He had expected to see Mia's body after looking over the opening, but the surface of the goop was moving. Vibrating, lapping up at the sides of its stone tank. Every pounding pulse from the nearby machines seemed to push the waves higher.

"That's... weird," Reggie said.

"It's *really* weird," Ben said. "Trippy. The noise from the machines is causing it to vibrate."

Evgeni cleared his throat. "And the vibration of it — whatever it is — is causing the high-pitched sound we are hearing."

Everyone turned to look at Evgeni. "The 'acoustic levitation' thing?" Freddie asked.

"Yes," he said. "I do not know if they are trying to levitate something, but they are most certainly using the machines to create a pressure wave that perfectly vibrates *this* material, causing it to elicit a sound as well."

"That's great, Evgeni," Reggie said. "And what's the point?"

"Well — and this is what Ben was referring to — this is an ancient technique that has been wrapped in myth and legend. And like all myths and legends, it has grown into something that is out of reach of reality. But there is an actual, provable scientific truth to the underlying idea: that sound, emitted at a strong enough decibel level at the correct frequency, or pitch, can actually *move* a large object."

"And this frequency we're hearing," Julie said, "is the proper frequency to do what, exactly? Not levitation, I'm assuming?"

"No," Evgeni said. "I did not think it could be possible, but now... now I am unsure *what* is possible. The things I have seen in the past few days, starting with the ship, and —"

"Evgeni," Ben said. "Please, we need to hurry. We need to know if we are going to be safe here. What do you think Luka's ultimate goal is?"

Just then, the ground beneath Ben's feet fell away.

He stumbled, feeling the stones rising and meeting his legs half-way, causing his knees to crack. He groaned in pain but noticed that everyone around him had experienced the same thing.

"And what the hell was *that*?" Reggie asked, picking himself up from the floor. Sarah had made it through standing, but she was shaky. She was holding Reggie's shoulder, trying to regain her balance.

It happened once again, this time with a deeper, harder jolt.

"Shit on a shingle," Freddie said, "the whole place is coming down on us."

Ben didn't want to be anywhere near this central atrium when that happened. The vat of vibrating goop, the corkscrew-like shape, the fact that it was dead-center in the city — it all added up to his belief that whatever it had been designed for, it was about to be ground zero.

And the machines, lined up in a circular fashion, all facing in at this space.

"Move," he said. "Now! Try to run, get inside a room and as far away from here as possible."

"Ben —"

"No, we're not arguing about it. Do it, now. Whatever's about to happen, this place is the epicenter."

No one seemed to want to argue with that assessment. They ran, dodging around the smaller hallways and threw a few open rooms that had not been closed off by metal doors added by the Russians. The ground continued to rock; the tremors changing in size each time, sometimes manageable, sometimes forcing the group to stop and hold on to a wall for support.

Ben and Julie ran side by side, each moving quickly enough to get away from the central area but slowly enough to keep each other upright. It was rough, but doable. The earthquake-like jolts were sporadic and unpredictable, completely separate from the machines' perfectly rhythmic timing.

"Whatever he's doing, it's waking this place up!" Reggie yelled.

"I'm not sure that's a good thing."

"Oh, it's most definitely *not* a good thing."

"Let's just get as far away from it as we can," Ben said. "Then we can figure out what it means for us." He hoped his words came out as encouragement, rather than the way they'd sounded in his head. Something more akin to terror, disbelief, resignation.

Julie reached the edge of the wall before Ben, their unspoken destination. Ben got there a second later, smacked his hands against it like he'd won a race, then turned and watched his shaking, tripping team and Evgeni fall into the room.

He didn't like where they'd ended up — by his calculation, they were still too close to the central atrium and the machines one level above, but there was nowhere else to go. This wall should be a structural exterior wall, but again, he was no architect. And he certainly wasn't a *Minoan* one. He had no idea if this room would crumple first or not at all.

But it gave them time, for the moment, to breathe. To figure out their next steps.

He checked his watch, but he didn't have to read it. Freddie and Reggie were ready with their update. "Time's almost out," Reggie said. "I'm thinking eight minutes, maybe less."

"I have seven minutes, nine seconds," Freddie said. "My uncle's going to be on time, too. Unfortunately."

"That was another thing I never really liked about the military," Reggie said, smiling. "Always so anal about being on time."

"It has its perks," Freddie said.

"Is dropping a bomb on Antarctica that will kill your own nephew and all his friends one of them?"

Ben turned to Evgeni, hoping to change the subject one last time. "Evgeni, you were about to tell us what you think is happening here. Do you know?"

The man's nervous, broken exterior had hardened into a cold, empty shell. He was calm, looking around at each person as they spoke, taking it all in. When he spoke, his words were even, calculated. "I do," he said. "And I am sure of it now. All of it — everything we have been talking about, speculating on. It is all true, and it is all related."

"Related how?"

"It is all related to the theory of crustal displacement. That the earth's crust is sort of like an orange peel, connected to the mantle but only by weak structures. It is, essentially, floating on top of it."

"And it can move around?" Sarah asked. "That's the premise, right?"

"Yes, precisely. As we have discussed prior. The idea is that the crust can move over the mantle of the earth, sliding about during cataclysmic shifts."

"What kind of cataclysmic shifts?" Reggie asked.

"The poles," Evgeni said, without missing a beat. "The earth is magnetic — it has poles. North and South. But they are not always in the same place."

"They're not?"

"No," he said. "They most certainly are not. We have seen proof of this played out in just about every scientific field, but the fact is that the poles of the earth move."

"That doesn't sound good," Reggie said. "Sounds pretty messy."

"It can be quite devastating," Evgeni said. "And, I believe, that is exactly what is happening now."

CHAPTER 53

EVGENI

"THEY MOVE, changing positions over celestial timeframes. Sometimes these shifts are massive, displacing entire continents."

Evgeni spoke like a record player, merely regurgitating information without actually having an opinion on it one way or another. To him it was fact, but he also could not react to it for a different reason.

He felt dead inside. The emotional fortitude he had been building had been worn away, finally blasted apart by Tatiana's death. She had simply ceased to exist, and a part of him had gone with her. He wasn't feeling anything right now, and it was simple enough to continue talking, to reason his way through what he believed was happening.

"You asked me earlier, Mr. Reggie, why I believe Antarctica has moved."

"Yes, I remember."

"Well, this is why: crustal displacement. I believe the continent, the two main landmasses that poke up from the plate holding them, used to exist in an entirely different location. They were farther north — *much* farther north."

"And a pole shift caused them to float away?"

"In a sense, yes," Evgeni said. "It was more complicated than that, and it probably happened over the course of a thousand years, but consider that a thousand years, in geologic terms, is a snap of the fingers."

Sarah jumped in. "And if that's the case, those thousand years would have been *massively* active in terms of geology. Volcanos, shifting plates causing incredibly powerful earthquakes, flooding everywhere —"

"Everywhere there was human life, yes," Evgeni said. "Or a 'Great Flood.'"

"Of biblical proportions," Sarah said. "We researched this in Egypt and Santorini. The cause of the flood that impacted ancient civilizations."

"Yes, but we also know that those civilizations may not have been *early*. Perhaps they were more like the 'middle' civilizations. Societies and peoples that came into existence long ago, but still long after their predecessors."

"So," Ben said, "you're saying that the people who built this place — the Minoans, or their predecessors — came here and built this city on the continent, but that the *continent itself* was not here at the bottom of the earth?"

"Yes, that is exactly what I am saying."

Reggie's eyebrows rose, and Evgeni stopped to look at him. "We have less than five minutes left, folks. Any last words?"

There was an awkward silence, and finally, Ben spoke up. "I, uh, I guess this is it, then. If we're dead, we're dead."

"'If we're dead, we're dead?'" Julie mocked. "*That* is your idea of 'last words?'"

"Well, I don't know —"

"How about, 'it's been fun,'" Reggie said.

Evgeni looked around at the CSO team, somehow joking about the end of the world.

"Has it been fun?" Ben shot back. "Everything we've been through — has it really been fun?"

There was another pause, and then Reggie chuckled. Evgeni and Freddie looked at him strangely, but then Ben laughed as well.

Julie joined in, and finally Sarah. All the CSO members were *laughing*.

"Wh — what is happening?" Evgeni asked. "Is this some sort of sick joke?"

Ben shook his head and spoke through tears. "No, I'm afraid not, Evgeni. No joke. We're just... taking it all in, I think. Seems like a fitting way to go, you know? Laughing?"

"But we all could —"

"Don't say it," Reggie said, still roaring in laughter. "Don't even say the word. You'll jinx it."

"I will what?"

"There's nothing we can do now — might as well have a quick laugh, if it's the last thing we do."

For whatever reason, the others seemed to think these words of Reggie's were especially humorous, and Evgeni looked from one person to the next, trying to decide what to do.

"Wait a minute," he said.

No one listened. He turned around, stumbling to the door through another earthquake-burst of movement.

"Hey —" Reggie shouted, still trying to hold back laughter. "Where are you going?"

"Five minutes left," he muttered.

"Five? Oh, yeah, right. Probably more like four."

"Four minutes," Evgeni said. "I need to —"

"What? Go back up to those machines?" Freddie asked. "Are you insane?"

But Evgeni didn't respond. He pushed against the wall, against the doorway, and then against the hallway itself. He followed the lights the Russian soldiers, Luka's team, had strung up. The hallway led to another, and then another, and he had burned through a minute before he knew it. Finally, he saw the somewhat brighter light of the main atrium. The path immediately began increasing in pitch, the steeper route heading toward the central area.

He could sense that someone was following him. One of the CSO members. But he was too focused, too driven, to turn around to find out who. He also wasn't sure his body's balance regulation would allow him to make that movement, with the world around him shaking so violently.

So he marched, carefully but quickly, toward the vat of semi-liquid in the central space. He saw that it was bubbling over, small portions of it rising and splatting over the edge, onto the level's walkway.

He turned, continuing to hold the stone walls of the path as it rose around the curved walkway.

He reached the second level and turned into the first of the massive rooms, saw the Russians seated behind their computer screens. He noticed that a few of them were holding the tops of the laptops, keeping them rigid against the shaking tabletops. Whatever they were doing, the earthquake they were causing didn't seem to affect them.

He saw a few soldiers, but they weren't paying him any attention. Two were sitting in chairs across the room, but one was holding his head like he had a migraine. Evgeni wouldn't have been surprised if that were the case — his own head was pounding from the outside *and* the inside.

Finally, with three minutes left on his internal countdown clock, he reached his destination.

The machines. There were no soldiers or technicians in here anymore — they had all gone into the other room or elsewhere in the facility, awaiting the results of this macabre test. No one had seen him enter, and now he was alone in the room.

He tried to recall what Luka had said about these machines. *They are all arranged in a very specific way,* or something like that. For a reason.

They weren't just haphazardly tossed in here — no, they had been placed in this room in a semi-circular arc, and in the other three rooms as well.

All in a circular arrangement.

Around the central space.

Around the vat of liquid that was now emitting a high-pitched whine.

CHAPTER 54

EVGENI

"EVGENI, WHAT IS IT?" Sarah asked. He looked up, seeing that she was the person who had followed him here.

The sound in the room was deafening, but thankfully they only had the high whining drone to deal with — the rhythmic thumping from the machines in succession was still on a five-second schedule. Plenty of time to talk between crashes of the massive mechanical monsters.

Evgeni watched as she was joined by the others, all the CSO team, and they were standing behind him now. He turned to face them.

There was no sign of laughter on their faces.

"You have a way to stop this?" Reggie asked.

He nodded, a single quick toss of his head.

"Good," Ben said, "because we're obviously all out of ideas, and we've got barely three minutes left."

"It's the machines," Evgeni said. "If we can turn them off, we can —"

"We can stop the pounding," Reggie said. "Right, but how can we get to the other rooms? We can't shut them all down in —"

"No," Evgeni said, shaking his head now. "No, we do not have to shut down *all* of them. In fact, we should not try to. Just *these.*" He pushed his hand out, just as Luka had done when he was showing them off.

"Why?"

Evgeni strode over to one of them, looking for buttons or knobs or some sort of controls. He waited until the machine smacked down once, then dove in toward what looked like a control panel. He tried to press the screen to turn it on, but it wasn't responding.

No, this has to be —

"Evgeni, look out!"

Ben shouted at him, and he ducked out of the way just as a huge boot crashed through the air, landing on the screen.

"What are you doing?" Evgeni yelled.

The boot retracted, then crashed again. The screen cracked, then a light flickered from it. Freddie pulled the boot back again and then kicked the screen a final time. This time, the screen lit up fully, flickered, then died.

And the machine died with it.

Evgeni's heart leaped. "Yes!" he said. "Yes, that is it! We need to do that!"

But the others were already in motion. They spread out to the seven other machines, focusing on their weak spot — the control panel. Freddie had guessed correctly: they didn't need to shut the machines down or assume control of them.

They needed to *break* them.

They had no interest in turning them back on later.

The CSO team, with barely a minute left, smashed the controls on the machines, one by one. As they worked on the final machine, the two soldiers Evgeni had seen in the other room entered. They seemed unstable, the man with a headache actually drifting on his feet.

They raised their weapons when Reggie smashed through the screen of the final machine.

Evgeni saw the scene before it unfolded in real life. He knew what was about to happen. He yelled, but the machine smashed down at the same time, the noise of it alone still loud enough to bury Evgeni's voice in the room.

No one heard him. They were all watching Reggie. All with their backs turned.

No one had seen the soldiers enter the room.

They lifted their weapons — both men simultaneously — as Evgeni started to run.

He aimed toward the space between the Russians and Reggie, just as Reggie's foot came down a third time on the machine's control panel.

No, Evgeni thought. *Not like this. Not when we are so close.*

He picked up speed, hoping it would be enough. Reggie's foot contacted the screen, the cracking sound reaching Evgeni's ears, the others cheering as the machine sputtered and began to die.

The rattling fire of the guns, both blasting to life simultaneously, was louder than he thought it would be. But he couldn't hear it clearly, as his mind was registering *another* sound, this one from inside.

It was screaming at him, begging him.

He was in the air, diving forward, trying to reach the space, but the damage had already been done.

His mind was telling him it had been hit. He knew it to be true, but his nerves had registered no pain yet.

He went down, flopping onto the stone floor, his lung destroyed and his other having to play catch-up to keep him breathing. The fall didn't help, and he saw a smattering of blood that had come from his mouth, landing a few feet away.

Someone was running, their feet pounding, jumping over him. Aiming for the guards.

They were a haze, a blur. He saw a skirmish, a brief fight. They overcame the guards, the five of them taking the Russians down with little trouble. He could hear their voices, barely. Couldn't tell what they were saying, but they sounded excited, upset.

He heard the pounding of the other machines, the ones across the city in rooms just like this one. It was quieter though, dimmer. The high-pitched whine faltered, the same frequency but now weaker, as if it had been cut in half.

His eyes closed, then opened. He wanted to stay alive, to help them fight. But it would be only seconds now. For him *and* for them if he was wrong.

The room darkened. He felt something, a deeper tremor than what the machines were pumping out. A terrible, ominous feeling. Was that inside of him?

It began to shake everything, and the others fell. He saw through the open doorway into the larger room, the scientists and technicians now paying close attention to the walls and floor shaking, the debris falling and landing on their computer equipment.

The bomb, he knew. *The bomb had been dropped and detonated.*

It may have been far above them, but they were absolutely feeling the effects down here. He drifted in and out again, finally opening his eyes and seeing the others around him, hovering. They were holding their ears, screaming against an unknown pressure he couldn't feel.

Or could he? He wasn't sure anymore, but there was pain all around him. He knew that much, at least. He felt his heart racing, preparing to explode out of his chest, saw things flying. The CSO team fell to the side, still clutching at each other and their ears, one of them trying to grasp for him but missing.

He felt the sensation of sliding, of being pulled by an imaginary force away from the central atrium area, away from the noise and terror of it all. The others were there too, sliding with him.

He closed his eyes again, and this time it felt right. It felt *complete*.

He had finished his job here, and he knew it was time to sleep.

He tried his best to put on a smile. The others would find him here; he was sure of it. He didn't want them to think he wasn't satisfied with his final play, his final contribution to this team he so wanted to be a part of.

He drifted off as he slid, thinking of Tatiana and Luka and the others, thinking of what he had done.

Thinking of home.

"HE SAVED US," Sarah said. "He saved us all."

There was debris falling all around them, the dust from cracks in the stone sliding and slipping and finally giving way, some larger pebbles drifting down toward the floor as well.

The rumbling had grown and receded, and while there were a few aftershocks every ten seconds or so, the damage from the bomb detonating far above their heads was done. They were alive.

"Wh — what even happened?" Reggie asked her.

She shook her head, still trying to piece it all together. She saw a few Russian scientists or technicians, stunned and trying to grapple with the fact that their plans had been foiled. Two of them were talking excitedly, but the others were standing near their tables, shocked and confused. She even saw a couple of bodies, larger stones near them.

These scientists hadn't fared so well in the cacophony of the bomb and the machines' final thrust.

The Russian soldiers who had fired on Evgeni were dead on the floor as well, their weapons laying harmlessly at their sides. Freddie picked one up, examining it and checking the magazine.

She felt the headache forming, finding it ironic that it had waited until *after* the insanity was over. She remembered the last moments — the noises, the rhythmic thumping and crashing of the machines from elsewhere in the city, the gunshots, Evgeni screaming at them.

And now he too lay lifeless on the stone floor of the ancient city. *Dead.*

All because he'd wanted to save their lives. All because he'd wanted to prove that he was not like Luka; that he was on their team.

"He jumped in front of a bullet," Freddie said.

"Four bullets," Julie added.

"What about before that?" Reggie asked. "The machines — he ran up here to turn them off? Why? He knew he wouldn't be able to get to all of them."

"He didn't need to," Sarah said. "I figured out what he was trying to do and look — it worked."

She pointed to a section of the wall that had completely disintegrated in the blast, chunks of stone crushed and spilling outward into the great hall. Behind it, another icy wall stood watch, the actual Antarctic continent preparing to reclaim its territory. As she looked, Sarah felt the cool air rush over her skin.

"He... blasted a hole in the wall?" Reggie asked.

"He *directed* it. The combined pressure wave of the bomb, plus all the machines, it was originally supposed to be targeting the vat of stuff that Ben fell into — whatever it is — at the center of the base. All that pressure literally heated the liquid material and caused it to vibrate, which was the root of that high-pitched whine."

"So he stopped it by destroying these machines?"

"Yes," Sarah said. "That's exactly what happened. By only destroying *these* machines, he was able to, in a sense, direct that pressure wave *here* — against this stone wall. The culmination, the bomb dropping up above our heads, it created a huge blast that would have otherwise caused something to happen in the central area, with the weird liquid."

"And that is?"

She shrugged. "I have no idea."

"*I* do," Ben said. He stepped closer to Sarah. "Crustal displacement."

No one spoke. Sarah looked around, clearing her throat. "Um, Ben, are you saying the Russians were trying to..." she couldn't finish the sentence. It was too crazy. Too unbelievable.

"It has to be the answer," Ben said. "Luka said these machines were built as modern-day versions of what existed here before, remember? That the Minoans, or whoever they were, built machines that were trying to do the same thing."

"And the liquid stuff that was vibrating?"

"No idea what it is," Ben said. "Some kind of oil, or metal that's liquid at room temperature? Some of it's still dried onto me, so we can possibly have it tested later. But that's not the point. Whatever it is, it works the same way as acoustic levitation. The Egyptians may have used it to move the massive stones from their quarry hundreds of miles away. By subjecting this liquid stuff underneath a stone to a certain pitch, the stone vibrates, effectively making it lighter."

"And you think that's what the Russians were doing here?"

"I don't think there's another possibility that makes more sense," Ben said. "Think about it — we know the Minoans built this place, and there was no way to bring all of these stones over that amount of ocean. So they built it using stones that were here *already*. Meaning this place was hollowed out of Antarctica itself."

"But Antarctica itself was in a different place," Reggie said.

"Exactly. It literally moved during a polar shift. The plate of crust it's sitting on slid over Earth's mantle, eventually landing here."

"And by turning on this... machine, or whatever it is," Julie added, "we think they were trying to do it again?"

"I don't know," Ben said. "It seems far-fetched, but we've all seen stranger things."

"I don't know, man," Reggie added. "This one might take the cake for weird Earth-stuff."

Ben laughed. "We're alive, for now. That bomb might have sealed us all in here, though. Let's think about a way out, then we can discuss what happened here."

"Any ideas?" Julie asked.

Freddie cleared his throat. Everyone turned to look at him, and Ben raised his eyebrows. "You got another secret, Freddie?"

He chewed his lip for a second. "My uncle likes to clean up," he said.

"Meaning?"

"Meaning he'll most likely send a team down here to check out the damage. Make sure no government secrets are lying around."

"Like us?"

"Well," Freddie said. "I'm hoping we'll get a pass. He didn't *want* to drop a bomb on us, after all."

Ben snorted. "Yeah, well, he did. I'll take my chances with his cleanup crew, but only because it's our only option."

"What about these other Russians? The scientists and techs, and the rest of the soldiers that should be around here somewhere?"

Ben shook his head. "I don't know. They're not our problem. I bet a few of them left with Luka, wherever they are. Maybe your uncle will be able to intercept them, too. I've got a few choice words for that Russian asshole."

"You and me both, buddy," Reggie said.

"Okay," Ben said. "We're not out of the weeds yet. Let's get moving. Time to go *up*, I guess."

Sarah waited for someone to ask a question or argue, but it seemed the five of them agreed. They would start walking up the corkscrew pathways until they reached the top of the base, where they would — *hopefully* — find an exit that hadn't been destroyed.

She took a deep breath, held it for a moment, and then started forward, following Reggie upward.

CHAPTER 56

BEN

THE WALK WAS UNEVENTFUL, which made Ben feel even more uneasy. There was nothing jumping out at them, nothing trying to attack them, nothing trying to kill them.

Which meant something was wrong.

He wasn't sure what it was, or if he was just getting in his own head, but there was a distinct feeling of restlessness, a feeling that their mission here was not over.

He thought about what they had just seen, what they had just been through. Evgeni's death was weighing on Ben's mind more than he thought it would. The man had chosen specifically to die, to make his dying wish saving people he had barely known.

Why? What good could come of that? Why were his and his friends' lives any more valuable than Evgeni's? He was thankful he was still alive and grateful to Evgeni for it, but he couldn't understand why the man had done it.

There had to be something more. There had to be some *reason*.

Ben walked in silence, ignoring the whispers of the others behind him, excitedly talking about what they would do and what they would eat the moment they were free from this place. He didn't want to think about that yet — the truth was, they *weren't* yet free. At any moment, a group of —

He held up a hand. He had heard something from around the corner, and he wasn't convinced it was just their footsteps echoing back at him.

"You hear something, boss?" Freddie asked.

Ben nodded, and the big man stepped up next to him, holding the subcompact machine gun he had taken off the dead Russian soldiers. Ben kicked himself for not grabbing another one or two weapons when they had had the chance.

Freddie pulled up the weapon and aimed it down the hallway.

"Hold steady," Ben whispered. "We don't know who —"

A woman stepped into view. She had a terrifying frown on her face, a look of general disdain. She was flanked by two men, each holding assault rifles and pointing them directly at Ben and Freddie. She raised a fist and the men stopped like trained dogs.

"Easy," she said. Her voice was southern, with a thick drawl. "Got ourselves some live ones."

"Who are you?" Ben asked. "Who are you with?"

"Name's Rogers," she said. "The rest is classified."

"You don't sound Russian," Ben said.

"Neither do you, big boy. You been having trouble with some, I hear?"

"I guess that means we passed the test?"

"Far from it. We're here to get you out, but don't for once think we're on the same team. As far as I'm concerned, you're all hostiles."

Freddie snickered. "Yeah, sounds like my uncle. 'Trust but verify,' but then only trust a bit and never stop verifying."

"Your uncle, huh?" Rogers said. Neither of the men next to her spoke. Both continued pointing their rifles forward, ready to pull the trigger at a moment's notice.

"Okay, let's get to it, then," Ben said. "I've been on edge since we got here."

"Why's that?"

"Plane got shot out of the sky," he said without hesitation. "That sort of thing can get to you, you know?"

"I don't."

Ben waited, trying to read this hard, frigid woman, but coming up wanting. She was obviously in charge just about everywhere she went, and from the looks of her men next to her, she didn't need to use her rank to prove it.

Finally, she flicked her head. "Walk, fast. Keep moving, keep up. Exit's about half a mile from here, straight up. We took out a few generators up top, but we don't think the light will stay on much longer."

"Got it," Ben said.

"Any injuries?"

"Just my pride," Ben heard Reggie mutter.

Rogers didn't respond. She simply turned, waited for her men to push forward in front of her, and then started walking briskly up the inclined hallway.

Okay, Ben thought. *Now we're getting somewhere.*

He was about to look at Freddie and smile when he heard another sound. This time it was voices. The two men in front had slowed and were now whispering to one another. They had heard it, too.

Without warning, one man's head exploded in a shower of blood, and he fell.

Rogers yelled, dove forward, and extracted a pistol from her side holster. She used the dead man's body as cover, lifting the gun and pointing it down the hall. The second soldier dropped to a knee, pointing his own rifle in the direction the shots had come from. Neither seemed to notice or care that their man had been killed in cold blood, inches from them.

Freddie snuck up and stuck his own weapon out, but Rogers turned and gave him a frown. "No," she said. "We got it."

Freddie motioned to the downed soldier. "Yeah, looks like it. Don't turn down a free soldier, lady."

She grunted something, but Ben couldn't hear it. They were all on their knees, crouching in the hallway, waiting to see if there was any movement. Ben couldn't see anything, and for five seconds they waited, nothing but the sounds of their breaths, rising and falling out of their lungs.

He was about to whisper something to Freddie when he saw a flicker of light. A tiny, flashing image of a round object sailed through the air. He wasn't sure if anyone else saw it.

"Hey, did you —"

The object clattered to the ground and then rolled.

"Grenade!" Rogers yelled. She dove sideways, landing on the man to her right. Freddie ducked backward as well, nearly crashing into Ben.

It didn't matter — they were too late. The grenade flashed an intense orange, and the entire space inside Ben's head seemed to go still. The white-hot searing light caused him to fall, but then the world above his head exploded into a million colors.

He felt his body being lifted, pushed backward and toward the intersection with the hallway behind them. He smacked his head against the floor, tumbling end over end.

He couldn't even scream or shout for help — it was all happening too fast. He grasped at the air, feeling the same useless weightlessness he'd felt when falling into the vat of liquid before. Nothing gave him purchase. Nothing gave him any help.

Finally, he found the back wall of the intersection. His back hit it first, then his head and backside. He moaned and then tried to open his eyes just as the wash of fire flew over his face.

He screamed now, loudly and for as long as his breath would allow, until the fiery intensity subsided.

Except, by then, there were gunshots.

A lot of them.

And they were landing all around him. He heard one hit something soft, something other than stone. He couldn't tell if it was him or someone else. Someone yelled something directly into his ear, and he felt his body moving once again. He was being dragged.

He knew now what was happening, and he knew why.

CHAPTER 57

BEN

"THEY'RE ATTACKING," he said, spitting a mouthful of bile onto the stone pathway. Rogers was there, along with her soldier. The others were as well. Julie and Reggie had dragged Ben out of the line of fire, and then they'd gone back to get Freddie.

They were all currently hiding out around the corner, taking stock and preparing to attack once more. Rogers said something about not enjoying a defensive position; that she would rather take up the offensive, and Reggie was arguing with her.

Ben could only hear a bit of it. The inside of his head was still on fire, still screaming and trying to gain his attention. He couldn't push it away.

"They're attacking," he said again.

"We know," Rogers and Freddie said simultaneously. Rogers scoffed and turned back to her argument. "Tell me something I *don't* know."

"I wasn't talking to you," Ben said. "I was trying to figure out why the Russians just... left. After Luka, their boss, ditched them, and then their little science experiment failed, they just started to disappear. All the soldiers, gone. All the scientists, clearly preoccupied with getting out of here."

"And you know why?" Julie asked. She had her hand on Ben's head, feeling for his temperature. It wouldn't do any good — if he had a fever, it would be hidden beneath the already-sweltering heat of his brow.

"I think so," Ben said. "I was trying to figure it out on the way up here. We were hoping to find you guys — Rogers and your team — but I couldn't quite place why everything was so *quiet*."

"And?"

"And we were under guard from the moment we came here, right?" Ben continued. "Not anymore. The only explanation is like Freddie said: the government wants to make sure there aren't any loose ends."

"I was talking about *our* government," Freddie said. "My uncle."

"Sure," Ben replied, "but I'd bet the Russians are thinking the same thing. Get everyone out, then burn the rest to the ground. Your uncle's bomb probably didn't even scratch the surface — literally. So they're sending out more teams to finish the job."

"That doesn't matter," Rogers said. "What matters right now is I got a dead sergeant and a handful of ragtag civilians, and I'm stuck in a damned Antarctic... something. What the hell even *is* this place?"

Reggie grinned. "Speak for yourself, miss. We've been here for a bit longer than you. We'd love to see the sun again, even if it is frozen and covered in ice up there."

"And," Freddie added, "I'd bet you guys have some cool vehicles up there, too. With *heaters*."

Rogers sniffed.

Ben reached out a hand. After a few seconds, she took it and shook it in a crushing grip. "You were probably told we were just civilians. That's technically true, but there's a bit more to it. I'm Harvey Bennett."

Her frown deepened, her eyes scanning Ben's. Trying to place the recognition. Finally, she grinned. "You're *Harvey Bennett?* That guy who runs around and..."

"Saves the world?" Reggie asked, laughing.

"I was going to say, 'gets himself into all sorts of trouble,'" Rogers said.

Ben chuckled. "You know what? That's probably more accurate."

"Okay, so I'm down in a stone graveyard with *the* Harvey Bennett," she said. "How special. Yet that doesn't change the fact that we're still under attack, and if they're like the Russians I know, we do not want to piss them off. Anyone got any ideas?"

Reggie lifted a hand. "Well, it's been a while since my range days, but if you'll be so kind as to get me one of those nice rifles you're toting around, I could lend a hand."

"You've been trained with one?" Rogers asked.

"You worried I'm going to hit you in the back?"

She didn't answer.

"How about I just stand in front of you the whole time?"

Finally, she shook her head. "This is ridiculous. I was sent here to get you all out, not to crack jokes and give you weapons to blast through an army of Russians."

Reggie shrugged. "We do what we can."

He moved toward the edge of the hallway, peering around the corner where the dead soldier lay. Ben moved with him, expecting him to pause and work out a plan Ben could convey to the others. Instead, Reggie suddenly darted out on his hands and knees, crawling toward the soldier.

"Reggie!" Ben whispered. "What the hell, man?"

Reggie didn't turn back. He crawled on elbows and knees all the way to the soldier, about halfway down the hallway. He reached the weapon, lifted it up and over his shoulder, and then poked around on the soldier's body for extra magazines. Finding three of them, he turned and was about to crawl back when Ben saw him stop.

"What are you doing?" he whispered. "Get back here. I'll get Rogers to cover you."

Reggie ignored him, then slid over once again to the soldier's side. He reached out and plucked something off the man, then finally turned and started back toward Ben.

When he rounded the corner, Ben let out a breath. Rogers was already scolding him, but the others — including Rogers' second — were smiling.

Reggie held up the weapon, the magazines, and — with a flourish — the grenade he'd taken from the dead man.

"Sorry about your man, ma'am," Reggie said. "Never feels okay to lose a soldier. But I figured this could be a little consolation prize."

He placed the grenade down and checked over the rifle.

"You have a plan?" Rogers asked.

Reggie looked at Ben, then back at her, then nodded. "I sure do. I figure we can start with a taste of their own medicine, then I do what I do best."

"Which is?"

Ben laughed. "Oh, you should probably just wait and see. It's better that way."

CHAPTER 58

PETROKOV

PETROKOV HAD NOT FELT this good in a long time. The drugs likely had a lot to do with it, but if not, the alcohol was the trick. Either way, he couldn't help smiling. The woman had returned, and their night was every bit as fantastic as it had been the night before.

He couldn't help but wonder if she might actually be truly into him. He had not had a lover — a companion — in a long time. He thought he might not ever again. Now, he wasn't so sure.

The events that had led to his current state of euphoria were slow at first, then more and more exciting. The mission, ultimately, had failed. He had started to drink because of that. Any failure of any Russian was a failure to him. That was a fact.

But then he had heard about the specific *kind* of failure that resulted from it. So far, no United Nations country had suspected any foul play in Antarctica other than the Russians' presence. They would launch an investigation, but Petrokov knew Mikhail's defense team could easily keep them off the actual path to the truth. That much would not be a problem.

And the Gorod project had been laid to rest in the most spectacular of ways. The Americans, as always, had come in, guns blazing. They had actually *bombed* the site. Petrokov and Mikhail, and everyone else involved, could not have been happier. The Americans looked to be the aggressors, and they would be tried in an international court for their actions.

They had also cleaned up Luka's mess quite elegantly. The Gorod project and facility were effectively sealed off from prying eyes, and no eyes would pry, since no eyes suspected there was anything left to pry into. No one suspected that the Gorod facility was actually *under* the ground — that was a secret that would be taken to Luka's grave.

Not that Luka would have a grave. When Petrokov had learned of his sniveling comrade's fate, he had drunk nearly half a bottle of the finest brandy he could find in the hotel bar. He had gotten mostly through a few glasses before offering a glass to his companion.

Luka and the few soldiers he had escaped with had been accosted by the Russian cleanup crew of special forces, where they met with a quick and sudden demise. Their bodies were cast into the sea, where they would likely freeze or become shark food somewhere on their long float home.

A fitting end for an arrogant, cocksure Russian. His team — the Motherland — would still win, and that was all that would matter.

They would have to pivot in order to stay on track, but their ultimate goal — the ultimate victory for Russia — was still in sight. It was still possible, and Petrokov would likely get the promotion he longed for that would allow him to oversee a small portion of that project.

And he knew far better now how to play the game. He had come out of this alive, which meant everything. He was a survivor, and if there was anything the Kremlin appreciated as much as loyalty, it was survivorship. Petrokov had played the game admirably, and he would now graduate to a higher circle, starting over with a new game, the one he *truly* wanted to play.

Russia's time was coming, and he would be there to see it.

He would achieve the greatness none in his country had seen in over fifty years. He would help usher in an era of Russian dominance that would take the world by surprise. *By storm,* to be poetic.

He smiled, hardly noticing that the woman was taking her clothes off. They had retired to his room once again, this time skipping the pleasantries and small talk and heading straight up after their bottle of brandy at the bar.

But he almost didn't care. There was time for that — there was always time — when his credit card was paying for it. Now, he just wanted to bask in the victory.

The Americans would call this a victory for their own country, and that was fine. The strange American civilians who had stopped Luka from ultimately achieving his own victory would also consider themselves victorious. And, arguably, they were.

But they were shortsighted. They couldn't see this whole game for what it was. They didn't know enough to know that they had been played from the beginning.

Petrokov had needed Luka to fail, but in a very particular way: he had needed Luka to fail while thinking he was succeeding. By getting close to success, but not getting all the way.

He had needed Luka to die, and he had needed him to think the Americans were to blame.

It had been a bit difficult to pull off, but Petrokov was no fool. He had done his job admirably, keeping even Mikhail and the others out of the way while he maneuvered. The emails, the phone calls, the subtle hints and web links — all of it had been his doing.

The CSO had bought it, taken it in and made it their own little pet project, just as he'd intended. He had gotten the US military involved, just enough to make it plausible that they could be blamed for the outcome. But the CSO's involvement, that strange compartment of civilian Americans who often bit off more than they could chew, had jumped at the opportunity to play worldwide police, eventually choosing Luka as their target.

Just as he'd designed it. Just as he'd hoped they would.

Leaving him, Petrokov, completely out of sight to continue his mission.

To continue *Russia's* mission.

His smile grew as he placed the glass of liquid — he wasn't even sure what it was anymore — down on the bedside table, stood up, and took the woman's hand.

"Good evening, my love," he began, all in Russian. He knew she couldn't understand him. "It is time I pay you the attention you are due."

CHAPTER 59

SARAH

"YOU'RE TELLING me you fought your way out of a maze full of Russian soldiers, all with five magazines, three guns, and a grenade?"

"Two grenades, but we only used one," Reggie said. His smirk was almost as ridiculous as the conversation. Sarah had always preferred the more sentimental version of the man she loved to the over-the-top, machismo, puffed-chest version she saw now.

The same version that had fought through the last of the Russians in the Minoan city and emerged, victorious, out of the top.

They had been airlifted to a ship waiting offshore, given something to eat and a warm shower, and they were now debriefing — or trying to — in the general's private office.

General Rollins was shaking his head, the look on his face telling everyone in the room how he felt. "That was reckless, and unnecessary."

"Was it?" Reggie asked. "We're alive."

"*Most* of you are alive. And that's on the American side. There's not even a single Russian we can take to court. No one to throw the blame at. The Luka fellow you targeted was found dead, floating face-down off the coast. It was sheer luck one of the boats had found him. And Rogers' team — "

"She lost her man because of an ambush. I decided to go with my plan *after* that, to be fair."

"To be *fair*, you would be court-martialed if you were still in my ranks, soldier," Rollins said.

"Probably a good thing I'm not, then."

Sarah stood up and tried to rescue the conversation. "What he's trying to say, sir, is that we felt we had exhausted all of our options."

"I *gave* you more options!" Rollins said. "I sent Rogers and her team down there to get you —"

Freddie stood up, his head nearly touching the ceiling, and towered over all the rest of them, the general included. "You sent a *bomb* down there," he said. "May I remind you that we were not even supposed to *be* alive? You sent Rogers as a way to clean up the mess. 'Plausible deniability,' all that bullshit."

"It's not bullshit when it works, son. And it's necessary. A necessary evil, but necessary nonetheless. You failed the mission according to the pre-established parameters. We moved to the alternative plan — also something we agreed upon — and then sent Rogers down there to ensure *that* part was taken care of. Finding you all alive was a great bonus."

"A 'great bonus?'" Freddie asked, incredulous. Sarah saw Ben release Julie's hand and stand up, walking toward Freddie. "I'm a *bonus*? That's what a life — a life of your *family member* — is worth to you?"

Rollins clenched and unclenched his jaw. "I am extending you the unique privilege to speak to me this way *because* you are family."

"I don't want your damned privilege, man," Freddie said.

Ben reached his side and put a hand on his shoulder. "Look, uh, General Rollins. I am sorry — we've had a hell of a time the past few days. We're obviously tired, on edge. We need some shuteye and then we can —"

"We don't need jack squat," Freddie said. "*We* are done. *I* am done."

All eyes in the room turned, including Rogers' and the other man with her, a man named Abernathy. No one spoke. Rollins and Freddie stared at one another for a long moment before Freddie spoke again.

"You're my uncle. I always looked up to you. I believe what you're doing is good, overall. You represent *good*, as far as you're able. I wanted to be like you — hell, I wanted to *be* you. As a kid, you're all I would talk about."

Rollins swallowed. "And now?"

Freddie took in a deep breath through his nose. "Now? I don't know. I guess — I guess I think the world's different. Borders aren't as strong as they used to be, and I'm thinking there's some good in that, too."

"What are you saying, son? Just spit it out. I'm a big boy."

"I think I'm done with the Army."

Sarah felt the air in the room leave. It was like someone had silently popped a balloon and immediately expunged all the oxygen, creating a vacuum. She was still seated, but she shifted and straightened her back.

"*Done* with the Army?"

Freddie nodded.

"This isn't Boy Scouts, Freddie. You can't just quit it when things get tough."

"Actually, I can. And I have no plans to make things easier — I *want* the going to get tough. I *want* to fight for the things I believe in. I just... I just don't think the Army is the best way to do that, anymore."

"And what is?"

Freddie turned to Ben, and he placed an arm over the man's shoulder. "Well, I haven't really discussed it with them much, but — maybe the CSO?"

The general scoffed. "The Civilian Special — son, are you mad? There will be a discharge, and it will not be favorable. Leaving the military after your career? After your record? To join a civilian phil-anthropy organization? They're not going to let you off the hook easy."

Freddie nodded. "I can take what's coming. Would be nice, though, to have a little backup. That sort of thing might go a long way."

The general looked like he was about to pop, and Sarah wanted to look away. She couldn't help it, though. She was rooting for Fred-die; a man she knew now she could trust with her life. And the general — a man who was supposed to be related to Freddie but had betrayed him — was about to be taken down a peg. It was the sort of justice she always wanted a front-row seat for.

"Harvey," the general said. "What do you think of all this?"

Ben sniffed, then looked at the others and then back to Rollins. "Well, sir, I'm not really one for speeches. I like to keep things short and sweet."

"As do I."

"Very well," Ben said. "Freddie's an asset to whatever team he's on. You already know that, or you wouldn't have sent him along. I understand what you did, and why. Doesn't make it suck less, but it is what it is. If he wants to join our ranks because of it, we'd be lucky to have him."

The general turned and walked back around his desk. He peered out, looking through them all, through the door and the hull of the ship and through the continent itself, it seemed. Sarah waited, antici-pating something she wasn't sure she was ready for.

Finally, he spoke. "I joined back when the Army was synonymous with 'the good guys.' We were fighters, warriors. Some of us still are. But the politics changed. The red tape came in, the suits showed up, the beancounters and power-trippers and the corporate evangelists. It's difficult to keep it all straight, honestly, and that's my job.

"I'd love nothing more than to see the old Army again, but I'm afraid that ship — I hope you'll pardon the pun — has sailed. It's too late for me; I'm already in it too deep, and I'll die that way. But for you — Freddie — it's not too late. You can't make the Army what you want, and you shouldn't change to make it fit who you are. But you *can* still have an impact."

"What are you saying, sir?"

"I'm saying if you want to join these guys, fight for what you think is right, keep your head on straight, you'll find some balance. You'll find some fights, but you'll probably also find some satisfaction in what you're doing. That's worth everything there is because it's how we maintain our character. Our integrity."

Freddie grinned, and Sarah felt tears welling in her eyes.

"I may not be able to get you a company salute, but I can at least get you apportioned to a 'darker' division — one where people won't ask questions. Anyone looking in under the layers will find a man who's doing the kinds of things we all wanted to do, the reason we all joined up. You'll be doing it, but not with the Army. On paper, though, you'll still be here."

Freddie nodded. "Thank you."

"I mean it when I say — you're a good man. A good soldier, and you've got a good heart. Those are the raw materials for becoming great, but you have to earn it. I think you will, but if you leave, I won't be there to keep an eye out for you. You understand that, right?"

Freddie thought for a few seconds, then walked up to his uncle's desk. "I do. Yes, sir." Freddie stuck out a hand.

General Rollins' face shifted, the stark frown softening and a smile appearing on his face. He stood up, then reached across the desk and grabbed Freddie by the shoulders, ignoring his hand. He pulled him into a bear hug, the two men crushing the desk between them.

"I would tell you to make me proud, son," the general said, "but you already have."

"SO," Ben said, holding up a glass to toast, "here's to the CSO, and its newest member."

Freddie held up his beer, and they all clinked their glasses together. Reggie and Ben were splitting a small bottle of bourbon, one that Sarah had purchased from the barman. She'd opened it and poured for them, chastising both men about not making this a big deal like the last time.

They had laughed and claimed that it had worked out just fine and that she should just keep pouring.

She and Julie were splitting a bottle of wine, some red blend that looked promising. Freddie had stuck to his guns, opting for a cold draft with a lime in it. The Argentinian bartender had seemed to appreciate that the most.

"Anyone want to explore a little while we're here?" Reggie asked. "The US dollar goes a *long* way in Argentina."

"We've only got a day here before we're supposed to be back on the plane," Ben said. "Not really much time to do anything."

"I thought you were like the boss of this thing, or something," Freddie said, sipping the foam off the top of his beer. "Like, you should be able to say when we go home."

"That's what *I've* been saying!" Reggie exclaimed. "This guy doesn't understand that R&R is a *crucial* part of my development regimen."

"Your 'development regimen' went out the window the day you met Sarah," Julie said.

Reggie feigned a hurt expression. "Look, just because I hit the jackpot with hot ladies and you ended up with this lug doesn't mean you have to take it out on me."

"Doesn't it?" Ben asked. "You know you're always stealing glances at Jules' backside whenever you can."

Julie's and Sarah's jaws dropped simultaneously, and Reggie's hands went up. "No, what? Me? Come on, that was *one time,* and it was *long* before I met you —" he looked to Sarah, but Ben knew she wasn't having it. "Come on, *Dr.* Lindgren, I swear —"

"Don't suck up, Reggie," Sarah said. "You know it gets you nowhere."

Reggie placed his elbows on the table in the outdoor seating area and stuck his head down, his chin nearly hitting his chest. He drooped his eyes, furrowing his brow, and then looked up at Sarah. "This 'sad puppy' routine always seems to work, though."

She tried to look angry, but then burst out laughing. Ben joined in, the sight of his friend's ridiculous face too much to hold in. They all toasted again, and then Freddie cleared his throat.

"Hey, uh, I was thinking. This whole mission, the stuff down in the city. It all seems to have been wrapped up too nicely."

"*That* was nice?" Reggie asked.

Freddie chuckled. "You know what I mean. Where are the UN investigators? Where's the public outcry, asking the Kremlin to explain what they were doing there? Heck, what about the US side of things — we dropped a *bomb* on Antarctica."

"I don't know, man," Ben said. "It's politics. Government stuff. Way above our pay grade. The CSO has a board made up of military folks, and they're pretty good at protecting us from stuff like that."

"Still... it seems odd. I just feel like it all ended too abruptly. Like, it's been pushed under the rug and that's it, you know?"

Reggie licked his lips, staring down into his glass of bourbon. "I feel that."

"Yeah?"

"Yeah," he said. "Freddie, you're not wrong. This one feels *unfinished.*"

"Why is that?"

"Your guess is as good as mine."

"Maybe it's not," Ben said.

Everyone looked at him.

"Yeah, I mean, think about it. Why would the Russians care about Antarctica? There's nothing there. I mean, sure, a city and some weird machines that *supposedly* could cause 'crustal displacement,' and move Antarctica somewhere else."

Julie smiled. "That does seem like something you'd want to get your hands on if you were a greedy country."

"Yeah, but *why*? I mean, what's the purpose of doing that?"

"You have an idea?"

Ben shrugged, taking a sip of bourbon. It was harsh, but it was cold. He appreciated it, but he mostly appreciated the weather — it was in the high eighties, the sun was shining, and there was no snow, ice, or stone in sight. "Maybe. I was thinking about it a lot on the way back up. And then again in Rollins' office. Why they were so quick to pull out, and why they killed Luka and the others and just forgot about them."

"And?"

"Well, I couldn't help but think of the geographic distance — I mean, you can't really get farther away from Russia than *Antarctica*. They already have the majority of the *Arctic* covered, but the Antarctic is like the farthest you can get from the Kremlin."

"Unless you move it," Reggie said with a raised eyebrow.

"No," Ben said. "Even then, what's the point? Then, it's still a couple of huge landmasses, slowly coming out of their ice-covered shell, that you have to protect. If they wanted more land, why not invade a nearby country?"

"And they already have far more land than one country needs."

"Exactly," Ben said. "But yesterday I saw a news report talking about global warming again. Say what you will, whether or not it's human-caused, it's happening. I tend to think it's just one of the many cycles of cooling and heating the earth has gone through, but that's just me."

"What about it?"

"Well, all that land on their north coast is frozen. Has been forever, as long as they've been a country, at least. But if you were able to cause something massive, like a massive polar shift that changes the landscape of the earth's crust, literally moving a *continent*, then..."

Julie picked up the thread. "Then you'd probably *melt* a lot of the ice up there, and what's on Antarctica, because it will all move and shift around. Some other places will be covered in ice that had never been, and other places that were *always* cold would no longer be."

"Oh my God," Reggie said. "You're right, man. Yeah. Russia would have an entire *coastline* of new seaports. They've been bolstering their Navy for decades, but they'd basically have unfettered access to the world's oceans, because sea routes that have *never existed* would be adjacent to their land."

The table sat silent for a moment. Freddie drank his beer, and the others waited for someone to speak. It was a crazy thing to believe, but Ben wasn't sure there was a better option.

Finally, Freddie smacked his empty bottle on the table. "This what it's like all the time for you guys? Solve one problem, then find something bigger?"

Reggie laughed. "Yeah, pretty much."

Freddie thought about it, then nodded. "Okay, sure. I can get used to that." He lifted the beer bottle and shook it around. "But first, I'm going to need a few more of these."

AFTERWORD

If you liked this book (or even if you hated it...) write a review or rate it. You might not think it makes a difference, but it does.

Besides *actual* currency (money), the currency of today's writing world is *reviews*. Reviews, good or bad, tell other people that an author is worth reading.

As an "indie" author, I need all the help I can get. I'm hoping that since you made it this far into my book, you have some sort of opinion on it.

Would you mind sharing that opinion? It only takes a second.

Nick Thacker

BOOKS BY NICK THACKER

Harvey Bennett Thrillers

The Enigma Strain (Book 1)
The Amazon Code (Book 2)
The Ice Chasm (Book 3)
The Jefferson Legacy (Book 4)
The Paradise Key (Book 5)
The Atlantis Artifact (Book 6)
The Book of Bones (Book 7)
The Cain Conspiracy (Book 8)
The Mendel Paradox (Book 9)
The Minoan Manifest (Book 10)
The Napoleon Job (Book 11)
Harvey Bennett Mysteries - Books 1-3
Harvey Bennett Mysteries - Books 4-6
Harvey Bennett Mysteries - Books 7-9

*For a full list of novels by Nick Thacker, visit him online at www.
nickthacker.com*

ABOUT THE AUTHOR

Nick Thacker is a thriller author from Texas who lives in Hawaii and Colorado. In his free time, he enjoys reading in a hammock on the beach, skiing, drinking whiskey, and hanging out with his beautiful wife, two dogs, and two daughters.

For more information and a list of Nick's other work, visit Nick online:
www.nickthacker.com

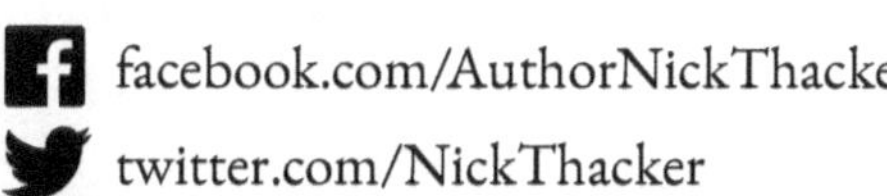

facebook.com/AuthorNickThacker
twitter.com/NickThacker
instagram.com/TheNickThacker